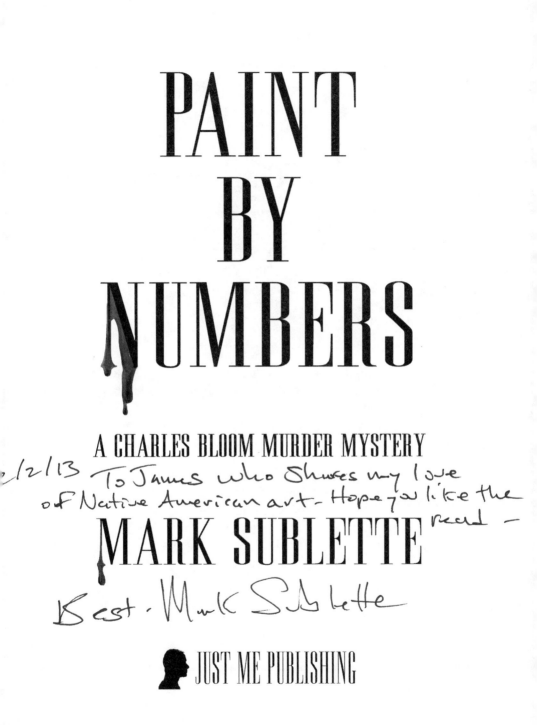

PAINT BY NUMBERS

A CHARLES BLOOM MURDER MYSTERY

MARK SUBLETTE

2/12/13 To James who shares my love of Native American art - Hope you like the read -

Best - Mark Sublette

JUST ME PUBLISHING

Published by Just Me Publishing, LLC.

Library of Congress Control Number: 2012939897
Paint by Numbers / Mark Sublette
ISBN 978-0-9855448-0-5
1. Fiction I. Title

Quantity Purchases
Companies, professional groups, clubs, and other organizations may qualify for special terms when ordering quantities of this title. For more information, contact us through www.marksublette.com.

Cover painting: Francis Livingston
Jacket and book design: Jaime Gould
Author photo back cover flap: Kathleen Sublette
Author photo back cover : Dan Budnik
Logo Photo: Tori Sublette

Printed in the USA by Bookmasters
Ashland, OH · www.bookmasters.com

Author's Note

The books in the Bloom murder mystery series are all works of fiction. Excluding a few well-known deceased artists and historic figures, all the books' characters are fictional; this includes the main character Willard Yellowhorse. The events surrounding all characters are complete figments of my imagination. Some historic dates, events and places have been incorporated to add to the realism of the story, but the circumstances surrounding such events are complete fiction. All art galleries, artists and art dealers are fictitious, although twenty years as an art dealer have given me a keen insight into the type of individuals who make up our unique community.

All the descriptions of various Native American rituals have their basis in fact. I have changed some of these rituals to be non-specific descriptions in respect of the Navajo culture. All the Native American people in my books are fictional and any resemblance by name, clan or description is pure coincidence.

The Toadlena Trading Post, a central component of all the Bloom books, is a real working trading post. This historic post specializes in Toadlena/Two Grey Hills weavings and is well worth the effort to visit. I would like to thank its proprietor, author Mark Winter, and his wife Linda, for their invaluable insight into the world of the weavers and their land as well as for putting me up in their trailer and feeding me volumes of good home-cooked food.

No book is complete without a great cover and I'm most appreciative to Francis Livingston for so graciously allowing me to use one of his paintings and to Jaime Gould for her graphic design skills.

I would also like to thank both editor Wolf Schneider for her energy, time, and immense ability in helping me shape the final outcome of this story, for which I will forever be grateful, and James Sublette and Sally Herfurth for their editing prowess.

Finally, thank you to my muse Kathleen, and my children, Charles and Tori, for without their encouragement and love my writings would not have come to fruition.

PROLOGUE

YELLOW AND RED DON'T MIX. 15 YEARS AGO. NEW YORK CITY

Willard Yellowhorse felt the noose tighten against his throat. Breathing was labored now. His life force was slipping away and there was nothing he could do. The last of the thick red paint that once covered the upper two-thirds of his body had slowly dripped off and was now captured on the fine linen painting canvas below. The swirl of red color formed rivulets of viscous paint on the covered floor. The image mirrored Willard's own bound torso, which stood precariously on a chrome barstool. An odd yet symmetrical pattern was taking shape: his death shroud. The image was compelling and not altogether dissimilar to his expensive artwork that contemporary art fans clamored for, but never in a million years would he have chosen to make this painting. Inexplicably, Willard had seen this image before: not suspended here in a cold-storage unit in a dicey New York neighborhood, but in a much more comforting surrounding. *The same composition had been drawn two weeks earlier by his grandfather, a powerful Diné medicine man.*

Hastiin Sherman, Willard's grandfather, had foreseen Willard's current predicament during Willard's curing ceremony on his last trip back to the Navajo Reservation. Sherman had sternly warned his grandson of an abrupt end in the sacred sands, his life path line stopped. "Change course or suffer the will of the gods," cautioned the old man. A bad coyote spirit, Ma'ii ni, had Yellowhorse's scent and soon would capture his prey.

Now Willard Yellowhorse wished he had listened. He had known the power of his grandfather's visions—they were legendary. But Willard had become too much like the whites he now lived among in New York, not listening to Mother Earth's rhythm. It would cost him his life. Too late now. His neck was securely in the spirit coyote's jaws with no way out.

Drip by drip, the last holes filled in from white to red, the canvas nearing its completion. Willard's nude body shivered uncontrollably, his handcuffs tinkling like a glass chandelier, sending small, faint red-paint droplets splattering along the canvas edges. The cadence eerily reminded Willard of his grandfather's scattering of powerful sacred corn pollen during the end of the curing ceremony.

Willard knew death was approaching and considered trying to write some note with the last little drips, maybe the initials of the man who had taken his life. He was paralyzed, yet in awe of the image below him that had miraculously come to life. The design was complete, the exact one his elderly grandfather had formed earlier with his sand painting on the brown Arizona dirt floor of his ancestral summer hogan. Willard's mind regressed to when he was sitting in the hogan watching the intensity of the old medicine man's execution of the complicated sand painting. Its beauty and intricacy had impressed Willard, a respected artist who understood creative talent when he saw it. The feat had taken Hastiin Sherman a full day.

Willard's consciousness drifted back to the present, realizing the slightest movement on his part would cause him to lose balance and die. He fought the death *chindi*, even though he innately understood the now-finished design had already sealed his fate. His toes gripped the stool, valiantly fighting gravity. Each rapid heartbeat was visible along Yellowhorse's carotids. The accentuated neckline was tangled in long, flowing black hair caught in a tight hangman's noose, the coyote's jaws. Only his superior balance and muscular legs prevented strangulation. Legs that had grown strong running the backcountry of his Navajo homelands herding his grandmother's sheep now fought death.

Time stood still for Yellowhorse. In the background, music erupted. He could hear the old Eagles tune "Seven Bridges Roads" playing in the distance, muffled yet the words were clear: "There are stars in the Southern sky." The imagery of stars in the sky, and the number seven intermixed with an eagle flying overhead. Yellowhorse wondered what death would be like and which ancestral spirits would be meeting him at the sacred Canyon de Chelly cliffs. His shivering body began to warm and a peace slowly engulfed him. Like his mind's eagle, he would fly soon, though only a short distance.

As the second verse began and the words reverberated in Yellowhorse's sweat-drenched ears—"There are stars in the Southern sky"—Willard Yellowhorse's balance finally gave way and with a loud snap of fracturing cervical vertebrae, STRUGGLE was complete: his final death-star painting, drips of red paint and yellow urine mixed on a white canvas. It would be worth millions.

CHAPTER 1

NO SALES. PRESENT DAY. SANTA FE, NEW MEXICO

Winter smells in Santa Fe are subtle mixtures of burning piñon wood and roasting green chiles, a fragrance unique to northern New Mexico. The more-than-mile-high air is cold and crisp, with skies deceivingly crystal blue, never betraying the next hidden snowstorm crouching behind the surrounding mountainous landscape. Except this year the snow hadn't found its way to the mountains, so Santa Fe's ski and retail season had been a bust. Charles Bloom was struggling.

"Today's temperature, 15 degrees, a 70% chance of a late afternoon snow squall and near-record low temperatures," the radio announcer dutifully reported in a singsong northern New Mexican accent, a reminder of his five-hundred-year-old conquistador bloodlines.

Charles sighed. "I remember when the snow used to come early and heavy! Now we have snow squalls and ice," he said out loud to the radio. "Don't forget the ice, Diego," Charles told the radio announcer,

4

whom he often ran into at Sunflower Farmers Market in the evening. The ice was why Charles couldn't do his morning runs any more before opening his contemporary art gallery, and this winter he couldn't afford a gym membership either.

He knew the forecast meant he might as well have not even shown up to open this morning. The frigid weather would insure no traffic and zero money today, once again. Tourists rarely ventured off the money-making Santa Fe Plaza when the cold winds blew, and if they did they would only walk up half of Canyon Road, never finding his little gallery, Bloom's, which was just past the critical halfway point. He was having his worst winter in the over-twenty years since he had launched Bloom's.

Doing the math in his head, Bloom started his countdown to survival. "OK, I've got five months of minimal sales. I've still got a few good pieces and my bank note won't come due for six. I can turn this puppy around. I just have to focus on selling, not the fact that I'm in fairly serious trouble. Sell, sell, sell." Bloom was an optimist at heart and was giving himself a pep talk, trying to prepare for the bleak day's prospects.

Bloom's was located on Canyon Road, one of the great historic streets in America, designated as a must-see by all the television travel shows. The address was important (and expensive), but unfortunately Bloom's was not exactly located on the main road. It was hidden down a small alleyway in an old re-done adobe. The original owner who had made it into a gallery started in the fifties: Agnes Sims, a hard-driven artist who also dabbled (quite successfully) in real-estate sales.

The little adobe structure had been modified numerous times by unknown Hispanic residents, each of whom had added their own little rooms before Sims took possession. A real-estate agent would now describe the gallery as Santa Fe funk—charming with an exceptionally odd layout and unbearably cold in the winter. The worn, wooden ponderosa pine floors squeaked with the slightest foot pressure so no alarms were necessary to alert when a potential client came through the doors. The ceilings were dreadfully low for contemporary art, which always shows best in large, open spaces with lots of room between paintings. The luxury of space in a Santa Fe gallery meant you had plenty of capital, not something the Bloom

Corporation enjoyed, but for Charles Bloom the space worked. The thought that the wooden planks underneath his feet had been worn by generations of retailers—first apple buyers, then artists, now him, was a comforting connection from past to present. And he loved his small wood-burning fireplace; the warm fires in the small shop made it feel less like a retail operation and more like a reflective nook.

Bloom had decided early on to specialize in contemporary Native American art. Not the traditional squash blossoms, silver jewelry, and black two-toned pottery, but modern Native American art. This set Bloom apart from all his competitors, which is important when you have 200 galleries all vying for a piece of the art-sales pie.

Very few Native artists truly were modern, for most of their roots in painting and sculpture were steeped in a realistic tradition, not abstraction, and their artwork reflected this. Bloom determined that Indians, as they are called in Santa Fe (Native Americans refer to themselves in this fashion, as do others) celebrated their heritage in almost all things they produced. Most had a difficult time straying very far away from their ancestral bonds.

Bloom had discovered early in his career if he tried to handle strictly modern paintings and sculpture with no hint of realism he would starve. The limits of what Bloom considered modern were therefore slightly broadened. His favorite artwork was complete abstraction, but Bloom's also carried a few artists that tended toward realism and social commentary.

Specializing in only Native artists allowed Bloom to represent the big names in the world of modern Native art, something that would never had happened if he hadn't found such a focused niche. Being one-sixteenth Cherokee himself somehow gave Bloom a bond with his artists, even if it was more mental than physical. Bloom's art was reasonable in price for the most part, starting around $1,000 and topping out at $75K.

Like so often during quiet times, Bloom's thoughts circled back to the contemporary Native artist Willard Yellowhorse, whom he had represented for five years in the early nineties, and had helped turn into an art superstar. In those days, Bloom's was a must-see destination by serious art buyers, and he and Willard had made terrific money. Charles had considered looking for that ideal spot on

Canyon Road itself, one of the few with high ceilings. But he and Willard had built their careers together in this old adobe, Willard so often sitting on an old wooden chair he pulled up by the fireplace, lost in his own thoughts.

Bloom had discovered Willard Yellowhorse at Indian Market during the third week in August over twenty years ago. Willard's work stood out from his peers' in a way Bloom had never witnessed before. Paintings with unique abstract designs and symbolism intertwined, primary colors using odd combinations that only Willard could make work. Natural elements were often woven into his large canvases: dirt, grass, insects, and even occasional animal scat. Yellowhorse told Bloom his inspiration came from his roots as a Diné, the religious sand paintings that his medicine-man grandfather made, and the weavings of his maternal grandmother. Yellowhorse would never elaborate on the designs other than to say, "You can be sure they are important to the Diné, but you are free to interpret them as you see fit. I don't want my Indian beliefs to influence the viewer." Nothing more or less, let the viewer decide.

The judges at Indian Market did decide: they did not get the importance of Yellowhorse's work and dismissed it as "not good," "not pretty," and "definitely not Indian," as Bloom heard one judge tell a fellow judge during the annual opening.

Indian Market for Willard Yellowhorse was no awards and no sales, but the Indian painter found a true believer in the young Charles Bloom. Bloom *got* Yellowhorse. They bonded immediately.

Bloom offered a prime spot to the young Yellowhorse in his gallery. He promised the then-unknown artist the main wall in his front room. This was the area that was usually dedicated to the dead guys, who brought the real money and paid the rent. For Bloom to give up the space to a virtually unknown artist was shocking to say the least. It was a gut response, one you can't explain, you just know. Very risky, though. If the clients never got past the front room because they didn't like Yellowhorse's work, they would never see Bloom's expensive dead guys—his bread and butter—just around the corner in the Santa Fe funk part of his gallery.

It was a simple arrangement. Bloom would promote Yellowhorse, pay for his entire advertising, do an annual show around Indian

Market-time in August, and they would split all the profits. Bloom would have an exclusive arrangement in the West, but Willard could have other gallery representation east of the Mississippi. Quite frankly, Bloom really didn't worry about losing him to an Eastern gallery. Those guys never got the so-called Indian Art, even if it was contemporary.

The arrangement worked well, and Charles and Willard had both flourished and the money had rolled in after only a couple of years. No more Indian Market booth on the street for Willard Yellowhorse, who could rely on gallery sales instead.

The thought of Willard on this cold, unproductive February day made Charles incredibly sad. Charles remembered how they had developed their careers together, how Willard had introduced him to other Indian artists and how Charles had given Willard feedback on which of his painting series were most popular—had encouraged him to do series, for that matter. Bloom's had become an impromptu gathering spot for Willard and his Indian artist friends. The notoriety and money Bloom's had received was especially important for Bloom, who had risked his entire savings on this gallery.

Charles' eyes teared up at the thought of the now-dead Yellowhorse. He wondered to himself as he had countless times before, "Why would he kill himself? I still don't get it. He was full of life. And he never left a suicide note, just that short statement, `My greatest and last artwork, STRUGGLE. All arrangements of my death to be handled by my dealer.'" Willard Yellowhorse's last horrific art project and the note's final statement about "my dealer" hurt Bloom the most, as he was no longer Willard's dealer. That honor went to a big-time gallery owner in New York who had the exclusive rights to all of Yellowhorse's work.

Charles had been thinking of Willard's last artwork ever since he read it was about to come up for the first time in 15 years at the spring sale at Sotheby's, its estimate $2.5 million to $5 million dollars. As shocking as that number was, it was even more amazing that none of the proceeds would go to Yellowhorse's family, but all to his New York City dealer who owned the copyrights for Willard's work, including the last very disturbing piece, STRUGGLE.

Willard Yellowhorse's prices had skyrocketed after his premature death 15 years ago. A recent auction had brought $1.5 million for a nice but not terribly large Yellowhorse. The death piece, as it was now referred to, was considered to be a masterpiece. As far as Bloom was concerned, it was hype and not true Willard. It had none of the soul of his early pieces. This piece was almost calculated, even though that was impossible due to the unusual circumstances in which it was produced.

Willard Yellowhorse had been stolen from Bloom's gallery after being heavily recruited by a premiere Eastern gallery, leaving Bloom's stable of artists two years before his death. Willard had moved to New York City to become an artist in one of those "serious galleries," as Yellowhorse had called his new gallery. Finally New York City *got* an Indian artist and it had killed him off. At least that was how Bloom saw things.

New York had changed Willard Yellowhorse. No more Friday night art-walk openings in the summer in Santa Fe with his pals. His openings were productions in Chelsea, impressive displays by invitation with many of the rich and famous making their tributes to the Indian wunderkind.

Yellowhorse's new gallery, The Cutting Edge, had cut its teeth by handling edgy works in the late eighties and early nineties. It had started handling Warhol's work shortly before his death. The timing couldn't have been better. It had acquired a sizable portion of Warhol's work and made a killing after he died. At the time the consensus by Cutting Edge's competitors was the gallery had overpaid on a prolific artist whose prime had passed, but in retrospect it was truly genius.

The Cutting Edge pushed Yellowhorse not only to produce more work, but also work much more extreme in its nature. No longer was it good enough to just make a piece of art, it also had to be some sort of performance piece as well. The gallery owner bought all of Yellowhorse's paintings outright at huge money—nearly retail—a rare thing in the art world. Almost all art is given to galleries on consignment and the gallery acts as the agent for the artist and makes anywhere between 50 percent on a young artist to 30 percent on a very well established one. Rarely did a gallery buy all the artwork an artist produced, especially not at prices close to retail.

This aggressive maneuver pretty much eliminated any other galleries from even thinking of trying to poach the artist.

The Cutting Edge had raised Yellowhorse's prices aggressively and had used this as the carrot for the artist to dump Bloom's gallery. Bloom could still hear Willard's words: "Charles, you need to buy my artwork outright. I'll still give you wholesale prices, much less than what I can get in New York City. I like you very much and you helped me get started. You're like family. But it's hard for me to pass up 100 percent sure sales to my New York gallery, especially when they want to raise my prices substantially."

This was of course the kiss of death for Bloom's. No way to purchase Willard's art at high prices and then hope to resell it in Santa Fe. Charles was amazed at the prices The Cutting Edge would pay for paintings and then just sit on the inventory, letting out only a few pieces at a time or none at all. Anyone trying to buy a Yellowhorse at auction had to contend with the owner of The Cutting Edge, who fiercely protected the price structure of Willard Yellowhorse's paintings. When they would occasionally come up at auction, The Cutting Edge would aggressively pursue each piece, including the minor ones. If you wanted a Yellowhorse painting, it was clear you would have to either go through his New York galley or pay dearly if you didn't. Charles had tried on several occasions to buy pieces for clients at auction, flying out to New York, looking at the painting and making recommendations regarding a fair price to pay for the Yellowhorse. Each time he was embarrassed when the pieces sold for double his recommended price.

The last time after being miserably shut out, the client blurted out, "Next time I'll deal with The Cutting Edge, they are obviously the market maker in Yellowhorse."

"That was then and this is now," Charles said to himself with a sigh, his voice the only one heard in his gallery for weeks. "I have to pay my rent, and I don't own any Willard Yellowhorses anymore, except a small piece he did for me, and it's not for sale, at least not yet." This was the first time he had contemplated selling his prized possession and it sent a shiver down his spine as he realized his serious predicament.

CHAPTER 2

HEADHUNTERS

Surviving February and losing five pounds, Charles hoped March would bring springtime. It didn't. At six-one, Charles Bloom usually weighed 195. He had a head of brown full, thick hair, green eyes, and sharp features. Unfortunately, his new leaner physique was secondary to a mixture of poor calorie/nutrient intake, lack of monetary funds, and mild depression. Cutting out fast food to save on money has a funny way of helping to keep one trim. The ironic thought of losing weight from mild starvation made Bloom consider writing his first art book, *The Art Dealer's Diet: How To Lose Weight Without Trying*. Main ingredient: no retail sales. It's just that easy. The thought should have made Charles laugh, but there were still four months to go before the July opera season and he doubted his book would make Oprah's book list before then.

March looked grimmer than last month if that was possible. The snow had rarely come to the Santa Fe Ski Basin, only a thin sheet of continuous ice. Even his favorite chile peddler from Chimayo hadn't ventured by the gallery as everyone was staying off the roads, which were coated with black ice. A large ever-growing icicle was draped along one corner of Charles' pitched-roof gallery. Charles knew it was a real danger if it fell when someone happened to be near the massive ice block, which was growing like a steroid-induced stalactite of frozen water. But it wasn't like customers were flocking to his door. Charles' inquisitive nature just loved to see the ice sculpture mature. So every day he watched the progress, wondering if the ice extremity would fully extend to the frozen ground or if Mother Nature would have its way and destroy the only visitor Charles seemed to have these days.

Finally, on a rare sunny day with the afternoon temperature hovering around freezing, the answer came. Two white-necked ravens had landed on the top of the roof and were helping themselves to a little drink of the thawing water, when a huge crash broke the calm of the day. The smashing sound of the ice breaking into a thousand pieces on the frozen ground below and the two screaming birds whose own lives had been startled echoed down the empty Canyon Road side street. Charles wondered if anyone even heard the huge noise, or if all the art gallery owners were in Arizona for an early spring break.

Normally, Charles loved Canyon Road. Santa Fe's legendary art lane was like Facebook on mezcal, with its odd connections formed by artists, collectors, locals, gallery owners, and tourists all with one thing in common: a deep appreciation for art and creativity. But this March it was still bone-chilling cold and activity on Canyon Road had largely ceased. No artist would ever send new artwork to a city in hibernation. The narrow street leading into the entrance of Bloom's was icy with a permanent slickness that never seemed to relent no matter how much salt was applied. Charles' 15-year-old Mercedes had started rusting badly this year, and was the only thing the salt seemed to have worked on. The Mercedes was the last remnant of glory days gone by, when Bloom's represented the premiere modern Native artist west of the Mississippi. Looking at his old car just reminded Bloom of how far his business had tanked.

The one sliver of good news was that the fall green chile crop had been a banner one. No shortage of fresh cheap chile. That was actually excellent news for Bloom, who loved fresh chile in everything he cooked, especially the variety from Chimayo, a small town north of Santa Fe. Chimayo was better known for its weavings and famous church, El Santuario de Chimayo with its healing dirt, than its chiles. Chimayo green chiles have a very distinctive flavor that is absorbed from the sacred thick brownish-red dirt they grow in. They are particularly hot, christened by the locals as "tourist killers." Having grown up in New Mexico and lived in Santa Fe for so long, Bloom had become accustomed to the extreme heat found in Chimayo green chile, not the mild stuff out of Albuquerque or Hatch. For a white kid, he could hang with his toughest Hispanic friends when it came to eating ass-burning green chiles.

The thought of the unique aroma of roasting fresh chile made Bloom's mouth start to water, but even cheap fresh green chile was a luxury. It wasn't that Charles Bloom was poor. It was that all his money was tied up in the form of art. Not a particularly liquid asset unless you want to blow the inventory out, so you waited. In March, you waited a lot.

The winter routine for the gallery was unchanging. First order of business: get a fire going to keep electric and gas usage to a minimum. After the old adobe gallery was warm enough to function, emails were answered, and new ones sent out to potential clients. Charles Bloom's limited inventory of dead artists and the few fairly new paintings had been sent to every possible name in his database, so email time was now more surfing the web and checking the weather channel on canyonroadarts.com.

Noon was a quick phone call to his best friend, Brad Shriver. Charles and Brad had met at a Santa Fe Gallery Association meeting, when Brad was new in town. Charles had given Brad plenty of advice over the years about Santa Fe's best realtors and restaurants and magazines in which to advertise. Upon opening his Upper Deck Gallery on the downtown Plaza, overlooking the Palace of the Governors, Brad had become Charles's barometer of tourist action.

The Palace of the Governors is the longest-occupied government building in the United States, since 1610. It's a huge adobe building prominently positioned on the north side of the historic Plaza, and it's where all the territorial governors made their residence. The country of occupation changed every 100 years or so. First it was the Spain, then Mexico, and finally the United States, but all kept the same central building as their home office.

The Palace of the Governors has a huge overhanging roof, or portal, which is used as a shelter for the Native American artist vendors allowed to participate in a daily outdoor arts and crafts show there. To get one of the coveted spots under the Governor's portal, you first had to be a New Mexico Pueblo Indian and secondarily you had to basically inherit the position, not be some one-sixteenth Cherokee whose family had only been in New Mexico for 60 years. These Indians had been around New Mexico for 1,000 years. No spot for the Bloom lineage ever, unless he managed to marry one of the vendors. These individuals looked like real Indians and the tourists ate it up.

The Indians often would dress in traditional clothing and turquoise jewelry, bundled in colorful Pendleton blankets with their backs against the building's warm south-facing wall. On a cold day the Native vendors would all huddle together. For most of the Indians under the portal, this is where their life played out. First it would be as a young child not ready for school, sitting next to a parent trying to make a living, dressed identically in traditional clothing and jewelry. Once in school, it was a summer job helping the family. Now those same children were adults with their own children following in the ancestral footsteps, taking travelers checks from the Japanese.

Watching the tourists negotiate with the Indians for their wares never got old for Bloom. When business was good, Bloom would go to lunch with Brad at the Plaza Café, getting a good window seat to watch the Indian opera. The tourists always seemed to flow the same way, east to west. There was no reason, no signs saying "go this way," but it was always the same. They moved like the sun. Many of the tourists were from other countries and loved to take photos and negotiate with the best negotiators in the world. The tourists always felt they had taken advantage of the poor Indians, but in reality many of the Indians drove better cars than their clients did.

Today's phone report from the Upper Deck Gallery was fairly bad. Just a few overweight European-looking tourists, probably Germans (they loved the West).

"Sorry Charles, just a few stragglers passing through. Be thankful you don't have my rent to pay. Why don't you just shut down for a couple of weeks and take a break. Now's the time, you won't be losing any business."

Charles pondered the option. "I'm just burning through the last of my capital staying open. Maybe I should. If I took off, would you want a nice Scholder painting and a decent Cannon woodblock for a month? See if you can have better luck in your overpriced Park Avenue gallery?"

"Sure thing," Brad quickly agreed. "Is it the Scholder with the large, dark, brooding purple Indian from the late seventies, with the shitty frame?"

"Yep, that's it. Not sure why it hasn't sold, it's a great piece and the seventies were an excellent time period for his work. It's probably the frame. I wish I had the money to put on a frame worthy of its price tag. I've got $68K on it. We could split over my cost, which was $35K. That would give you plenty of room. The Cannon is the one with the Indian sitting in the living room. It's got a small tear on one side, but I had it conserved back when I had a little money and you can't see the repair hidden under the mat. It's worth about $12K and I've only got $2K in it. We could split anything over $6K. You unfortunately would still have to sit here in frozen land hoping for a live one and continuing to waste your electricity."

"Hey, I never turn down free quality inventory. Let me know when you want to come over and I'll clear a wall. Any problem if I were to put them on my website?"

"That's fine. I could take them off my site. I would be shocked if anyone has visited that site in a month, unless it's the other galleries checking to see if I have finally gone out of business and wanting to poach my gallery's Canyon Road address."

"Charles, you've got the retail blues. I get them sometimes, especially when your dick clients offer you less then what you paid for a piece and you start thinking about taking it. Speaking of offering you less than what you want for something, you don't happen to have any Yellowhorse pieces stuck away? I have a serious buyer who just wants an example for his marginal collection, headhunter-type guy and it's pretty much a sure deal."

Charles knew all about headhunters. Headhunting is when a collector buys paintings for the signature on the piece, not for the art. These individuals are not serious art connoisseurs, even though they can spend a lot of money. Usually a headhunter would fill his own order at some second-rate auction in which a dealer dumped a crappy picture by a good-named artist. The collector is proud he has such a great artist in his collection and the dealer can't believe he got so much for the piece. But due to his premature death, even a marginal Yellowhorse would still bring a ton at auction so it was hard for any collector to fill his need for mediocrity.

"Sorry, Brad. I haven't had any of Willard's work since before his death. I have one little painting left, but it was done for me so I'm hanging on to it. You know I really liked him and would never be able to replace it."

"Yeah, I know. He was just a terrific artist. What a shame he died so young, barely 30 if I remember right. How about that dick dealer who stole him from you in New York City? Any chance he's got anything squirreled away?"

"I don't talk to him, but my understanding is he ran out a few years ago except for the infamous death piece he's selling at Sotheby's contemporary sale in May. Everything now is just what comes on the secondary market or auction. I could make a call or two and see if I can break something loose from one of my old clients. Your collector is a sure thing? I would hate to burn one of my few remaining clients who still have a Yellowhorse I sold them. You can understand my hesitancy on a maybe sale?"

"Yep," Brad assured, "this guy's a classic headhunter. Could give a shit about what it looks like. It just has to be signed and real. He probably maxes out around $50K."

"Won't get much of a piece at today's prices, you realize that?"

"Yeah, I know Yellowhorse has gone through the roof. Sorry I didn't get a piece when he was still showing with you. You kept telling me I was missing the boat. Same old thing, seemed like there would be time enough to get one later and I knew his only dealer well."

"I know the feeling, Brad, I didn't put any away other than the one he gave me. Who could have predicted Willard Yellowhorse would have dumped me and then offed himself? I never saw that coming. It still seems unbelievable. It always was fishy to me. That last so-called

16

piece STRUGGLE is nothing more than a morose artifact of Willard's death."

"Yeah, pretty trippy the way he killed himself. Insured him a place in the art-history books though. You going to New York to watch the big boy sell?"

"I doubt I'll have the cash. New York is so damn expensive and the only way is if one of my clients wants me to bid on it or my Scholder sells. I got one client, a multimillionaire, who called and I told him I would be happy to go for him, preview the painting, but he just wanted a free over-the-phone assessment. I told him it would probably be a very good investment but in my opinion very bad karma. Something was wrong mentally when Willard made that piece. It was just not a Yellowhorse in the truest sense. My client thought I was full of shit and told me in a condescending voice that karma was for fools, not businessmen. All he cared about was what it was going to be worth in five years." Talking about Willard's death made Charles even more upset. "This collector is your worse nightmare! He buys a painting from some dealer or little auction, then gets worried he overpaid, or the piece wasn't right, and the phone calls and emails start with images of his latest find. God help you if he gets an answer he didn't want to hear, like he overpaid for the piece. Then he wants to know who the expert in the field is. Anytime a Yellowhorse came up for sale at auction he always called and grilled me about the piece. After the auction, if it sold for too much or less than what I thought, I would get another call, 'Why don't you know your own market?'"

"Bloom, that Mr. Dick Head client probably won't be paying your meal ticket to the big city. Don't you know as a dealer you are supposed to kiss ass and tell the guy what he wants to hear even if it's bullshit? Then charge him to go to the auction, stay in a great hotel, eat at expensive restaurants, and bid the damn piece up so he has to pay more for it then he should have!"

Bloom sighed, "We are getting cynical—and only in our forties."

"You're right, this fucked-up winter has me on edge too and if a live one comes in here, he's toast. So come over here with your secondary shit, and get out of town for a few weeks! Hey, good news, a bus load of Orientals, probably Japanese, just got dropped off in front of the Plaza. Maybe I'll go down and see if I can round them up. Get that Scholder over here now!" Brad hung up.

Charles' first thought was maybe he should run the damn paintings over there right now. Might get lucky. The yen was high against the dollar these days. But Charles Bloom was a responsible man who always looked for the good in others, and he was going to take his time making any big changes.

CHAPTER 3

A DECISION IS MADE

Grateful to have the chance of a sale, Charles Bloom spent the next three days calling every client to whom he had ever sold a Yellowhorse. Surely one would want to let go of something, which would mean a payday for the client, for Charles, and for Brad. The first client he called said, "Can you get me another one as good or better if I sell this one? You know he's not making any more." Yes, Charles certainly knew that.

The next nine conversations went something like this:

"Hi, this is Charles Bloom. I was wondering if you want to sell that Yellowhorse piece I sold you. I've got a buyer looking for one."

"I'm afraid not, I love my piece. I'm so happy you made me buy it. You said I wouldn't regret it and I haven't."

Charles then would respond: "Yes, I love his work as well, but Willard's pieces are very valuable now so you will do extremely well. Twenty times on your money, at least."

"No thanks," was the answer from the first 10.

And then Charles got lucky. Number 11 was a good client who had bought lots of work over the last 20 years but was getting up in age. All the pieces he had collected could be described as average. Most were minor works but some were from good artists. It was a collection that would never be important, but would be sellable in a good economy. Unfortunately, this was not that time. It was a recession and off-season, but the Yellowhorse was always sellable.

This particular Yellowhorse was a nice drawing. Decent size at 16 X 20 inches and fully signed. He had done it 18 years ago. The paintings that have the entire Yellowhorse name on the piece were determined to be of more value. Often on drawings Willard would simple put his initials W.Y., which collectors took to mean Yellowhorse thought the piece was less important, thus not fully signed. The truth was he often forgot to sign pieces, especially drawings, and when this occurred he generally just put W.Y. as he was in a hurry. Charles knew this for a fact as Willard had once said as much when Bloom caught that he had forgotten to sign something. Drawings brought relatively little during his early career, so who cared if it said W.Y. or Yellowhorse. The client had paid almost nothing for the drawing Bloom was hoping to pry out, but now it could be worth a month's hiatus to Bloom.

The image was a classic Yellowhorse: black background with lines in parallel, a hint of an animal in the background, most likely from some Diné mythology. Charles was sorry he hadn't asked Willard more questions about his work at the time, but it never seemed that important. And it was hard to get him to open up about his work. When he originally sold the drawing, Bloom was still getting plenty of pieces and he could sell anything and fast. He barely remembered the drawing. It had come in and gone out the same week. It was the preliminary drawing for a painting that ultimately was made quite large. Bloom was pretty sure the big painting was in a museum collection now. If right, he could get an additional 20% for the drawing, especially if it was one of those museums that had a recognizable name. Something with the word Modern in it or one of those unpronounceable names before the word Museum.

Bloom negotiated to sell the piece on consignment for a 15% commission, low by anyone's standards but he couldn't take a chance of not getting the piece. Once a client decides to sell something, even if you instigated the idea, the piece will be gone fast. Bloom was afraid the old client now seeing the value of the piece might shop it around and get an outright sale. Bloom couldn't afford to buy the drawing outright, but he could sell it and fast. This way everyone would profit. The drawing should fetch close to $30K even in a bad economy. This would give Brad enough room to make something with his headhunter client.

Bloom's client agreed to the deal. It didn't hurt that the original cost for the drawing was only $1,500. His profit would be well over $20,000. Bloom would make $4,500 and Brad could charge what he felt was fair to his client. Brad would be happy to get the piece and a quick sale.

Bloom's had never been closed for anything, especially not a vacation. The thought of not going to work was hard to imagine for Charles but also thrilling. The cash he would receive from the sale of the Yellowhorse would give him enough to live on for a month and pay all his bills.

The more he thought about a hiatus, the more he liked the idea. Emails could be checked remotely, if there were any, and since Charles had no girlfriend or pets there was nothing really keeping him from leaving. Keep the heat barely on so the pipes don't freeze, lock the doors, and put a sign up that says, "By appointment or chance." Put his cell number on it and go somewhere. But where?

Calling all those Yellowhorse clients had brought up repressed feelings. Something was still gnawing at Bloom about Willard's death. The concept of bad karma had been eating at him for more than a decade. There *was* bad karma, he knew it. Or maybe his Santa Fe sensibilities were kicking in. Santa Fe is known for attracting those who believe in other lives and karma. After all, it is home to Shirley MacLaine. But in his gut, Bloom knew there *was* something wrong about Willard's death. It just didn't fit the man he had once known and called a friend.

Charles started a conversation with himself, not caring that he was talking out loud. "That death painting seemed staged, not Willard's work. I just don't believe he would kill himself to make some monumental historic art piece. And why in the world would he let a New York dealer who could care less about a Native artist handle his estate, much less his burial? It just doesn't make sense. He came from a traditional Navajo family, for God's sake." Bloom's vocalization of his unresolved issues made him shiver even more acutely then the five-degree mid-day Santa Fe temperature outside. Karma. *Chindi*. Whatever you wanted to call it, it was blowing through Bloom like an icy wind.

The Navajo talk very little about death, burying their dead quickly. But Bloom knew there were definite rituals surrounding death. If those rituals were ignored, there would be repercussions to the family and entire social order. Things would be out of harmony. Yellowhorse knew this even better. No way would Yellowhorse disregard these most serious of traditions, leaving his body to some Anglo wheeler-dealer New York gallery owner who knew nothing of life in Navajoland. If the Navajo death rituals are not observed, the Navajo believe that the deceased can return to their former dwelling in spirit form, haunting the living. The way Bloom had heard it, the rituals were very specific. Didn't they call for men to wash and dress the corpse? Hadn't he heard that if a person expires in their home on the rez, the home must be abandoned or destroyed?

Bloom had vowed to forget about Yellowhorse years ago, but he never really had. His connection with Yellowhorse had been stronger than any bond that he had ever had with any of his other artists. Maybe it was time to find out why. Maybe there was a reason for that connection, and it hadn't ended with Willard's death. Bloom couldn't repress his inner voice any longer. Willard had had an innate gift, Charles had been the first art dealer to know it, and now Charles knew that STRUGGLE was just not the lasting legacy by which Willard would have wanted the world to remember him.

Charles locked up his gallery, having finally made a decision, one he should have made years ago. He made a quick visit to Brad Shriver with his meager inventory in tow and watched as Shriver hung them on a prominent gallery wall. Somehow they looked more important hanging on the high eggshell-white walls of the Upper Deck Gallery. Maybe Charles would get lucky and have someone else sell something for him. A great thought, but probably unlikely. Still, Charles optimistically left Brad three bank deposit slips, one for the Yellowhorse drawing and one for each of the artworks he had left, just in case they did sell.

Back at his own gallery, Charles resolved not to look at this winter's lack of sales as an omen of doom, nor even as a let-down of the artists who still believed in him enough to show with him. No, it was simply a reaction to the freakishly cold, dry spell. As Willard used to say, Mother Nature will have its way. Well Charles Bloom was going to have his way, too.

Charles placed his little hand-printed sign telling of his new office hours into the cracked multi-pane historic front glass window, and poured a little extra salt on the front porch so nobody would slip—if anybody ever came. He then turned to his old beat-up Mercedes and yelled out to the world, "Time to make that trip to the rez!" The two ravens that had set up residence in the last remaining piñon tree on the property cackled back at him in raven, "Good luck but we'll miss your Ramen leftovers."

Charles Bloom had always wanted to meet Willard's family and see their world in winter. The rez was dirt cheap by Santa Fe standards. His $4,500 would go a long way. He kicked each worn tire on his 15-year-old gray Mercedes which had a chameleon-like appearance due to the peeling protective paint sealant, and decided he would leave tomorrow morning for Gallup, three hours away from the city lights of Santa Fe. It was time to resolve some unanswered questions.

CHAPTER 4

MAKING A DOCTOR

Fredrick Alexander Marsh III was born in 1957 to a well-to-do doctor's family in Brooklyn, NY, an only child. The last two Fredrick Marshes had been well-respected surgeons. It was a given that Fredrick Marsh III would follow in the family footsteps regardless if young Fredrick had other dreams.

Fredrick's father, Dr. Marsh II, was a tall man who spoke quickly and had little patience for his son. Time was money and he made his money cutting bodies so he was never home. The hospital was his castle. This, as it turned out, was fine by young Fredrick, as he hated the smell of his father's clothes almost as much as he hated his father. A sickening antiseptic odor seemed to adhere to anything that came in close contact. If his father would hug his son, which was rare, Fredrick would smell of the sickening residue for hours.

Dr. Marsh simply told his son he was to be a surgeon so he better get used to the smell and study hard, otherwise his life would be for shit. Young Fredrick always wondered why anyone would want to be a doctor. He never saw his father and when he did, he always seemed to have a tall vodka in his hand and be angry. Fredrick monitored his father's drinking habits closely. One drink and you could still safely talk to Dr. Marsh. This didn't last long, as number two came quickly. This was the point where you stayed out of the way and didn't speak unless spoken to. Three drinks usually meant trouble and you hid in your room. Four beverages, or three very tall ones without ice, and the whole family was in peril.

Young Fredrick Marsh III didn't like to think about one night when his father had definitely had four drinks. Dr. Marsh was stumbling about the house looking for his son. Time to have a man-to-man talk, learn how to stand up to bullies. Fredrick knew all too well about bullies and it started at home.

Fredrick was young but very intelligent. He sought refuge in the one place his father wouldn't look for him: his own home office. When Marsh senior couldn't ferret out his son by screaming, "Come out and be a man," he turned his attention to a different prey, an easier target... Mrs. Marsh.

Catapulting her on top of his office desk as if she were a corpse thrown onto a cold metal slab in the hospital basement, Dr. Marsh aggressively began his sadistic patient evaluation: a four-drink special examination. Or as Fredrick referred to them later on, a Smirnoff Surprise.

Mrs. Marsh had regrettably played doctor before with her husband and knew better than to scream. She grabbed the nearest thing she could to bite down on to help ease the forthcoming pain, intent on keeping his rage to a minimum. In this case it was her son's teddy bear, lying in the office chair she was straddled over. She never realized her son was going to witness the brutal rape at the hands of a deranged alcoholic.

Fredrick was in a fetal ball lying behind the desk chair, which was starting to sway with each forceful thrust of his very visible father's hips. Fredrick focused intently on one of the many medical posters of humans in various stages of dissection that his father so proudly displayed on the office wall. The anatomical depictions kept Fredrick's mind distracted so he never fully heard the live pounding flesh just a foot from his head. Muffled screams of pain and his father's groaning seemed to disappear as if in a human vapor as the graphic anatomy charts became all-encompassing in the boy's subconscious.

It wasn't until the pounding sound stopped overhead and a bloody semen-soaked teddy, now a cleaning rag for his father, was discarded back to earth, that Fredrick came out of his self-induced trance. Seeing his crumpled bear on the floor directly in front of him broke his spell and like a baby gazelle sensing a moment of escape from a lion's mouth, he quietly scrambled out from underneath the table and chair, and slipped back to his bedroom, his odd-smelling teddy tightly in tow.

Once safely under his covers, Fredrick's hands, still noticeably shaking, somehow found the dexterity to take a pair of round-tipped scissors and cut off teddy's right arm. The amputation gave Fredrick access to peel off Teddy's outer covering like he would an orange's skin, discarding the multicolored fur forever. Like Fredrick, a new teddy emerged that night, one with clean, cream-colored fabric but dangerous to the touch, sharp feathers poking out. No more bear eyes, no more smiling mouth. Fredrick hugged his bear tightly, oblivious.

In his daytime existence, Fredrick's conscious love was art. He liked to draw and felt he was good, especially as his mother told him he was gifted in this respect, although her advice was he should follow his father's wishes and not think too seriously about art as a career.

Fredrick never inherited his father's statuesque genes. Instead he got his mother's Ukrainian traits: short, stout, with oversized Popeye calves. At 16, Fredrick had reached his adult height of five-foot-six. His black curly hair never seemed to fill in completely and started receding just as puberty finished. His dark black eyes were magnified by the thick glasses he wore to correct his severe myopia. The pupils looked like puddles of mud against his blanched white skin.

High school for Fredrick Marsh was like a prison. He hated everyone except his art teacher, whom he would ask for endless tips on drawing and becoming an artist. Mr. Wells, an older man with a noticeable lisp, encouraged young Marsh. Wells promised, "Fredrick, if you really, really work hard, I'm sure you could be famous someday." Fredrick loved hearing this from the old, odd man who could recognize Fredrick's dream of becoming a famous artist. Fredrick studied and doodled. His notebooks were filled with images of the human torso in grotesque forms. Often he would take the human anatomy and add a face of a particularly hated person to its body. The face would be in detail and drawn well enough to recognize the individual.

Good grades came easily for Marsh, but as hard as he tried to perfect his artwork, he never seemed to get to the level he could see in others' work.

When his high school had an art contest his senior year, Fredrick worked for two months on a gigantic canvas of skinned humans embracing. It was his masterpiece. Fredrick finally felt he had conquered the art of drawing. The hours of practice seemed to be finally paying off.

On the day the winners were announced, Fredrick's name was missing. The trauma of not even getting an honorable mention damaged Fredrick Marsh III's self-image permanently. He had assumed he would get recognition. After all, he was "gifted." His mother had told him as much. And Mr. Wells was one of the judges. He couldn't look at Wells the rest of the year as the thought of his betrayal made him seethe with anger. "I am a great artist. The world is not ready for me yet. They will be someday," Fredrick pronounced to the mirror.

Getting out of Brooklyn was all Fredrick cared about. His acceptance letter to Boston College was his ticket out. Boston was colder than Brooklyn, but it still had great art museums. There were two factors that had determined his college selection. One, it was away from his family. Two, the city had great art. A city with an exceptional cultural matrix was critical to nurture Fredrick's artistic aspirations. The university also had to be acceptable to his father's standards and Boston College would suffice. It wasn't Harvard, his father's first choice, but close enough. Boston had great medical schools and this was a good stepping-stone. Fredrick figured he could do a couple of years in the pre-med track, then make the break to the art department. He needed the time to build up his courage or hope his father died of cirrhosis. He hoped the latter came first. Fredrick just had to wrap up high school, and he'd be free.

CHAPTER 5

BLOOD AND GUTS, RAH, RAH, RAH

For most seniors, the end of high school is a time of exhilaration, reflection, and some sadness. Adult goals, careers to be discovered, new lovers, and friends that will never be again. It's the end of life without responsibility, the final chapter of childhood. These are the normal feelings of the high school graduate.

Not for Fredrick Marsh. Graduation only meant escaping the daily humiliation of seeing Wells—"The bastard traitor who told me I was to be great, then stabbed me in my back." Senior year offered no friends to say goodbye to, no teacher to miss. No notes in the yearbook or prom-dance parties. Dating was exceptionally rare and sex was nonexistent. The only real things in Fredrick's life were the surgical photos he had started to accumulate and use as models to improve his drawing. His father actually encouraged his son's fascination with gross human anatomy as he thought this would help him in the quest to become a great surgeon. If Dr Marsh understood how deep his son's obsession ran, he would have sought therapy for him instead.

After Fredrick had been accepted into a good university, Dr. Marsh decided he would let Fredrick accompany him to the surgical theater. "Time to become a physician," his father announced to his socially immature son. The operating suite was theater to Fredrick. Though he hated surgery, the thought of humans being dissected alive was fascinating.

The surgical theater was a small, gray-colored room with sterile white tiles. Stainless steel furniture perched above the operating suite as if it were an ultra-contemporary home. It was the same feeling an owl must have on top of a pole looking at its prey. A feeling of power. The area was designed so medical students and residents could watch live surgeries without having to be sterilely gowned or get in the way, yet still get practical experience. By all rights Fredrick should not have been allowed, but he was the great Dr. Marsh's son, so he got a pass.

The actual process of scrubbing in to participate in a surgery is laborious. The most important aspect is becoming sterile before ever entering the surgical room. Each doctor and nurse has to be covered head to toe in a sterile gown, mask, hat, gloves, and shoes. Before rubber gloves are donned, a 10-minute finger-to-elbow scrub with a nauseous soap is mandatory. This smell becomes bonded with the surgeon's skin and was the same odor that made young Fredrick so sick to his stomach. It was his father's smell.

The surgical theater above the operating suite had none of the limitations or cumbrances of real surgery. Fredrick only had to watch his father, not listen to or smell him. He could watch as live human bodies were slowly dissected in front of his very eyes. Each patient represented another secret camera shot for his growing portfolio of human subjects: the basis for what he hoped would be his lifelong field of study as a painter, and help Fredrick achieve his dream of becoming famous.

Fredrick was surprised at how much he enjoyed seeing exposed human skin slowly sliced open with a shiny scalpel, then the nurse with her hot cautery needle zapping the small blood vessels as they squirted their precious bright-red liquid. The occasional gusher of highly aerated blood that would explode into the surgical field when a large artery was unintentionally severed. The frantic nurse's chaotic response, the cautery wand zapping wildly, and the wisps of blue-white smoke that occurred due to the obliteration of copious amounts of fresh, dying red blood cells called "a new pope."

After the initial skin layer had been breached, it exposed the underlying subcutaneous fat tissue, which Fredrick found beautiful. It would glisten like a fresh snow under the hot operating lights. Below the fat was a fascial sheath enveloping abdominal muscles. Finally, muscle. Deep red, beefy, with little striated lines of twitching fibers. When sliced, the meaty muscle parts simply separate, falling to each side, no different than cutting into a good rib-eye steak. With the muscle disposed of, the inner sanctum of the human body is revealed to be a deep, dark cavity, the soul of the body. Many would say that a human soul is one's brain or heart or even eyes, but for young Fredrick it was the organs that make us what we are.

To experience live, pulsating organs even from a distance for Fredrick was somehow sexually exciting. Fine steam would sometimes emerge off the organs in the cold surgical suite below, drifting upwards to the window. Fredrick would press his face against the glass to get as close to the drama below as he could, the human moisture collecting on the window like dew on a leaf in the early morning fog.

Fredrick liked to take his tongue and gently, secretly lick the operating viewing window as if it were a special lover, hoping those around him didn't notice his repeated tongue thrusts, his erect penis, or hear the faint sounds of his hard-pounding heart.

Afterwards, Fredrick would assemble the multiple images he took with his small box camera into different groupings to help him understand his subjects better. He was always nervous when he had them developed and told the processor of the film these were for his father's medical classes and to be very careful with them as they represented specific cases that could never be reproduced.

When a new set of the photos would arrive, Fredrick would run home inspecting each photograph for hours and play with himself as he had once seen his father do. But now Fredrick imagined he had the scalpel and was the doctor, the patients' lives in the balance. Fredrick often worried about his behavior. It seemed aberrant from others. Yet each additional package of photographs only added to his heightened climax. The worries faded away after time.

CHAPTER 6

BOSTON COLLEGE, CLASS OF '78

At Boston College, no one seemed to ever notice the small, balding college freshman that spent hours in the university medical library. For Fredrick, the library was a sanctuary, a place to draw his figures, which were so beautifully illustrated in the Netter Atlas of human anatomy. There were no personal computers yet, so to learn, one still had to haunt the library and leaf through paper books. Netter's illustrations were gorgeous, drawn in every detail, no blood vessel or nerve too insignificant, they were his bible. Fredrick would try to reproduce the essence of what he saw in the atlas in making his own radical images of skinned humans often intertwined in deep kisses or intercourse.

The senior Marsh had given his son, the surgeon-to-be, an ivory-handled surgical scalpel. The instrument was an antique from an 1860s Civil War surgical kit. Fredrick created vivid images in his mind of all the bodies the knife must have entered during its tumultuous career. He found by just stroking the blade's shiny surface he would become sexually aroused, which helped him immerse himself in his cadaver drawings.

Time passed quickly and soon the undergraduate became a senior at Boston College. Fredrick only had one art class in his first four years: Art Drawings I. The class was a disaster worse than with Wells. The second week of class, Fredrick shared some of his best drawings with his professor, an elderly, almost-deaf professor who had a distinctive Slavic accent.

Dr. Shawinski had taught at Boston College for nearly 50 years and obviously hated freshman art class but was stuck with it every two years. This was his year and his class was particularly obtuse. He had only seen one individual that even cared about the class, an odd-looking, partially bald student whose age was undeterminable: Fredrick.

The professor was shocked and slightly frightened by the portfolio of naked zombie people Fredrick shared with him. While well executed, their grossness was beyond description and physically bothered the old man. He sternly warned Fredrick never to show these to anyone and recommended Fredrick should probably get some psychological counseling. He did commend him on his artistic ability, but the perverted subject matter was inappropriate at any aesthetic level. Fredrick's line of thought should be immediately abandoned before it damaged him permanently. Dr. Shawinski considered reporting the disturbing imagery to the dean but felt his harsh admonishment would suffice. It wasn't like Fredrick was some maniacal murder; he was just misguided.

Fredrick was again crushed by a professor's cruel interpretation of his work. "Couldn't he see the beauty in the human form taken down to its most basic components? How can these individuals be allowed to teach, much less live, on the same planet as gifted artists that put their trust into their care?" Fredrick muttered.

The art class cemented Fredrick's course. He would never take an art class again or listen to any other person regarding his art other than his own inner voice. That voice would decide what was good or not. Marsh got his only B at Boston College in Art Drawings I in his senior year, his final humiliation by the so-called art world. Upon receiving his final grade at Boston College with its outlier grade of B in Art he was livid: "If this is what so-called art professionals do to aspiring artists then the world needs a different kind of person to make judgment, me! I will be the decider of who is good and not, and I'm great. The world will see, I will control my own destiny," he vowed.

Fredrick Marsh III easily got into Boston College Medical School. He despised the thought of becoming a doctor, but he could not face his father's wrath, and needed his money. Unfortunately his dad's health somehow was still good, in spite of his severe alcoholism.

The art world had not found Marsh and it seemed it might be a long road to success in his chosen field, so a few years of medical school would be in order before switching course. Anyhow, Marsh was excited about the thought of gross anatomy his freshman year. He would get to cut into human flesh, even if it was dead. He planned on using his abalone-handled scalpel. This was exciting and gave Marsh the idea for his first-ever job the summer before medical school.

Boston has the distinction of having the first cemetery in the country, Mount Auburn. The cemetery was founded in 1831. It was Boston's first tourism site and the inspiration for New York's Central

Park. The cemetery was named for the highest point of its seven hills, Mount Auburn. Many of Boston's greats were buried at the park, including Longfellow, Winslow Homer, and the founder of the Church of Christ, Mary Baker Eddy. The cemetery was also Boston's first art museum. The great sculptures and monoliths that arose to honor the wealthy became the cornerstone of art for the city. Museums didn't widely exist at this time so cemeteries became the art exhibits of the day.

Fredrick loved to wander through the stone graves and visit the great artists of the centuries. He wished he possessed x-ray vision to see through the mausoleums of stone to the bare bodies entombed within. Death had not taken away from their artistic greatness; in fact only through death was their place in history solidified. Loving the surroundings led to the thought that he would enjoy working on the grounds.

An older black man named Levin Day managed the landscaping and had for nearly 20 years. He was puzzled by the young white man who wished to clean gravestones, especially one who was obviously over-educated for a manual job that paid minimum wage. Fredrick's obvious excitement about working in the cemetery overrode Day's gut hesitance, and he gave Marsh a summer job of cleaning poison ivy that outlined graves, sweeping leaves, and removing dead flowers and sundry items left behind by visitors.

Fredrick found solace walking throughout the grounds with their numerous antique wooden bridges that connected the massive cemetery to the surrounding little hills that were referred to as mountains, seven in all. This was sacred ground to Fredrick. Ponds filled with mature plants and multi-colored fish dotted the landscape. Huge headstones were everywhere. Fredrick swept up carefully, gently arranging the climbing vines so as to support their growth. He loved to watch the pilgrimages that patrons made to various parts of the cemetery with flowers. Some were obviously relatives of the deceased, but many were just fans of famous people. Maybe these great individuals had been lonely in their lives too, and only in death had become so popular.

It was the fans that intrigued Fredrick the most. There was a steady stream of people to the round mausoleum that was the resting place of the Church of Christ founder. He would see people cry and hug, and become very emotional upon visiting the gravesite. This was comforting to Fredrick. The fact that people were remembered for deeds long after their deaths gave Fredrick hope he too might have a following some day as a famous painter, even though his genius might only be discovered years after his death. All Fredrick Marsh cared about was that he was able to produce a lifetime of art that got distributed to the great art collectors. These graves and their followers gave him hope. He planned to someday buy a plot in his new home and final resting place, Mount Auburn.

CHAPTER 7

MEDICAL SCHOOL WITH AN A IN ANATOMY CLASS

What medical school tries to do is stamp the life out of those who attend, especially in the first semester. The goal of the school is to make it so challenging so as to weed out any of those that don't have the stomach or stamina for extreme work. It accomplishes this by requiring massive reading and memorization of minute facts, especially with regards to human anatomy. For Fredrick, this was a fun review and not challenging at all.

He would spend extra time in the human anatomy lab for the enjoyment of cutting on real humans and examining them. His expertise was so impressive that the other lab groups requested his assistance in dissection and identification. For the first time in Fredrick's life, he felt a sense of accomplishment. He was somewhat liked, even if it was only to get his help. He finally started to develop social skills.

Fredrick slowly came out of his shell and began interacting with his fellow live human beings. The semester went fast. Sadly, before he knew it, he was back to being the nerdy guy who loved bodies. Yet the positive initial interaction had helped Fredrick develop a sense of self he never had before. He still hated the thought of ever practicing medicine as it would require real interaction with sick people, but for now medical school was fun.

The four-year grind of medical school is painful yet goes quickly, primarily due to the little free time one ever has. No time for anything other than studying and the occasional dinner on the town. Fredrick took what little time he had and continued to work on his drawing skills. The gross anatomy class had helped him develop a sense of dimension in his drawings he never had and for this reason he was glad he had attended medical school. But the last two years of school turned into torture, with daily rounds with doctors like his father, the antiseptic smell covering them all. Fredrick found himself scrubbing repetitively after rounds to remove any trace of the hospital smell that made him physically ill. The excess washing caused his arms to develop a lobster-like appearance, which he was forced to hide by always wearing a white medical jacket. The long sleeves trapped the antiseptic smell that only added to his mental angst. He looked and smelled like a doctor.

Fredrick realized it was only a matter of time before he had to drop out. He finally decided he would have to tell his father that he wasn't going to continue on, when what Fredrick could only describe as heavenly intervention occurred. His father, Fredrick Marsh II, died of a massive heart attack while performing a routine cholecystectomy. He just keeled over and fell head first in the open body cavity, dying literally inside his patient's belly. When hearing the story of his father's demise, Fredrick's first thought was, "If only I could have gotten a picture."

For Fredrick Marsh III, life had just become much, much easier. A huge trust set up in his name immediately kicked in upon his father's death. Work was no longer on the agenda.

Fredrick withdrew from medical school the week after his father was buried and just two weeks short of receiving his medical degree. "A first," he was told.

"One of many, I can assure you," he replied to the astounded registrar as he proudly walked out of her office after tossing his Externship badge on her desk.

CHAPTER 8

NAVAJO COUNTRY

Leaving Santa Fe early in the morning on March 7th seemed to take a burden off Charles' shoulders. The gallery usually brought Bloom joy and allowed him to exercise his creative juices in arranging the displays and coming up with new shows, but the last year had been brutal. Working long hours and not making enough money to pay himself had started to take its toll on Charles Bloom, now 46. The thought of sitting in a lonely, cold gallery with nothing to look forward to but March's frigid west wind was just too much this year.

Most people love coming to Santa Fe, "the city different," and hate to leave. They dream of making it a permanent home. It has great art, architecture, and international cuisine. Cultures intertwine and it has an old-world charm that is not like any other Western city. But looking in the rear-view mirror of his Mercedes at the early morning smoke rising off the wood-burning chimneys, and seeing the tranquil scene disappear into the distance, made Charles smile for the first time in a long while. Charles found himself saying, "*Hasta luego*, my old friend. This may be the last we see of Bloom's, another Santa Fe gallery that just didn't have the right stuff to make it. Gave it a good try. Lasted longer than most, but just missed somehow...."

The grin got large and then something he hadn't heard in a very long time—a deep belly laugh—came out of Charles' mouth. Not forced as when he was trying to close a sale, but a real heartfelt laugh. The thought of just saying "fuck it" to the grind of the gallery world truly made Charles feel better about his life, even if it would mean he had failed and didn't have a profession to fall back on. Somehow it didn't seem to matter. He was out of the gallery, the heat was turned down low, and the inventory was miraculously still working at the Upper Deck Gallery, a good location with a great salesman. Maybe if the art gods were shining on him he might have a decent March, or even April if he so deemed. Hell, he might even go up to New York City and watch Willard Yellowhorse's painting STRUGGLE get auctioned off at Sotheby's. Maybe the artist-stealing dealer would be hiring after having made a cool two or three million dollars off the artist Bloom had discovered and he had stolen from Bloom.

For now, the thoughts of work were starting to fade and streams of images of what to try to accomplish next on the impromptu vacation to the rez were filling Bloom's mind.

Everyone who lives long enough in the Southwest will sometime or other refer to the place where Indians live as *the rez*, short for the reservation. It's like some hip way of saying, "Yeah, I'm from the West and know my way around the real Indian world, the rez."

The truth was, Charles Bloom didn't know shit about Indian life on the reservation other than what his Native artists told him, and many of those individuals didn't really know much either. They were Native by blood; artists who fit his niche but were from Eastern tribes whose heritage had long ago been lost and was now primarily relived in history books. The place Bloom was headed was very much alive. A land dominated by Navajos where whites were only visitors and often felt uncomfortable.

To ascertain what had led to Yellowhorse's seeming abandonment of his people and heritage, Bloom would have to infiltrate into that culture. What he knew so far: The Navajo—or Diné, as they call themselves—live in an area as large as many of the smaller states in North America. Over 200,000 Navajo live on the Navajo Reservation and it covers wide tracts of spectacular beauty but often open, inhospitable land through a variety of climates in three states: New Mexico, Arizona, and Utah.

Willard Yellowhorse was from the Bear Clan. His maternal ancestors were some of the great weavers of the early 20th century. They wove in the style of Toadlena/Two Grey Hills, known for its fine weavings of natural browns, blacks, and grays. The Toadlena/Two Grey Hills weavers are scattered in a 25-mile radius in New Mexico around two posts: the Two Grey Hills Trading Post and the more active 100-year-old Toadlena Post. Toadlena was the post with which Willard Yellowhorse's family had always done business. They were known for their fairness and dealt with some of the best weavers in the entire Navajo nation.

Charles had never been to the Toadlena Post but was thrilled to finally visit it. He had heard Willard speak of it, fondly remembering his grandmother selling her rugs to the white trader at the post for money and canned goods. Bloom had even handled a piece Yellowhorse had done remembering one of those moments called TOADLENA DAYS. A large 4 X 4-foot canvas of hundreds of little bricks that represented the post and three stick figures engaged in some kind of conversation with the sky raining Navajo rugs down on the people. This would now be classified by those who have written books on Yellowhorse as one of his early formative pieces, those images where he was still using recognized Western forms like rugs in his works before he moved on to his mature stage of abstraction and collages that were primarily produced in New York.

Charles remembered the painting when Willard brought it in to his gallery—the paint so wet he had to carefully store it for a week so no smudges were added. He could visualize Willard's interaction with the piece, explaining the history of the old trading post at Toadlena and how it had impacted his earliest memories. These were fond memories because selling a rug that had been woven over many months and then receiving a big chunk of money was a time of family celebration: new clothes, food, and a trip into Shiprock or Farmington. These rug sales only happened once or twice a year so it was always a big deal in a young boy's life. It had made an impression in Willard's mind and helped him produce TOADLENA DAYS.

Bloom had displayed the painting for a month before it sold and he also had fond memories, but they were of Willard's interpretation of the old post he had never seen before. He remembered selling the work for nearly $10,000 almost 20 years ago. It would probably be worth close to $500K now. Not huge money for a Yellowhorse as it was not his so-called prime abstraction/collage work, but still an amazing price. The fact that what this one non-iconic Yellowhorse painting would bring was more money than that generated by the entire weaving production of a generation of Bear Clan weavers seemed wrong. That the value of hundreds of Navajo weavings which took tens of thousands of hours of work over generations would not equal the same value of a painting completed in maybe six hours seemed way out of whack in some karmic viewpoint. That was art though. If the New York crowd blessed the artist, then it had to be the best and worth a great deal of money. Bloom wondered to himself if he was in the right profession or if it was a deeper issue, an ethical conflict with regards to how one values humanity.

"Am I just so pathetic when it comes to my own shortcomings as an art dealer," Bloom questioned as his Mercedes churned up the miles heading south on I-25, "that I can't deal with the fact that I made $10K and my client will make half a million? Maybe I'm like the weavers; I will never be recognized for my true worth."

Good dealers never think about these things because it's a lost cause to do so. If you are an art dealer for any period of time and any good at your trade, this will happen to you repeatedly. The fact that a dealer can buy something and make money on it is why your clients listen to you when you tell them the hype about how this guy is a good investment. Often they really are great investments and they do go up in value, sometimes a whole lot. Yet it still comes as a bit of a shock to the dealer when it really comes to fruition as it did in Yellowhorse's case.

Thinking deeply about Willard Yellowhorse gave Bloom chills. It brought up repressed feelings, many of them about his own inadequacies with regards to Yellowhorse's career. Launching Willard's career had catapulted Bloom's own gallery into a different league. Never did either of them flaunt their success. Charles had always been in awe of Willard's art. He viewed it as an innate gift, not something that could be taught. Willard seemed to feel the same way about his art; it was never a commercial entity to the artist, but his best expression of his life's view. Which brought Charles' thoughts around again to the same nagging issue with Willard's untimely death. It still didn't sit right. Something was wrong. He could feel it. Maybe the whole vacation bit was just an excuse to get some closure in his life and move on. Do a little legwork, meet the relatives, find Willard's sister Rachael, and maybe things would seem better. By the time Charles had finished evaluating his poorly composed vacation plans, Santa Fe had completely vanished in the rear view mirror and so had Albuquerque. He was heading due west on I-40 to find answers to disturbing questions he knew he must ask.

CHAPTER 9

GALLUP, NEW MEXICO

Charles Bloom had been in Gallup many times. The first time he was 10, and his father decided the family needed to see real Indians. Born in Portales, NM, Charles had grown up in that small cattle-farming community that also had a university, which was why the Blooms had ended up in such an isolated place, Charles' father being a college professor.

Charles had always liked his hometown but never felt he quite belonged. If you didn't talk cattle and wheat prices, you were an outsider. College professors' kids didn't really count as natives. They almost always left Portales and never made it back home, a generational commitment gone by. Portales was a great place to grow up and left him with happy memories, but Santa Fe was his home. Its active art scene and busy social schedule upgraded small northern New Mexico town into a metropolitan environment. He always knew after college at the University of Arizona he would settle back into the Land of Enchantment.

For Charles Bloom's father, an anthropologist, visiting New Mexico's Native haunts with real Indians was a must and Gallup was at the top of the list.

Charles could still remember his first visit to Gallup, expecting to have wild Indians surround the family station wagon and start hollering. What he found instead was poverty, alcoholism, and uninterested Indians—and yet at the same time, a raw honesty.

As Charles' old Mercedes pulled into Gallup now with its row of pickup trucks, all with local radio station stickers on their bumpers, the feelings of his first trip flowed back. The town seemed unchanged. The routing of I-40 around the heart of the old Route 66 had killed off many of the hotels and local restaurants and brought in the Taco Bells and McDonalds, but the flavor of the town remained intact. Luckily Lotaburger, a New Mexico favorite for locals, was still in town. He pulled into its inviting red and white sign.

Pawn stores, Indian arts and crafts, and of course lots of bars. Alcoholism in Gallup is a well-known problem. Books of dead and drunk Navajos showing the heartache of addiction can be found in any bookstore. Even one of Bloom's own artists—a Navajo named Ernie Begay—had often portrayed the sorrow of booze inflicted on his people. For Charles, Gallup and alcoholism seemed to be intertwined, yet something about the town also spoke to him of authenticity.

Yellowhorse had given him his perspective of the city and how it shaped his own artistic being. These interpretations had changed and enlightened Bloom, and had made the way he saw the town more mythical. For instance, Yellowhorse saw the fighting drunks as demons that affect all society. He believed the Diné were lucky to have most of their demons captured in one place so it could remind those on the right path to follow the old ways and not be pulled into the white man's nightmare drug, alcohol.

Reflecting back on Willard's observations made his death even more baffling. "*Old ways.* How could Willard say that to me, then go to New York City to make money and kill himself just for the sake of art?" Still thinking about the mystery of what had happened, Bloom decided this trip would be his own awakening into the Native world.

He would spend time with Willard's family if they would talk to him. He would become the link between Navajoland and New York City.

Bloom remembered meeting Willard's younger sister on a few occasions. Rachael Yellowhorse. He hadn't seen her but once since her brother's death, when Charles went to her graduation from IAIA, the Institute of American Indian Arts in Santa Fe. IAIA was known for its great alumni including T.C. Cannon, Fritz Scholder, and Willard Yellowhorse. Charles had watched Rachael's progress. Like Willard, she was gifted. Her medium was sculpture, a type of art Bloom's sorely needed, but she was not interested in representation from any Santa Fe gallery.

Charles could still remember 10 years ago, congratulating her after the graduation ceremony and inviting her to see his gallery. He would love to represent her as he had Willard. He vividly recalled Rachael's face and how her generous burgundy lips quivered and quickly said, "No thanks." Her dark brown eyes had filled with tears at the thought of her deceased brother's dealer's brazen attempt to entice another Yellowhorse into his lair. This was how Charles interpreted Rachael's obvious gut reaction to reject him.

Now remembering her strong facial attributes, her deep passionate eyes with their long lashes set against the most perfect high cheekbones, brought back strong feelings for the girl he barely had known.

The smell of his double-meat-and-cheese green chile Lotaburger made him salivate. Charles hadn't splurged on meat in over three months and the thought of biting into one of his favorite fattening foods was just what the doctor ordered for mild starvation. Blake's Lotaburger had always been a Bloom tradition—an original New Mexico chain opening its first hamburger stands in Albuquerque in 1952. Charles' dad's greatest gift to his kids was taking them to one of Blake Chanslor's Lotaburger stands. You could get a great homemade hamburger for 35 cents. It stated the fact right on each Blake sign. Charles' dad would tell his kids in his professorial way, "The Lotaburger is for the everyday man who works hard and deserves a good, cheap meal every once in awhile. Nothing wrong with quality food at a good price."

For Charles, no burger, even a Lotaburger, had been cheap in quite a while. As he bit into the first juicy chunk of Angus beef, the green chile flavor lighting up his deprived taste buds, Charles remembered his dad. He decided it was time once again to see Rachael Yellowhorse—to take action like a real man would.

"I am going to find Rachael Yellowhorse and get some questions answered. She won't like me showing up, but I've got nothing but time. I bet at 30 she's turned into quite a beauty if she hasn't gone to seed and had too many kids," he thought. "Yep, going to track her down. I could even consider it a business expense. She might show with me yet. I still need a talented sculptor. I better keep this receipt. My first expense of the trip; in fact, for the entire year." Now talking out loud to the grease-soaked receipt as if it were his best friend, Charles inscribed the words: *Rachael Yellowhorse artist invitation, day one.*

The Gallup Motel Six amazingly was still only $26 dollars, clean, and fairly safe by Gallup standards. It was near the end of the long Old Route 66 strip, one of the few remaining motels on the strip that was safe from drug dealers. A couple of run-down motels with big boot signs that permanently said "free coffee" were still standing and seemed to have life inside, their neon signs long ago having dissolved into an alphabet soup of letters with no recognizable words intact. No longer inviting, the once expensive neon boot signs now seemed more like warning signs not to come close or you might get your ass kicked or killed. The Motel Six was two blocks from the actual Boot Motel with its faded yellow outdoor pool furniture. Bloom's new housing had all the qualities he was looking for: cheap, a safe distance from danger, and a place to call home as he undertook his odyssey into the Yellowhorse family secrets.

CHAPTER 10

TOADLENA

It was amazing to Charles Bloom how tight the Navajo nation's social connections were, even with 200,000 tribal members. It only took a half-hour walk down Gallup's old main street and following the leads from two Indian arts-and-crafts stores before directions to Rachael's family were located.

The weavers of the Yellowhorse family were well known and sought after by high-end textile collectors, so all the Indian art dealers knew where the family lived. Yellowhorse's maternal side was Bear Clan, and those weavers had made fantastic chocolate-brown colored weavings in the tradition of the Toadlena/Two Grey Hills style for almost 100 years. Toadlena/Two Grey Hills weavings are unique to the reservation and have a very specific look. The rugs are almost always natural handspun wool from sheep the individual weaving families raise. The sheep that have the best wool and colors are highly prized by the weaving families. The colors can range from white to gray, brown, very dark brown, and camel color. The weavers spin and card their own wool to give each weaving a unique one-of-a-kind color composition, but always with natural colors. Sometime in the 1920s the Bear Clan started to use the darker colors in their weavings, even dyeing the brown with piñon pitch from local scrubby pines to give the color a very dark composition. The colors and patterns were passed down through the generations of Bear Clan weavers, making them very recognizable to dealers. This is important since the rugs were never signed and weavings that have an attribution bring more money, especially if they are as tight and well designed as the Bear Clan pieces. Unfortunately, in the last generation of the Bear Clan, none of the girls had taken up the art of Navajo rug weaving.

There was still one Bear Clan grandmother, Ethel Sherman, who wove, but she was in her late 80s and one rug trader had heard she had just passed. The last few rugs she had produced were small 2 X 3-foot rugs. Her granddaughter was Rachael Yellowhorse, who was very talented but, like her late brother Willard, chose a different form of art: for Rachael it was sculpture. Grandmother Ethel, as she was called by her grandkids, had hoped to improve Rachael's spinning and weaving techniques but her granddaughter was too busy to work much on her skills. Rachael was a teacher and active in the politics of her people. She also had family responsibilities. This was a new phenomenon for women to be interested in the world of Navajo politics as, like in the *bilagaana* world, the Navajo were changing.

Rachael Yellowhorse taught art class at Newcomb High School near Toadlena and was still making her own art, according to the well-informed dealer at Turpins.

Toadlena is one of the two trading posts in the area known for Two Grey Hills weavings, a grand old post still actively buying and selling the finest of the Two Grey Hills weavings. Rachael had grown up at the post, coming to the old red-rock building almost every weekend with her grandmother Ethel. Ethel Sherman, who was Rachael's maternal grandmother, lived very close to Toadlena so she decided to use the trading post as her base. Tourists would come and watch as Ethel spent hours at the old pine loom her husband of 60-plus years had made when they were first married. She would progress on the weaving an inch or so on a good day. Ethel would often get the rug sold before it was ever finished to some enchanted tourist. Half the money she received for the rug went to the owner of the trading post. For his half, he allowed Ethel free access to the post and his customers and he would handle the paper work and negotiation on price. Any tips were all Ethel's.

Tourists often wanted a photo of Rachael and Ethel. "Get a photo of real Indian weaving rug," Ethel would tell them in her broken English and then charge $1. There are hundreds of photos of Ethel Sherman and Rachael Yellowhorse and occasionally her brother Willard next to one of Ethel's weavings floating around the world. Many times the tourist would send a photo back to Ethel, who was never shy to ask if she could get one. Ethel had better photographic records of her weavings and her two grandchildren growing up than any of the other weavers on the reservation. The Yellowhorses, like almost all traditional Navajos, didn't own a camera.

Willard had told Charles about his early experiences as a "post kid" and how the interactions with international tourists who visited Toadlena changed his perspective. On some level, it allowed him to explore being a painter who didn't just paint "Indian imagery."

What Charles could gather from the Gallup storeowners was Rachael Yellowhorse had never married. She apparently had been serious with a white man, who had taught at the local high school, but her grandparents disapproved and she had ended it. All the traders in Gallup had hoped Rachael Yellowhorse would take up weaving like her ancestors. As a young girl she had made a few exceptional weavings and obviously had the talent.

Hearing she was still single and had at least considered one white guy gave Bloom hope. Tomorrow, Charles Bloom would be on a mission to find a girl whom he had originally seen in a 20-year-old faded color photograph of a great Two Grey Hills weaving made by the famous weaver Ethel Sherman. And he would begin delving deeper into the mystery of why Willard Yellowhorse had seemingly forsaken Navajoland, severing ties with his family, his culture, and the influences that had inspired his art.

CHAPTER 11

FINDING RACHAEL YELLOWHORSE

The first road to Toadlena Trading Post is easy to miss off of old 666, now known as Route 491. It's halfway from Gallup to Shiprock. The old post had never been good at advertising. They just figured if you didn't know where to turn you would find out or you weren't that interested.

Today the sign—the size of an apple-crate—was almost completely hidden by a large chamisa plant that still had its yellow, now-dead flower heads attached. The sign simply had an arrow with the words *Toadlena* written in faded-red hand lettering. The first language of the person who had painted the letters could not have been English, as some of the letters were capitalized while others were not. The sign was a great piece of folk art and spoke volumes about what the post must be like and what Bloom could expect from its inhabitants.

Bloom slammed on his brakes as he passed that sign that pointed at the dirt road turnoff at the same exact time you needed to turn left.

The great obelisk mountain of Shiprock just peaked over the horizon due north of the turn-off.

The old road to Toadlena was desperately in need of a grading. Its washboard jolts became increasingly uncomfortable as Bloom's old Mercedes with worn shocks lurched along. Just as he was having second thoughts about the whole idea and thinking the road must be some kind of short cut, not the main drive, and he should go farther up Route 491 to find the real road, he came across a teenager herding a group of chocolate-brown sheep.

"Excuse me. Is this the road that goes to the Toadlena Trading Post?"

Looking as if a Martian had just asked him a question, the boy replied, "Well yeah, didn't you see the sign?"

"Um yes, I did see it, but it was so small and the road is so rough I just wasn't sure. You don't happen to know if Rachael Yellowhorse lives nearby?"

Thinking about the question for some time, the boy looked him square in the eye and replied, "She's my aunt. Who are you, and why you want to talk to her? You from the government or something?"

Apparently a white guy that travels in a Mercedes down dirt roads on the reservation is not an everyday sight. Bloom didn't look like a tourist. He was asking for particular people, and the kid had never seen this *bilagaana* before. His aunt must have warned the boy about white men and how they can kill you if you spend too much time with one.

"I used to be friends with her brother Willard. I was his first art dealer from Santa Fe, and I was in the area and just wanted to say hi. That's all. I'm not from the government," Bloom explained.

"I see. Well I'm Willard's son, Preston, and you must be Bloom. My grandfather told me about you. He said you were smart to recognize my father's talent, but the big city killed him. If you want, I will take you to see Aunt Rachael. I just have to put up my grandmother's sheep. You can pull up to the next road and take a right to the end. I'll meet you there."

Bloom was dumbfounded. The first person he stopped to talk to turns out to be Willard's son! Was this luck or maybe some unknown force guiding him? He had no idea Willard ever had a child. Nothing was ever mentioned by Willard and even his biography on all the websites for famous painters said nothing. Was it possible? Or maybe the term *father* meant something different to the Navajo. "OK, Preston, I'll take the car up and wait for you," Bloom agreed.

Slowly working with his herding staff, the young man pushed the group of 20 or so sheep through the snakeweed and chamisa toward the corral. The weather was 18 degrees, but for Bloom it seemed warm and refreshing, out of the gloom and doom of winter in Santa Fe.

At the waiting spot, Preston Yellowhorse jumped into Bloom's Mercedes, his feet covered in frozen mud, and told Charles to go back to the main dirt road and head west toward the post. As the two bumped along its tortuous path, no words were spoken. Charles, because he was still in shock, and Preston, because it was the Navajo way. Nothing fast, it was rude to rush things. Let it happen.

Finally Charles got his nerve up: "So Willard was your father? It must make you and your mother proud to have had such a famous artist for your dad."

"No, not really. He ain't famous out here and my mom's dead. She died right after I was born."

The next 10 minutes were void of any conversation. The only radio station, 660 AM, filled in the silence with general reservation news, mostly in Navajo, though something about a scremo band that didn't quite translate in Diné was mentioned. Preston then said the only two words he spoke till they got to his house, "Cool band." His head beat to the music in his head.

Rachael Yellowhorse's house was a small hogan made out of aluminum siding and prefab windows with a typical Navajo octagonal shape. Its orientation was traditional, with the front and only door facing east to greet the morning sun of Father Sky. The original hogan was made for Changing Woman, the deity where all subsequent Navajos originated. Most of the old hogans around Toadlena are both rock and wood, with the cracks filled with mud.

Rachael grew up with her brother Willard in a traditional hogan, but after his death her family moved out and into a modern prefab hogan. Most of her neighbors had moved out of the dirt-floor hogans and into trailer homes. Rachael could not imagine giving up her heritage that was handed down for generations. She kept to the eight-sided building minus the rocks and juniper logs.

Rachael had moved from her childhood home in keeping with tradition. The Navajos believe if someone dies in a hogan they should be buried in the hogan's dirt floor and the entrance sealed up or the north wall of the building opened up for removal of the body and the hogan burned. Though Willard had not died at home, his visit just a few weeks before the bizarre suicide and the fact that his body was buried away from tribal lands had made living in the hogan feel wrong and thus it was abandoned. Rachael's mother and father, both deceased now, had moved to her maternal grandparents' place: Harold and Ethel Sherman. Her grandfather was just known as Hastiin Sherman, a very powerful medicine man. Hastiin Sherman now lived near his boyhood home not far from Canyon de Chelly. Rachael had chosen to build a new hogan that was much closer to her work at Newcomb High School, located between mile markers 58/59 off Route 491. Her grandfather was two hours away, but Rachael usually kept her late grandmother's sheep near her place. The grazing was better and secretly her late grandmother Ethel hoped that their presence would sway Rachael to start weaving again. Rachael was gifted at the loom but had not seriously woven anything since she was 16.

Rachael's small front yard, filled with odd and wonderful sculptures made out of local car parts, set the house apart from all its surrounding neighbors. Preston Yellowhorse bolted from Charles' car, slamming the door as if it was some old pickup truck, not a gently used Mercedes. Bloom cringed at the squeak of the door's frame being ever so slightly bent for eternity.

"Aunt Rachael, Aunt Rachael. That art guy from Santa Fe, the one you said was cute, is here."

Charles Bloom was stunned to hear that he had been called cute by Rachael Yellowhorse. It had seemed to him at their last meeting that she had considered him a nuisance, a bad reminder, not someone to be noticed. Bloom exited his car, gently closing his door as he still smarted from his passenger's less then gracious exit.

Walking past Rachael's sculptures, Charles was reminded of Willard's paintings that had similar figures but in two dimensions. The three-dimensional quality of Rachael's sculptures brought Willard's paintings to life in retrospect, even though it was all Rachael. For Charles, these were also the first exciting artworks he had seen in two days. As an art dealer you become acutely aware of your physical surroundings, especially in Santa Fe where every corner has some over-life-size bear or modern sculpture peering at you. It is the norm to be engulfed by art in Santa Fe, and the distinct lack becomes apparent in rural settings. These complex sculptures of Rachael's immediately made him feel at ease.

Rachael Yellowhorse pushed open the slightly bent door screen, another apparent victim of young Preston's excess testosterone level. Rachael extruded half her body out the door jam. Her beauty had accelerated since the last time Charles had seen her eight years ago. No longer the face of a young girl, but a full-fledged woman, her burgundy lips even larger and her full breasts impressive as they peeked outside the old frame door. Her hair was shiny, black, and completely straight, its full length reaching the mid-portion of her back. As Bloom approached, Rachael quickly brushed some strands out of her chocolate-brown eyes, leaving a trail of flour over the edge of her forehead. She had been making biscuits and had forgotten to clean her hands as she hurried to see what Preston was yelling about.

Upon seeing Bloom for the first time in more than a half-dozen years, a smile crept onto her face. She recognized him immediately. He too had developed nicely. Trim, with jeans that fit perfectly over his muscular lower body. She found herself staring at his butt that seemed to be perfectly shaped. Rachael was surprised by her immediate attraction to the *bilagaana* art dealer.

"Hi Rachael. Sorry to come unannounced." Bloom's breath seemed to freeze upon each syllable he uttered. "I needed a break from the dismal Santa Fe art scene this winter. And I wanted to visit you and see how you were progressing as an artist."

54

Rachael's smooth brown skin turned an immediate shade of crimson on hearing Bloom had tracked her down and come a long way just to see her. As she thought of the implications, it crossed her mind that maybe Charles Bloom just needed another Yellowhorse in his stable of artists and her face's skin color in chameleon-like fashion returned to its natural brown hues. "Hmm, Mr. Bloom, I don't know what to say."

Charles decided to take another approach, one that was more honest. "Please call me Charles and you don't have to say anything. I just needed to see you and talk. It was important to me. I kept thinking that I had to come. Besides, I've always wanted to see the rez," he sputtered on. Saying "the rez" sounded like maybe he was trying to be hip in some sort of Indian way.

Rachael seemed to understand, though. "Well Charles, that happens in life, when you are pulled in some direction and you don't know why. It sounds like you need a good sweat lodge to help you with whatever has driven you here."

"I'm up for anything that's warm right now." His teeth started to chatter in the near-zero late afternoon air.

"Excuse me for my rudeness. It's cold, please come in. I'm just making some biscuits for dinner. Would you like to join me and Preston, whom you just met?"

"Rachael, I actually would like that a great deal."

Rachael signaled for Charles to come in and opened the door slightly to let him in while keeping as much of the wood stove's precious heat from escaping as she could. Rachael's full body was for the first time in complete view: a short black cotton skirt clung to her thighs revealing great muscular legs, a small waist, and a terrific ass. As Charles Bloom scooted by her, his arm accidentally grazed the white tee shirt that said Rez Power, causing Rachael's breast to perk up. Seeing her full figure and erect nipples made Charles Bloom blush, her sexuality pulling at him. But how would she react when he started questioning her about her brother?

CHAPTER 12

EARLY LIFE SHAPES YOU

Jim Bernard Callahan II, born in 1953, was originally called Jim after his father's first name. This abruptly stopped after his 10th birthday. The family (minus the elder Jim) changed their first and last names in the winter of 1963. Being a Callahan was no longer a good thing. Their last name became his mother's maiden name, Phillips, and Jim Jr. became Bernard James Phillips. At 10, young Bernard was too young to understand exactly what had gone wrong, but old enough to realize that outsmarting others was an essential building block for a successful life.

The name change occurred the same year that Bernard's father, Jim Bernard Callahan I, was convicted of securities fraud. His punishment: Attica State Correctional Facility, a 20-year sentence. A particularly harsh punishment for a white-collar crime, but the judge had friends who had been swindled by the notorious Jim Callahan, so a pound of flesh was extracted. No one knew exactly why the stiff sentence, except the judge and his Sunday bridge group. Young Bernard realized his father had been taken for a chump.

It was an extreme reversal of fortune. Jim Callahan I had been a successful investment advisor for some of the rich and famous in New York City. To get Jim Callahan to handle your money was golden. He only handled large funds, usually for old money, and was known for his ability to constantly achieve steady yearly returns. The Callahan family lived in a nice brownstone across the street from Hunter College in Manhattan. The proximity to the college ultimately was the demise of the successful and ambitious Callahan. His undoing was a small but tasteful group of Pablo Picasso paintings that were exhibited at the college. Jim Callahan had stumbled upon the show and found the Picassos exhilarating. He visited the exhibit every day during its two-month run. Callahan was hooked on art and particularly Picasso. After the show he spent the next year visiting art galleries and museums around the city. Callahan became a fixture at all the galleries that featured modern art. Often he would drag his young son Jim Jr. around with him, exposing him to all the great artists of Europe and emerging contemporary artists around New York City. He explained to Jim Jr. that nothing in the world was more special than art and what it could bring to you. As a businessperson, he wanted his son to understand art was also an investment and a commodity.

After a year of looking at paintings and learning the market, Jim Callahan felt he knew enough and started to collect small, inexpensive examples of Picasso's work, his favorite artist. Little drawings and ceramics, those pieces he felt he could afford. Picasso was still alive and nice recent works could be had at fairly reasonable prices. Major works, especially older paintings, were extremely rare in the States.

As his collection grew, Callahan would upgrade to larger examples, making a nice profit on the pieces he had previously purchased. Known as a value buyer in financial circles, he found the pricing of art to be frustrating, the one aspect of the art world he hated. Being forced to pay the extra premium to get a desirable painting meant the piece had to go through two or three different dealers' hands before he wound up with it.

Because the art market is an imperfect market, price fluctuations of extremes are possible and often normal. Who's to say a piece is worth two times more? It is in the eye of the beholder. Most of Picasso's paintings were coming directly from Europe, generally Paris. When a desirable painting came out it would go to a New York dealer, then at least one more dealer's hands, before Callahan was able to buy the painting. It was as if the Picassos were a drug and each dealer stepped on the product to get their little taste before it made its way to the ultimate buyer. The true collector was stuck with the top price. The price doubling or tripling was not something a man who was known for being an astute businessman could easily brook.

Callahan decided the art world, like the financial world, was not that difficult to understand. Buy only established artists for subjects they are known for, and then find a buyer at two times the price. Callahan decided to travel to Paris and become his own buyer, with no more middleman run up.

Jim Callahan, who had spent a significant amount of his yearly salary in Manhattan art galleries, used his leverage with these same New York City art dealers as a guide to the Paris art scene. He gently extracted the names of European dealers who were the main source for all the New York galleries. A few of the dealers seemed to freely give out names of individuals who were known in the trade. One name that came up was Picasso Louie. He was supposed to be a great source for Picassos, thus the name. He was an American who had made his home in Paris to deal art. Louie's name had come from two separate dealers as being "a person who came up with things." They told Callahan if he wanted to be an art dealer then he should find Louie and see what he had; he could occasionally come up with amazing pieces.

One of the largest and most successful dealers in New York was very closed-mouth about his family's European contacts, and when Callahan mentioned Picasso Louie's name, the owner, Brit Currency, a tall, distinguished-looking man who always wore a tweed suit and black bowtie, curtly retorted, "Mr. Callahan, my recommendation is you would be well advised to let professionals deal in art. It can be quite a tricky business when it comes to acquiring the right piece. It is much safer and more fun to collect art from those who have been trained to understand its intricacies and pitfalls. I understand you're well heeled in the banking profession, but being an art dealer takes an entirely different still set—in my opinion, not one you're capable of navigating. Stick to what you know: pushing money, not locating fine art."

If Currency's tongue lashing wasn't humiliating enough, he then looked Callahan straight in the eyes and took off his glasses for added emphasis to make sure he, the mere mortal, understood that he was no art dealer and never would be. The thought that Callahan didn't have the expertise to buy and sell art was ridiculous. Callahan began to stew: "Didn't Currency understand that he was one of the top money managers in New York and he made daily multifaceted decisions regarding large amounts of money? He was an art dealer; soon enough Brit Currency would eat his words." It was at that moment that Callahan's life changed.

CHAPTER 13

PARIS

Picasso Louie was a fat, oddly dressed man in his mid-to late-forties whose appearance seemed much older than his chronological age. His clothes were always mismatched as if in one of Pablo Picasso's cubist paintings—blocks of red in his shirt against black-striped pants, over which Louie's prominent abdomen hung. He smoked non-stop. His favorites were Camels. A poorly fitted toupee covered his misshapen head. His English had a peculiar Parisian sensibility, as if he were a native to France but had studied somewhere in the Southern part of America, an occasional "y'all" slipping out during conversation.

Callahan met Picasso Louie in a small storefront on the third story of an off-street location not far from the Louvre. Callahan's first purchase as an art dealer was a small Picasso portrait that was from his early blue period. The piece cost half of what Callahan had expected to pay. It was a beautifully rendered painting and Jim Callahan was so stunned at the price, he didn't even negotiate.

On the flight home the next day to New York, the choice Picasso safely tucked into a briefcase, Jim Callahan devised his art future. Callahan was at first upset with himself for not trying to bargain with Louie, but the more he thought about it, he realized it was a stroke of luck. Paying Louise's asking price would help him in his new venture as an art broker. Louie would bring him better material expecting a better price from the eager American, cutting out the greedy New York City dealers completely. Callahan would wait for something of great value before playing hardball.

Callahan didn't declare the small Picasso when he entered the country, figuring he could argue it was a trinket, a copy of one of the great Masters. Once safely through customs, he immediately took the painting to a dealer who had sold him a Picasso in the past. The dealer inspected the painting closely. He asked about its history and Callahan told him he had purchased it from a private collection in France. The dealer agreed the piece was legitimate and fairly priced. It sold the same day, with a nice profit of $7,500. The portrait paid for his trip plus a hefty return, and Callahan would get a much better piece on his next trip for free. In fact, Callahan decided he would get a group of investors together and make a big hit, a new addition to his already lucrative stock advising and another level he would conquer in the pyramid of investing. He had been seriously collecting art for over a year and now was also selling. How hard could it be?

The pyramid was a classic model of investing. Like the Egyptian pyramids, the strongest architecture is a solid base that allows the structure to be built upon. The lowest and largest investments (the base) should be CDs, treasury securities, and US savings bonds. As you progress higher, each level gets more risky. The top of the pyramid or sixth level is the most risky: this is options, futures, and art.

Callahan went to his three top clients and explained he would be able to get them a 20 percent profit in a few weeks once the exact art piece was secured. Callahan had provided solid returns for years for these three investors, so they jumped at the chance to get such a windfall. Jim Callahan was able to get a total of $750,000 from the three well-to-do New Yorkers, not a small amount in 1962.

Next he called Picasso Louie and explained he was looking for a major Picasso, preferably from an early period—cubist and large. He would prefer an older piece as Picasso was still alive in 1962 and was actively producing ceramics, sculptures, and paintings. Callahan explained that he had half a million dollars to spend, and Louie should let him know when he had a piece.

Two months after Callahan phoned him, Picasso Louie called to tell him he had found an exceptional painting from 1941 done during World War II—a very strong and large image of the photographer/painter Dora Maar, one of Picasso's lovers. The piece was out of an old collection that had never been on the market. Callahan made the call to his investors and arranged to see it in two weeks... the time clock was now ticking.

Flying over in first class to spend close to a million dollars was a great feeling. Callahan had thoughts of completely getting out of the financial world, and just buying and selling paintings. He figured even if none of the big boys were interested in the piece for inventory, he could sell it at one of the auction houses. Worst-case scenario was he would make at least $150K, not bad in 1962.

The painting was everything Picasso Louie promised it was: huge and impressive, amazing in its composition of Dora Maar sleeping, her bent head looking so sad. A very compelling image. The price was $650K, non negotiable. Callahan made a halfhearted attempt to negotiate but realized he didn't have the stomach for it and besides it was a bargain. He would still have $100K for something else. Picasso Louie had another small painting for $50K, which was twice as good as the last piece. It was pricey but Callahan figured he could skim this off the top as a kind of bonus for being such a good negotiator on the large piece. He had a receipt made out for one painting at $700K; the little Picasso portrait just didn't exist.

The money was transferred into Picasso Louie's account and the painting was released to Jim Callahan. Getting it back duty free was a little more difficult. It was too noticeable to take on a commercial plane, so it was time for some real art-dealer work. A private jet was hired for $7K, first to the Dominican Republic, then on a boat to Miami. Presto, no duties.

The painting was easily smuggled back into the States. The $7K cost was still much less than duties on $700,000. Callahan was excited at such a magnificent masterpiece and he was the owner, just two years from when he had seen his first art show at Hunter College.

First stop, that pompous ass dealer on Madison Avenue who had told him he wasn't cut out to be in the art world. Callahan had decided he would charge him an extra $7K on top of the $1 million price tag. He could hardly wait to see Brit's face.

An appointment was set up with the gallery owner. Retribution time. Callahan wished he had a hidden camera to see the expression when Brit Currency's little mouth started to water.

Callahan carried the painting in a large art case that he bought especially for the Picasso. He waited until the owner came out from his inner sanctum. Brit escorted Callahan back to his private office to see the painting. He offered Jim some coffee and began the ritual of small talk before looking at what Callahan had brought to show. It was agony for Jim Callahan, engaging in drawn-out conversation with the man who had called him unprofessional, especially with a million-dollar painting just waiting to be rubbed under Brit Currency's pompous nose.

Finally his moment of victory arrived. Brit was ready to see Jim's masterpiece Picasso. Callahan extracted the painting from its expensive case at a slow pace savoring the moment. He watched the owner's face, locked onto Brit's eyes. It was the moment he had been waiting for... a heartfelt apology.

Brit Currency, the owner of Brit's Fine Art on Madison Avenue, never flinched. Callahan was amazed; his own mouth dropped open as if he were a cartoon character, disappointed at the lack of excitement shown by Currency. "This is one good poker player," thought Callahan.

Then came the worst words any person could hear after spending $650K: "Very nice copy, have you ever seen the original? It's in Madrid. Was this what you wanted me to see? Looks like Picasso Louie's work. Yeah, see the signature. He always changes the "O" just a bit, as a marker of his work. That way he can always say he was not trying to make a forgery. His work is starting to get a following. I've known of one selling for almost $10K. It was as good as this one."

All the blood drained out of Jim Callahan's face, his heart speeding out of control. He had been had. Money spent that wasn't his. He wondered if the bonus painting was a fake as well. He felt nauseous and thought for a split second he might pass out. Mustering all his inner strength and not wanting to fall apart in front of the despised gallery owner, he sheepishly asked, "I guess all the dealers know of Picasso Louie's work?"

"Yes, it's fairly common knowledge in the trade. Mr. Louie has been known to take advantage of neophyte dealers and collectors. Particularly unscrupulous dealers have been known to refer individuals to him if they want to inflict monetary damage. I've heard Louie will offer a dealer a kickback for the referral. They send some pigeon over and they split the profits. Quite a racket. But he is good at these copies. Very good."

"I thought you would like to see the piece. It's quite a lovely reproduction, don't you think?" Callahan mustered to the now immensely hated Brit Currency, the man who had just shattered his life.

"Yes, it's nice. If you want to sell it, I would be happy to give you $5,000, which would be a fair wholesale price. I always like to have these to put in the window as a come-on, and I don't have to worry about it getting stolen or damaged. I have quite a few collectors for Mr. Louie's work, usually monetarily challenged individuals who like their friends to think they are serious collectors. They know I am very discreet so they don't have to worry about me spilling the beans."

"No, I've got a little more into it, I'm afraid, Brit. But thanks anyway. I just wanted you to see it. I thought it was quite nicely done for a copy."

"Yes, I would agree. If you change your mind, let me know. It's fun to have these knock-offs around. I love to hear unsophisticated so-called collectors go on and on about how important the painting is, not knowing it's a second-rate copy. No offense, but you know what I mean."

"None taken." Callahan hated the man in the tweed suit. If he had had a gun at that instant, he would have killed Brit Currency and then turned it on himself.

Callahan was in serious trouble, down $707K counting the trip back to sneak in the fake. Ironically, the chartered trip cost more than the painting was worth and, worse, there was no record of how the piece got into the United States, no way to prosecute Picasso Louie or his U.S. conspirators. If Callahan tried to go after Louie, questions would be asked about how the painting got to the States. The small Picasso he had previously snuck in and sold would be discovered. He would go to jail.

This was the end of the beginning for Jim Callahan. To keep his head above water, he devised a plan to siphon off money from his clients' stock portfolios to pay off the painting investors' $750K plus 20 percent interest. Thus a Ponzi scheme was born out of necessity.

The term Ponzi comes from Charles Ponzi, an Italian immigrant who set up a pyramid of investors buying discounted postal reply coupons. His scheme was so successful that in 1920 he was making $250,000 a month. This of course would be nothing compared to

Bernie Madoff, who by 2008 had used a similar scheme to swindle $50 billion.

Callahan would have to take new clients into his investment holdings that now included both painting and stock portfolios. Their funds were used to replenish the original embezzled monies. He would use the testimonials of his original Picasso investors to convince new clients to invest in his fund. Each new client's money was automatically used as if it were interest earned on stock/painting deals. Ultimately, just as with Ponzi in 1920 and Madoff in 2008, Callahan's scheme blew up. The numbers needed to pay all the investors got too big and it only took a couple of clients pulling out their money at the wrong time and the whole thing collapsed. Callahan had no exit strategy and could not make enough on legitimate investments to cover the high promised rate of return he needed to keep the whole thing afloat. He never bought another painting.

Jim Callahan's world came crashing down on him September 7, 1963: $17 million dollars lost. It was a huge amount in the early sixties. The press coverage was intense, as many influential New Yorkers' wealth was taken down.

The New York Times headline screamed, "Fake Picasso brings down a Wall Street titan." Articles ran daily. As details were exposed, the articles increased in numbers. Dealers were interviewed, all of them shocked Callahan's art ineptitude. Eventually Picasso Louie was found and interviewed. His only recollections were of the small Picasso and a larger piece that he had clearly told Callahan was a reproduction of the famous piece in Madrid. He insisted Callahan's intentions must have been disingenuous, or why did he go through the Dominican Republic and then by boat to Miami? Louie postulated that Callahan had stopped in the Caribbean to deposit money he had stolen from investors. The press ordeal would have been worse, but President John F. Kennedy was assassinated in Dallas on November 22nd and everything newsworthy changed to the President.

At the time of Callahan's arrest, no Picassos were found other than the Dora Maar copy Callahan had gotten from Louie and a few lower-end ceramics and drawings. The small fake Picasso he secretly gave to his son, Jim Jr. Callahan told Jim the little fake Picasso was very valuable and to hide it and never mention a word of its existence. He explained he was going to be gone for a long time but he would be back by the time Jim was finishing college.

Unfortunately this was not the case for young Jim, who now went by Bernard. His disgraced father who had ripped off the rich and socially important was killed in 1971 at the Attica riots in New York's State Prison where 11 guards and 32 inmates lost their lives, including Jim Callahan I. The artist whose work put Jim Callahan in prison, Pablo Picasso, would live another two years, finally succumbing to old age in France in 1973.

The eight years since Callahan's imprisonment meant enough time had passed and most New Yorkers had totally forgotten about the 1963 front-page headlines. *The New York Times* ran a small obituary and article on Jim Callahan and his greed, ending the piece with the story of the fake Picasso and how naïve Callahan must have been with regards to art collecting. Brit Currency was interviewed once more and went into great detail Callahan's ineptitude, one final insult to the old family name. Bernard, now a teenager, made a mental note of the harsh words Mr. Currency had with regards to his now-deceased father.

The only money Jim Callahan's family ever made from his Ponzi scheme was posthumously, 26 years after his death, when the now-deceased inmate Jim Callahan was part of a lawsuit that forced the state of New York to pay $8 million to those who had died in the riots. Jim Callahan's family, now going by the last name Phillips, received $7,500 courtesy of the courts, the same amount that Callahan had made on his first and only real art deal, which set the wheels in motion for his death.

CHAPTER 14

GROWING UP POOR

It's harder to be rich and then become poor, than just being born poor, according to those who have experienced such fate. For Brenda Phillips, the widow of Jim Callahan, this was particularly true. She had been a social butterfly in the New York City scene until the demise of her husband, when she went from everyone's party list to everyone's hit list. The name Callahan became synonymous with greed, deceit, and worst of all, trying to profit off fake art. The first two defects some New Yorkers understood, but none of the social New York aristocrats could brook with stealing money by using art as the bait. It just was not done.

Changing her name had helped, but occasionally Brenda would run into an old friend who had invested with her husband and the whispers would begin again about how she was back in town and "the nerve of her showing her face."

The trauma had permanently damaged Brenda Phillips so she spent most of her time indoors and away from the public.

Bernard James Phillips, her only child, had to endure a name change in the fifth grade and a move to Brooklyn, a long departure from Manhattan's high life.

His father's love of the arts, even if flawed, had deeply affected Bernard. The constant references to his father as some bumbling art collector/dealer obsessed Bernard. He was determined never to be the naïve chump. He would make the world of art his profession and someday those who had screwed his father and belittled him the most would regret their pompous actions.

CHAPTER 15

SKINNED HUMAN BODIES DON'T SELL

It had been nearly 10 years since Fredrick Marsh had quit medical school to focus on his life as an artist. His quarterly trust-fund distribution was huge and the excess money had been building nonstop since his father's death. Marsh's actual needs were minimal. He had decided to stay in Boston and work on his painting skills. He found a little apartment near his favorite Mount Auburn Cemetery where he had once worked as an assistant groundskeeper. He loved walking through the endless pathways that traverse the cemetery's seven mountains. Fredrick Marsh never tired of seeing the parade of onlookers, most of who just enjoyed the cemetery's park-like feeling. Fredrick had become entranced with the cemetery's occupants. He took one entire distribution and purchased a large isolated plot of land that would be his mausoleum. Fredrick could envision people would come and find the isolated corner that held the remains of the famous artist Fredrick Marsh. He, like Winslow Homer, would be remembered for his great accomplishments in the art world. He would join the pantheons of famous American artists at Mount Auburn.

Unfortunately the discovery process for his art career had not gone as scripted. Ten years of struggle, working studiously every day at improving his human cadaver paintings, had not produced much interest. The portfolio of surgery photographs he had taken as a teenager in the surgery suite while watching his father was nearly worn out due to daily handling. Marsh had added additional images of cadavers in various states of embalming.

Marsh had made friends with one of the less affluent undertakers who occasionally visited Auburn Hills. Marsh had explained his art and how the human condition in its most basic form was what he sought. Fredrick was able, for a small art fee, to go in and take images of the bodies in preparation as long as the faces were covered. The excitement at seeing a fresh body with its organs exposed caused Marsh to become sexually aroused. His proclivities for the dead had become more extreme as time passed.

Marsh had no girlfriends and his only real sexual release was after visiting the mortuary. He would go directly to the side of town known for prostitution and visit Ms. E, as she was known. Her specialty was for the odd. Nothing was too abnormal for Ms. E and she encouraged her johns to speak freely about their fetishes. Marsh actually would open up to Ms. E. Maybe it was her complete lack of judgment, or that it simply made Fredrick feel good to talk to someone.

Ms. E had serviced many of Boston's finest and Marsh's necrophilia fetish seemed harmless enough and the pay was excellent. She pretended to be a dead body and Marsh would act out opening her body up. Using his penis as a scalpel he would slowly eviscerate her abdomen, which allowed him to reach sexual climax. For Ms. E, servicing the odd and sexually disturbed was all in a day's work.

CHAPTER 16

TIME FOR A CHANGE

Fredrick Marsh finally managed to get representation in a small second-tier gallery called Proof. The tag line read: "The Proof is in the Art." Marsh's intertwining cadavers were at the extreme end of the spectrum of what could be shown in a public forum. The gallery was off the beaten path but it was a bona-fide art gallery, much to the delight of Marsh. He had finally become a professional artist, even if he did have to pay a part of the gallery's rent for the honor.

Marsh found the only way the gallery owner would consider showing his work was basically a monthly bribe to keep his work hanging. Fredrick Marsh's paintings had been in the gallery for almost a year without a sale. Money, of course, was inconsequential but the fact that no one had bought a piece was beginning to disturb Marsh. He had assumed once his art was in a respected gallery, it would fly off the walls. Who wouldn't want his fantastic floating corpses?

Fredrick felt one of the main problems was the gallery was too small and would only hang one piece of his at a time. The art-buying public couldn't see enough work to appreciate his talent. The gallery had a stable of 20 artists and the owner explained even though Fredrick was contributing to the monthly rent, he had an obligation to the other artists, the ones who actually sold.

Marsh would come by the gallery once a day and look through the window at his one painting. It was one of his masterpieces, almost a year in the making. It was two women, both intertwined to make a heart design. Their strips of flesh hung from their decomposing bodies, dripping to the floor to make another heart design. He had entitled the piece simply LOVERS. It was nearly six-feet tall by five-feet wide. It took up the better part of an entire wall. The owner had pushed Fredrick to price the piece reasonably since he said Marsh was an unknown and that the subject matter was somewhat challenging. They had settled on $7,500, though Marsh wanted to put it at three times that.

Still no buyers. As the days turned into months, Marsh became increasingly upset. Finally one day he demanded a meeting with the gallery owner to discuss the poor progress.

The gallery owner, a man in his mid-40s whose heyday in the art world was well behind him, encouraged Marsh to try New York City. Maybe Boston was just not sophisticated enough for "his type" of art. It was 1986 and the contemporary art scene was on fire in New York. While Marsh's work was not anything like most of the contemporary art being produced, it was so unusual it could easily be the next hot thing. Or at least this is what Proof's owner told Fredrick.

Marsh liked the thought. It wasn't his painting, but the art venue that was wrong. He needed an art-savvy crowd and then he would be discovered. Boston was obviously not the place. It had a great cemetery but no real art appreciation. He would miss his walks at Mount Auburn, but he could come and visit and he ultimately would be buried there. For now it had to be the Big Apple, New York City, the number-one art market in America. Besides, how could he go wrong with a moniker like the Big Apple? Marsh loved fruit.

"I think you are right. I'm in the wrong city. I will keep my painting LOVERS with you because you were the first to recognize my genius and deserve the opportunity to continue to handle my work. I will move myself and the rest of my body of artwork to New York City and find an appropriate gallery," Marsh said to the obviously relieved gallery owner who wished he would take LOVERS with him as well.

"I think that's the right move, Fredrick. I'll give you a list of the big names in New York City. The sooner, the better."

"Right, I'll go tomorrow. The faster I get a gallery, the sooner I become famous. You know this will help you, as well. I think we should raise the price on LOVERS to $25K. These pieces will become very sought-after shortly."

"Sounds like a plan to me, Fredrick. Good luck."

"Thanks," replied Fredrick. "I don't think luck will have anything to do with my success, this was meant to be."

The next day when Fredrick Marsh had safely left Boston and a year's prepaid rent to Proof was in the bank, the painting LOVERS was stored in the art gallery's deepest corner, never to be shown again.

CHAPTER 17

FINDING A NICHE

Bernard J. Phillips' life had not been a storybook one. He had a very troubled teenage period. His mother, who had finally found another man, was now working as a secretary for a local construction company in Brooklyn. Bernard's new stepfather was not the loving type and hated art. It was all about sports; he lived for the Yankees and hated the Mets. This meant Bernard loved the Mets and hated the Yankees.

The final straw for Bernard living at home came June 8, 1969. Bernard walked into the living room where his stepfather was watching his favorite player's number being retired: Mickey Mantle, number 7. Bernard said nothing. He just sat next to his step-dad and opened his jacket up with a shit-eating grin. When his stepfather saw the custom tee shirt he went ballistic. He started choking Bernard, and if not for Brenda Phillips, Bernard's mother, he might have succeeded. The shirt had in bright, large capital orange lettering: MANTLE SUCKS! Bernard left the cramped house in Brooklyn that afternoon, never to speak or see his mother again. He was 16.

Bernard made his way to the city, where he found work at a fruit stand. He sold fruit for a local store and was given a free undersized bed in the basement. Survival required him to mature overnight and become a good salesman. No fruit sales, no money, no food. His daily struggles ingrained into Bernard that he never wanted to be poor. He would succeed, starting now.

Selling fruit is an excellent way to develop your people skills. Manhattan's inhabitants are busy and they don't like to be bothered with some kid selling a bruised apple. To get passers-by to buy required making an immediate connection. This could be a cute phrase or, in Bernard's case, he learned to juggle. He spent hours honing his God-given talents of balance and showmanship.

Bernard would juggle a pear, an apple, and a rubber ball. He would then put a handkerchief over his eyes (which he could see through) and start his act. Each time he would take a bite out of the fruit, missing the ball till the end, when he would have only cores and then he'd catch the ball in his mouth, a devoured fruit in each hand.

Pulling off the mask, he'd retort to the now huge crowd, "Who wants some fruit!"

The fruit stand allowed Bernard to made a decent living and put money away. As Bernard got regular customers, life became easier, but this was only the start. The thought of being rich as he'd been in childhood started to consume Bernard's every thought.

He knew he was destined to be rich and successful, and in the art business. Every day he would look at his little fake Picasso that his father gave him, his only possession, and announce to the painted image, "I will be a successful art dealer. I will show the art world what a Callahan is truly capable of." But how?

The years slipped by as he took in the fruit-stand proceeds. He aged into his 20s without even a GED. Education finally took on a priority. Work at the fruit stand became part time and education full time.

Four years later, Bernard Phillips graduated with a degree in fine arts from Hunter College, which had been next to his boyhood home. No one knew Bernard was the son of Jim Callahan, and as a child had visited a Picasso show that had ultimately doomed his father. The show had been pivotal in both the Callahans' lives.

CHAPTER 18

THE NEW HIRE AT BRIT'S FINE ART

Brit Currency's gallery had continued to flourish in the art world during the last couple of decades since Jim Callahan's demise. Pop art had arrived and Brit had seen the writing on the wall, literally. Brit's Fine Art moved heavily into the pop scene, specializing in such artists as Warhol, Lichtenstein, and Basquiat. Picassos were very hard to come by and exceedingly expensive. The switch to pop had been risky, but it paid off in spades. Brit Currency now had one of the largest galleries in New York and he was one of the most successful dealers in the country in modern art.

The gallery was known to have a staff of 10, large by New York standards. The big sales were all handled by the maestro, Brit Currency, but there was plenty of opportunity to meet other important clients and make good sales. Bernard knew that Brit Currency had been the main reason for his father's downfall. His father had explained how the arrogant Brit Currency had belittled him. Jim Callahan blamed Brit for his incarceration and so did Bernard. If it hadn't been for Brit Currency, his father would still be on Wall Street, Bernard would already be wealthy, and his father would be alive. As much as Bernard craved wealth, extracting reparation for his father's misfortune was his true motivator.

Bernard Phillips had his degree in hand, salesmanship skills honed from years in the trenches, and it was time to venture into the art world and make his mark. Taking some of his fruit savings, Bernard splurged on a custom-made suit in all black with gray trim. He wanted to look the part of someone with taste and money. Bernard understood people want to buy from those they can relate to. Acting and looking rich was important.

Walking into Brit's Fine Art was an experience in itself. To get through the first floor entrance required being buzzed in off Madison Avenue. The receptionist would inspect the individual waiting outside and make sure they were of sufficient merit to enter the rarified air of Brit's.

Once through the door, a gorgeous woman in her 20s would greet, meet, and triage the client. Was this a Brit client only? A looker? A wannabe collector? A few questions could usually filter out the important from the average. The VIPs were all known by name and face, no mistakes made when dealing with these individuals. No questions asked, just straight to Brit's office. For all others it was a game of 20 questions.

First: "Have you visited our gallery before?"

If the answer was yes then a follow up was, "Have you worked with anyone in particular?"

At this point if Brit's name was mentioned and if they had bought before, then it was a quick shuffle to the back room. Wine, champagne, or fruit juice was offered and the wooing process began.

If the answer was, "No, my first time," and they did not own work by any of the artists and were just looking, these individuals were forgotten and told, "Let me know if we can assist you with anything." These so-called clients were dismissed as looky-loos, just wasting time using the gallery as their personal art museum.

Bernard now entered Brit's as an adult. He could still remember being a child and visiting here at his father's side. There was an odd déjà vu when seeing it again so many years later. The smell was unchanged: sweet perfume and oil paint. The room appeared smaller than he remembered; he wished his father's hand were still next to his as emotions flooded in.

The sound of Brit's voice in the background brought Bernard back to the present and focused his mind on his task at hand. He hoped to be able to land a job and begin his plan to undermine the gallery that broke his father. He said he was looking for a position and was quickly told nothing was available, but after the young lady decided he was dressed well enough and quite handsome to boot, he was allowed to fill out an application.

Bernard took a seat and filled out all the pertinent information, using his stepfather's name under family ties. If Brit Currency had known it was Jim Callahan's son filling out the application, he would have been shown the door. Only in the art world would an application actually solicit information regarding who you were and possible connections. Selling art often was as much about who you knew as what you knew. Bernard realized after filling out the worthless application if he hoped to land a job and not have his paperwork simply thrown in the trash he would need to up the ante. The front receptionist simply wanted his phone number and would never show the application to Brit.

Then an opportunity presented itself, and Bernard knew instantaneously he would be hired. It was the stroke of luck he needed, and damned if he was going to let it slip by. Andy Warhol walked through the front door with his troupe of closest friends. Anywhere Andy went in New York there was always a small scene; he had a palatable vibe that was undeniable. Bernard had actually met Warhol at his fruit stand and knew this could be his ticket to a job.

Warhol was much more cautious since nearly dying on the streets of New York at the hands of one of his disturbed fans. After that shooting incident, he didn't let people into his inner circle of friends except those whom he knew very well. But being in his gallery, he felt comfortable even when approached by Bernard. Warhol figured Bernard was some rich collector who had been properly vetted. Warhol, who had been greeted by Brit and his own personal handlers, had stopped in front of a large portrait of Geronimo that he'd done.

Warhol's latest series was of the West. It included Chief Joseph, Indian shields, cowboys, and, of course, the most famous Native American, Geronimo. The series had not been very successful in comparison with his early work of Marilyn Monroe, Elvis Presley, and, of course, his Campbell's Soup Cans. Warhol collected everything. This included Indian art, photographs of Geronimo, and Navajo rugs. He was proud of his latest series even if the world hadn't figured it out; the East was always prejudiced against the West, even if Warhol did it.

Bernard walked right up to Andy as if they had been best of friends, standing directly between Brit Currency and Andy's little entourage of "yes" people and said, "Hi Andy, it's been a while. Do you still love pears?"

"Well, yes, they're my favorites. I'm sorry. I've forgotten how we know each other?"

As Brit looked on with a suspicious glare, Bernard took an apple out of his coat pocket and adroitly juggled it with his one free hand with the final throw landing in Bernard's mouth.

"Ah," said Warhol. "I remember you; you're my handsome fruit peddler. Do you still have my little drawing I traded you for?"

"I most certainly do," Bernard replied. "I always keep it close as it reminds me of what great art should be." With a dramatic flair, Bernard pulled out his wallet and retrieved a small clear envelope which contained one of Andy Warhol's cards with a drawing of a pear with the words PEAR/FRUIT on it, and then a pear drawn in simple but clean lines under Warhol's lettering. The drawing was undoubtedly executed by a brilliant artist who could make the simple stand out; even a pear on the back of a business card.

"I'll be. You really do still have it. I'm impressed, and I don't impress easily these days. What brings you to Mr. Currency's lovely surroundings today? Looking to add to your collection of Warhols?" Andy smiled as he teased his fruit peddler, knowing that it was highly unlikely Bernard was buying his work.

"I do hope to add a piece soon, but until then I will do the next best thing. I've just finished my academic training in fine arts and my first job application had to be to Andy Warhol's gallery, and thus the visit. I want to sell your art." Bernard then lifted up his application, still in his left hand, showing it to Andy and Brit as proof of what he had just told them.

"You don't say," Andy responded. "I hope Brit here is going to give you a job. I can't imagine anyone I would rather have act as my agent in selling my work. Other than you, of course, Brit. So Brit, what do you say? This kid got me to trade him an original Warhol drawing for a single fifty-cent pear. I would say he's a pretty good salesman, wouldn't you?"

"Yes, Andy, if this young man's credentials are as he says, and you approve, I'm sure we can have him selling some of your lithographs," Brit agreed.

"Oh that would be peachy." Laughing to himself for using the word *peach* to the fruit vendor, Andy said, "I would like that. But let's make sure he gets to sell the good stuff, no lithographs. I have a feeling about this young man's talent."

With that, Warhol and his troupe moved to Brit's inner office, Brit looking back over his shoulder wondering who the hell he had just hired.

CHAPTER 19

LEARNING THE TRADE

Like his father Jim Callahan, Bernard expected things to come easily. Unlike with his father, they actually did. Plus, Bernard would make it known he was nobody's fool. He was a natural salesman and had made sure he understood his product, art. He was put on a very short leash at first. Brit didn't trust the young hotshot. Brit was still miffed by Bernard's juggling antics that landed him a job, one that wasn't even available, but his talent on the show floor was undeniable. The first day he was allowed to sell, Bernard put down two $10K Warhols: a Red Marilyn and a Yellow Marilyn. Brit changed his tune about his recent hire. It looked like a smart move with $20K in the bank, half of which was the gallery's and the other half, Andy's.

Within two months, Bernard was second only to Brit himself in total sales. If Bernard had been allowed to interact with the big clients, he would have easily been at the top. Bernard had to make his sales by pure salesmanship, talking people into more painting than they had ever imagined they would purchase. For Bernard, it was much easier then selling fruit on a cold New York City street corner. The street was mainly filled with people who had little money and didn't like letting go of it under any circumstances.

Rich people only needed to be reassured that what they were purchasing had value and maybe would even go up over time. Bernard sold art by emphasizing the fact that artworks were investment-grade commodities that would be worth a lot more in the future. After all, artists die and then almost always the artwork instantaneously becomes more valuable. You simply had to outlive the artists. Bernard coined this very successful selling technique with his colleagues as "Paint by Numbers." The "Paint" represented those works by now-deceased artists and the "Numbers" the hefty increase in their value that occurs directly after their death. Every potential client was always reminded about the artist's age and how they could only produce so much more work in their life. It was a powerful sales tool.

CHAPTER 20

FINDING A GALLERY

The process by which an artist is accepted into a gallery is part talent, part connection, and often luck. For Fredrick Marsh, finding representation for his paintings of cavorting cadavers seemed to be impossible. Marsh had been painting daily for 10 years. Slow and methodical in his approach, he had always assumed that when his skill set got to a certain level, all the galleries would be after him. This was not the case.

Fredrick had a portfolio of his work photographed by the best in the business, and cards with his thin resume attached. He would make an appointment with a gallery to show the work. At each interview he would leave a hand-tooled brown leather portfolio of his images with 20 of his best paintings, all in expensive 4 X 5 transparency format, ready for publication. New York is the number-one art-buying destination in the country, with more galleries per square mile than any other city except maybe Santa Fe.

Buying his way into Proof in Boston had not been the method of choice for Fredrick Marsh. He had the means to be aggressive in spending his trust-fund stash, but hoped this would be a last-ditch option. He was, after all, a professional artist who had been painting all his life. Many galleries would be interested in his work, since New York was a sophisticated market, unlike Boston. Or so he assumed.

Marsh decided to attack the city street by street, setting up an appointment every day with one or two galleries, arranging an interview, and leaving each one his expensive leather portfolio. After two months of canvassing the city he had visited Fifth Avenue, Lexington Avenue, and Park Avenue. No luck.

He devoted the next month to re-canvassing those galleries to see if they had decided about his work. Most had thrown out the images and were now using the leather portfolio in some new gallery function. One gallery, RAD, had actually put one of their own artists in his leather book, using a magic marker to blot out his hand-tooled name, which was still vaguely visible through the black ink. Marsh made a mental note of the artist's name, Craig Lendskip, some hotshot sculptor. Enough was enough. "You'll wish you hadn't put him in *my* book," Marsh muttered. Nobody listened, but they should have.

Well, nowhere left to go but Madison Avenue. It was his last resort, as this was where the best galleries were. Marsh was egotistical but a realist, and knew his chances of getting in would be better at lesser-known galleries that were looking for breakout artists.

CHAPTER 21

CRAIG LENDSKIP

What drives an artist to create is a question that is invariably answered the same way: because they must.

Craig Lendskip could remember the day his life's inspiration began, even though he was only seven. His father was a corn and soybean farmer. The Lendskips lived in the small town of Darwin, Minnesota, population 200, not the kind of place one would expect to spawn an exceptional artist. Darwin had one unique individual who inspired young Lendskip: Francis A. Johnson.

In March of 1950, Mr. Johnson started to roll a ball of twine in his garage. He was driven to create something that was bigger than his own life: the largest ball of twine. Johnson worked steadily on the ball for 39 years straight, four hours each day, until his death in 1989. This became the largest ball of twine made by a single individual and for Lendskip it laid out his own path in life.

Craig's father's farm was next to Johnson's, and at the age of seven young Craig was brought to visit Johnson, who was working on his ever-expanding ball. Craig's father liked Johnson as an individual. His farming skills were above average and he was a neighbor on whom you could count. But he was also strange, not unlike his own son. Craig had started incessantly playing with Play-Doh by age three. He was always molding little objects from whatever was at hand. A typical dinner for Craig involved sculpting the mashed potatoes on his plate, adding peas and carrots as decoration, and then spending the meal changing the composition as it slowly was eaten. After dinner it was back to the Play-Doh for a couple more hours of sculpting before bedtime. The elder Lendskip wondered if his son might have some kind of mild retardation that required building things with his hands. But with the exception of his constant sculpting, he was a perfectly normal child. Craig socialized with other kids well and his vocabulary was exceptional. Plus he was a loving child. The only thing abnormal was his constant need to manipulate objects into three-dimensional configurations. Round structures were his favorite form.

Finally, in a desperate move, Mr. Lendskip decided to take his compulsive young son over to Francis Johnson to see what might come of it. He figured if his son saw the old man endlessly working on a worthless ball of twine he would see how his own life was going to turn out.

Little did Mr. Lendskip know he was setting in motion what would become his son's lifelong passion. Instead of being scared by Johnson's obsession, Craig was excited to see someone else who enjoyed building nonstop. Craig began his own balls of twine that same night. Unlike Francis, who would only wrap the ever-growing ball, Craig focused on hand-sized balls of varying size including multi-balls, all from the remnants of Francis Johnson's twine pile. Johnson loved the boy's gift of sculpting and shared little tips on how to work with the twine. He would occasionally take one of Craig's little balls and incorporate it into his own growing masterpiece, telling Craig, "You are now part of the Great Ball of Twine, something bigger than yourself, a legacy for Darwin."

Craig loved the fact he was part of something larger than his life; balls of twine immediately became his destiny, too.

The little boy grew into a wonderful young adult. His father still had great trepidation about his son's unique gift, but it was clear Craig Lendskip had became a sculptor of twine in the footsteps of his mentor, Francis A. Johnson, the creator and artist of the largest ball of twine.

CHAPTER 22

FOLLOWING YOUR DREAM

Unfortunately for Craig, growing up in Minnesota on a farm meant you would be a farmer like your father, and his father. The Lendskip men farmed the land. That's what you did. Being an artist was not an occupation. It was a hobby. Building twine balls was on your own time. Even Johnson worked his farm. Art was not a real job, but a curiosity.

Craig understood his role in life. He was content working the farm during the day and constructing small twine sculptures at night. He was an only child, so he would inherit the farm and the Lendskip legacy. His fate was cast. Craig would sit for hours in harmony with the elder twine artist, neither speaking. The twine was their words. Craig liked to dream of what might have been if he had been born in New York instead of the middle of Minnesota. He did not regret his life but still he wondered. Then his opportunity to leave came, but as with most of us, it was not ever how we imagined or wanted.

November can be dangerous in Minnesota. The most notable day that drove home the point was the Armistice blizzard of November 11, 1940 that killed 49 Minnesotans. A monster storm that caught most by surprise, it was a date Mr. and Mrs. Lendskip would regret not remembering forty-five years later. In 1985, the snow came early, and Craig's world diverged from his preordained farmer's path in one instantaneous moment.

Craig's parents were coming home from the feed store in the family farm truck. Craig was at Johnson's, with his latest ball of twine. Craig usually would make the weekly store run but his sculpture was nearly finished and his father could see in his son's intent eyes that his twine was calling. He yelled to Craig through the barn door, "Keep working, it's looking good. You finish by the time we get back home. Your mom and I got this one." With those final words of encouragement to his only child, the elder Lendskip and his wife made the trip instead. The weather wasn't bad when they left, a few snow squalls, but heading home it changed with a vengeance into a whiteout. The first blizzard of November became a fierce storm more typical of January. The old truck was filled to the top with this season's winter supplies and was traveling slow, more by instinct than visual landmarks. Taking longer to get home than usual, the Lendskip truck arrived at the railroad crossing the same time as the Burlington Northern heading to Minneapolis. The Lendskips never saw the 7 o'clock train barreling at them. The monochromatic conditions, overloaded truck, and rattling of the old vehicle obscured both the sound and image of the train as they crossed the rural farm route as they had a thousand times before.

Craig Lendskip suddenly lost his only family other than his close friend, Mr. Johnson. His life was upended. To succeed on a farm without the help of a committed family is nearly impossible. If your heart isn't into it, you're doomed to failure. Craig valiantly continued his father's dream of being a farmer for one more season. It didn't go well. Without his family pushing him to farm, Craig simply spent more and more time working the twine than the field. His last field of corn he simply let go to seed. "The birds need to eat," he rationalized as he labored to finish a particularly complex twine sculpture.

The family farm of three generations went on the sales block the week after he finished the twine masterpiece. He took the highest offer for the property and all its contents, excluding balls of twine, and made plans for his new life.

You would think leaving Darwin, Minnesota, for Manhattan is a huge step for a simple farm boy with a rural education, but for Craig the drastic change in environment was seamless. Maybe when you come from Darwin it's easier to evolve to the next level in life. There was no longer any connection to Minnesota other than Mr. Johnson's ever-growing ball of twine. Craig remembered having seen a LIFE magazine article on David Smith, an abstract expressionist sculptor, a Midwest boy like himself. Smith had worked as a welder on an automobile production line in South Bend, Indiana, where he discovered his love of sculpting. Smith's large sculptures of round metal elements intertwined, forming unique shapes that reminded Craig of his own intricate little twine sculptures.

Craig would follow David Smith's path, which had worked out so well for him. He would move to New York City to try to make a life as a sculptor. He wished he could visit Smith and get his insights, but like his own parents, Smith had died in 1965 in a tragic car accident, his artwork doubling in value overnight. Craig was shocked how much one of Smith's sculptures would bring. Craig Lendskip did art for art's sake, not money. In fact he had never sold any of his little sculptures, though he had given many away to friends, including a masterpiece to Johnson for all his encouragement. His hope was to live in New York City and find other individuals who were like himself and Francis A. Johnson. It was if he were looking for a separate race of people—those humans who were genetically coded to make art. In 1986, New York City was the Mecca for these individuals, with the largest congregation of artists in the country.

Arriving at 19 in the largest city in America with no friends, no gallery, and very little money, might seem foolhardy at best. The farm—after all the equipment and taxes had been paid off—was worth less than what one of David Smith's smallest sculptures would sell for. But youthful ambition somehow blots out all the overwhelming negatives one has to face. If one actually knew how tremendous the odds against succeeding were, there would be no artists.

Craig Lendskip's first stop after finding a small apartment was the Guggenheim Museum to see the exhibit *Transformation in Sculpture: Four Decades of American and European Art.* The museum show featured several of Smith's great sculptures. Lendskip thought seeing the great works in person would be one of those pivotal moments in his life, just as when he was seven and saw the great ball of twine.

The show was only sculpture and was the first exposure Craig Lendskip had to other artists' work other than Mr. Johnson's twine ball and the headstones in the Darwin Cemetery where his parents were buried. A guardian angel must have been watching over the young man as he looked intently at the exhibit's entrance piece: a monumental sculpture, an important masterpiece of stacked metallic boxes by Donald Judd. Peering at the shimmering steel geometric forms, Craig's robin's egg-blue eyes became almost black as his pupils dilated to their maximum width trying to take it all in. Then, as if the museum's walls were watching, he heard a melodic voice ask, "How do you like it?"

Without ever turning around, gazing motionless at the stainless geometric forms, the shadowy back light projecting an ephemeral design against the pure white wall, Craig slowly replied, "It's almost as if God's hand must have been guiding the artist. His ability to visualize such a heavenly concept is truly genius. I never knew sculpture could ever be so pure." Still staring intently at the sculpture, small tears flowed from Craig's face, melting onto the gray concrete floor. The obviously intense gut reaction in the young man deeply touched the gentleman who had asked the question, who at this point now also had tears flowing from his eyes, his tears mixing with Craig's on the floor to form their own geometric shape, appropriate for two gifted sculptors. The middle-aged man who had asked the question was none other then Donald Judd, the famous sculptor whose work Craig was staring at.

CHAPTER 23

FINDING A HOME

Craig, who was gifted but uneducated in the who's who of the art world, hadn't a clue who Donald Judd was. He introduced himself, at the same time wiping his flannel shirt across his eyes: "Hi, sorry to make such a scene. I'm Craig Lendskip. I make sculpture myself, or at least that's what I call it since I really don't know if constructing balls out of twine would be considered sculpture in New York. I just moved here from Darwin and this is the first museum I've visited in my life, and to see such a remarkable piece right off the bat caught me kind of off guard."

"You moved from Darwin, Australia?"

"Heck no. Darwin, Minnesota. I'm glad you can't tell, my new landlady said I've got a real strong accent. Anyway, sorry about that scene, I just couldn't help myself."

"That's quite all right. This sculpture also has a very special place in my heart. I'm glad it was the first piece your virgin museum eyes got to see, it must have been meant to be. It's nice to meet you, Craig Lendskip from Darwin, Minnesota. I'm Donald Judd from New York City." Judd then waited for what he expected would be another strong emotional response from the young man when Craig realized that he was the person who had made the sculpture.

But Craig simply said, "Nice to meet you. You must be knowledgeable about sculpture since you already know this piece. I guess it's by a very famous sculptor to be in such an important position. I actually only know of one sculptor, David Smith. That's why I came to the show. He's supposed to have some pieces here."

"Yes, I do know quite a bit about sculpture, and I am a fan of Mr. Smith's. In fact I do sculpture myself. I'm happy to walk with you and discuss some of the pieces if you like. We could start with Mr. Smith's monumental work. It's the finest sculpture in the show, in my opinion."

"Great! Even though I've been sculpting my whole life, I really don't know a lot about other artists' work. Would you like to see one of my pieces? Mr. Judd, right?"

"I would love to see one, but please call me Donald."

With that, Craig Lendskip pulled out of his heavy overcoat one of his latest creations he had just finished that morning. He was still keeping it close so he could marvel at his work. A very delicate piece, it was a ball within a ball, all constructed out of common twine and Elmer's glue. The entire sculpture fit easily in the palm of Craig's hand. The inner ball was a solid piece of very fine twine that was encased by another ball of slightly coarser twine with little octagonal windows just small enough that the inner ball couldn't escape, yet one could clearly see the inner ball in all its glory. "I call this work BALL BEARING. I particularly like this piece as it can make a neat noise." As Craig said "noise," he started violently shaking the sculpture and a small dull sound rang from inside as the inner twine sphere smashed against the sides. "Once the glue hardens a little better, the pieces should ping like a well-tuned tractor engine, thus my title BALL BEARING."

"That is marvelous!" exclaimed Judd, who was truly impressed with the young man's creation. "How on earth did you make such a wonderful object?"

"Well the inner ball is just finely woven twine. It takes quite a while to get the yarn this thin and requires the majority of the time needed to make the piece. The outer piece is much coarser twine and Elmer's wood glue. The hardest part was getting the outside ball's little eight-sided windows just right and to make it thick enough so you can get the desired noise out of it without it falling apart. It takes a lot of practice to get it perfectly round. And layers of glue. In two weeks, it should really ring when you shake it hard."

"How long have you been making these sculptures?" Judd inquired.

"Let's see, about 13 years, give or take."

"Either you don't show your age, Craig, or you started very young."

"I began sculpting when my father had me mentor with a great artist. I was barely seven, and have been working at it every day since then."

The obviously stunned Judd looked at what was clearly a remarkable individual who was at this point unknown to the world and was also working in a medium no other artist could have imagined. Judd then asked the question all artists ask of other artists: "Where are you currently showing your work?"

"Um, I did show in Mr. Johnson's barn, but I don't have a gallery. Do you know of any that might be interested in my little balls of twine? I know they're different and probably not very sellable?"

"Yes, as a matter of fact, Craig, I do have connections and I'm sure they would be very interested."

"Really? You like what I've made?"

"Oh very much. It's quite unique."

"Donald, I want you to have my little BALL BEARING. I've always wanted to share my work, so please take this. You are the first artist besides Mr. Johnson that I have given one to, and being a fellow sculptor, I can't imagine it will ever find a better home."

"Craig, that's a fantastic gift. If you don't mind, the only way I would feel right is if we did a trade. I will get you one of my little sculptures for your collection. It only seems right."

"That's great," said Craig. "I don't have any art yet other than my own and a David Smith poster. It will be exciting to see what kind of sculpture drives you. I'm sure I'll like it."

"Yes Craig, I'm pretty sure you will, it will display nicely against your Smith poster...."

With that the two went on to explore the rest of the show.

The next week, Craig Lendskip discovered who Donald Judd was. Donald had a smaller version of the same sculpture they had both experienced in the Guggenheim delivered to Craig. Its value exceeded that of his father's farm, though Craig would never sell it.

Judd made introductions on the behalf of Lendskip and by the next week Craig was part of a great little gallery just off Park Avenue. A total of seven days in New York City and Craig Lendskip was showing at a very good gallery and had a Donald Judd sculpture that came with Judd's personal phone number. Not bad for a farm kid from Darwin, Minnesota. But New York City has a way of seducing artists, and overwhelming them too. Nothing Craig Lendskip had experienced in his sheltered Midwest life was going to prepare him for what was coming his way.

CHAPTER 24

THE EAGLE HAS LANDED

Fredrick Marsh was down to the last major street in New York City. It was his final chance to find gallery representation and it was the most daunting of all, Madison Avenue. All the other galleries were not interested in his work. The comments had ranged from "interesting" to "vile." None were helpful but all liked his leather portfolio presentation and many recommended he go into marketing.

Walking into Brit's Fine Art, Fredrick had little hope of scoring a wall in the fancy and obviously pop-oriented gallery. He had a hard enough time just getting the staff to open the front door. The gallery walls were filled with large paintings that were images of famous people or words, like POW. "Nothing cutting edge at this gallery," he thought as he wandered through the exhibit space.

He had hoped to speak with Brit himself, but was exiled to some pretty young girl whose response to opening up Fredrick's leather portfolio was a sickly look of disgust. She slammed the book shut after viewing only the first image, making an audible thunk, and replied in a firm voice, "No thank you, wouldn't be a good fit."

Fredrick, who at this point was so distraught that another gallery was flatly refusing to even consider his work, countered, "How about if I pay you $5,000 to show my work."

The flustered assistant answered, "Mr. Marsh, we sell highly vetted art. Either you have what we want or you don't, and no amount of money you could pay us will ever change that. Good day."

Alerted by the slammed portfolio, Bernard Phillips, who was standing nearby, had listened in on the conversation and was stunned. This guy would pay $5,000 to have his work shown? He would actually pay the gallery? He must be really bad, crazy, or both.

Bernard quickly excused himself for lunch and followed Fredrick Marsh out, catching the short man with the poor comb-over just as he exited the front door of the building. "Hello there, Mr. Marsh. I'm Bernard Phillips, an associate at Brit's Fine Art." Pointing to his shirt tag that said as much, Bernard continued, "I happened to hear your conversation about wanting to show your artwork and thought maybe I could be of some assistance?"

"Do you make the decisions about who is shown or not?"

"Not exactly, but I am always interested in seeing a fresh artist. How about I buy you lunch and you show me your portfolio?"

"Well I guess it can't hurt, though if you can't show me, I don't see what the point is."

"Mr. Marsh, confidentially, I may be opening my own gallery shortly and I'm going to be looking for interesting artists, something different. You might be just the kind of artist I'm looking for."

"OK, Mr. Phillips. I'll be happy to show you my lovely floating nudes. It's nothing like anyone else's work, I assure you."

Fredrick Marsh and Bernard Phillips headed to a local coffee shop to discuss Fredrick's work. Picking an out-of-the-way corner, not wanting anybody to see him talking to somebody that was basically kicked out of the gallery, Bernard got to the point. "So if I heard you correctly, you would be willing to pay $5K to show your work?"

"Yes, every month if that's what it takes to get in the front door. I firmly believe once the art public gets to view my body of work in the appropriate setting, I'll take off. I know it."

"Hmm. Every month. Interesting concept. How about I look at your portfolio that my uneducated associate so rudely dismissed," Bernard suggested, as his mind processed the possibilities of integrating Marsh into a plan he had already been considering.

Marsh's face beaming, he slid the expensive leather book over to Bernard. Marsh observed Bernard's face intently for his reaction.

Bernard knew he was being watched and was careful not to show his true response. He wanted to say: "No way can I sell this shit." It was executed well enough, but not commercially sellable. Who wants dead floating cadavers that are partially mutilated hanging in their front hall? Bernard's Oscar-winning performance convinced Fredrick otherwise. "Yes, this is terrific! Mr. Marsh, this is something very original and extremely thought provoking, the kind of work I was hoping to discover. You have a gift that is quite rare. Unfortunately, few in the art world recognize true genius!"

Marsh's face smiling ear to ear, his mind racing, he couldn't help but think, "Finally." Someone had seen his work and understood it in all its glory.

"Fredrick," Bernard pressed on, his plan now formulated, "I think you have what it takes to make a stir in the New York art scene, and with your backing I can be the art dealer to get you to the top. I am the top salesperson at Brit's, which as you know is one of New York's finest galleries. I have the client connections, the art background, and the sales experience to be invaluable to your career. The one thing I don't have is the capital and it sounds like you do." It was true Phillips was the top salesperson, excluding Brit. What he failed to say was he had been there barely a year.

"Yes, money I have. What do you have in mind, Mr. Phillips?"

"I would first obtain a good but affordable space in Chelsea, an up-and-coming location in my opinion and I know just the right space. We can get lots of square footage for a minimal investment, something you can never do on Madison Avenue. Chelsea is where I believe the next hotbed of great contemporary art will be found. I will need a budget for serious advertising. People will need to know who we are and how to find us. Of course the majority of the advertising will be your work. Most of all, I need money to buy Warhol's work."

"Why in the world would I want to give you money to buy Warhols? I don't like his shit to begin with. No originality, just a glorified graphic artist, if you ask me. I don't want my beautiful figures next to some fucking soup cans."

"Yes, many would agree with your analysis of Warhol, but he has a following. You can't deny that. And his work sells. I know this for a fact because I've sold the most in this town. If Warhol will sell to me directly, we can make a sizable amount of money and bring his substantial clientele into a location that is still off the beaten path. You will share in the profit as well," Bernard reasoned.

"Money I don't give a shit about. I have more than I can ever spend. But if that white-haired, wig-wearing fake gets my work more recognition, I'm all for it. You can take all my profit and put it into advertising for the gallery."

"Could you come up with, say, $75,000? So we can get this off the ground? I will be giving up my current job security and pissing off a very powerful person in the art world when I borrow his client list and best artist," Bernard pointed out.

"No problem. I can get you the money tomorrow if needed."

"Excellent. We will need to put the gallery in your name for now until my non-compete clause is up in two years. Mr. Brit's lawyers made it quite clear I was not allowed to open my own gallery, but nothing says I can't work for you."

"Fine," Fredrick retorted. "Then I will name it, if that's OK?"

"Well, a name is very important, no doubt. What do you have in mind?

Marsh's face started to light up as he thought of viewing humans being slowly dissected: "The Cutting Edge. I believe that's a name befitting my artwork."

Bernard repeated, "The Cutting Edge. I like the sound of it, a good choice. We'll be known for those artists making art history, on the edge of what is known. Very good indeed."

Marsh thought to himself, "Yes, and also known for paintings of human bodies being cut open with the edge of a very sharp scalpel."

It might be a devil's bargain that Bernard was making, but the budding gallery director was nothing if not an opportunist. The next step was orchestrating his departure so he took what he needed with him.

CHAPTER 25

WHO NEEDS A LOCKSMITH

The inner sanctum of Brit's Fine Art was Brit Currency's office. The golden Rolodex was housed there, with only Brit and his personal secretary Lilly ever permitted access. For Bernard to screw Brit and get his own gallery rolling, he would need those precious names—a 30-year client list and the paintings they owned. Even if he could just get half of the information, he could be set for years.

Getting in was almost impossible. It was always locked and only Brit, Lilly, and the security company had access. Bernard had been in the office numerous times but only once without an escort. That one time Brit had asked him to find some papers on his desk that he needed to close a sale. The gallery was a madhouse at the time, with both Lilly and Brit in final negotiation on big deals. The door was opened and he was told exactly what to find. Bernard made a quite unauthorized stop at the Rolodex and quickly looked through. He couldn't help inspecting the C's for Callahan and found his dad's name. Written in red ink next to it was: Attica Prison, and next to that a smiley face. He realized he would need at least 30 minutes to get the main hitters. It was obvious it was the holy grail of contacts. Before leaving he pulled out his father's index card, and stuck it in his pocket. It was worth the risk. It was personal.

If Bernard were to get caught stealing highly classified information he could be in legal trouble, criminal most likely, and his family's reputation was already not the best in New York. Any serious investigation and his past would come out. The dreaded family history. Bernard decided entry was only possible through Brit's personal secretary, Lilly.

Lilly was a plain 35-year-old spinster who had worked for Brit since graduating college. The office gossip was she was paid a six-figure salary and there was no doubt she was second in command. It was also clear she found Bernard attractive, as he had caught her on more than one occasion staring at him. She always seemed to ask for his help when it came to hanging a painting or lifting a heavy sculpture.

Bernard was 30 and strikingly handsome with model-caliber looks. He was six-foot-two, 200 pounds, and all muscle. The years of juggling fruit and lifting heavy crates had given him amazing biceps and thick shoulders. His clothes always seemed in danger of bursting at the seams. Dark Mediterranean complexion, jet-black wavy hair, and a strong chin like Kirk Douglas. His white teeth were straight except for one bottom tooth that gave his mouth character.

For Bernard, getting a woman to do things for him came easily. Generally, females were just something to be used and discarded; finding a replacement never was an issue. Love was nothing he had ever experienced nor had any real interest in. He had seen his own mother used by his stepfather and he wanted none of it, even though with his own behavior he had fallen into exactly the same pattern.

One of his biggest problems working at the gallery was that his clients' wives were often attracted to him. It could be uncomfortable and occasionally led to a blown sale. It was blatantly obvious when they would flirt with him as Bernard tried to sell their husbands an expensive painting. In the art world, almost all the high-end art purchases are by men. The art business is very chauvinistic at times. Look at the top artists' prices. Almost without exception, they are male. Men are not better painters than women; it's just that men buy the art and they like men. When Bernard was in one of those awkward moments when the wife was killing his deal, he would try to separate the husband and talk golf to bring him back on his side before going in for the kill. On the rare occasion that it was the wife's money or she was alone purchasing the piece, if she was straight, Bernard always got the client. He always closed.

So Bernard needed the names and the prey was Lilly. He invited Lilly for drinks one night and put on the charm. He confessed how hard it was to work around her, as he was afraid it would be apparent to the rest of the staff how much he liked her. Lilly was, of course, hooked immediately and confessed her mutual attraction.

Bernard needed the list before he could jump ship, and now he had his fish on the line. But he also knew he had to reel her in carefully. This required finesse.

Bernard courted the older Lilly, waiting until she was beyond controlling herself before he slept with her. Once he had made love to her, her defense system ceased to exist. She was in love, the kind that hurt when she thought of him. It was critical at this point of complete submission to get the privileged client information before their romance became obvious to the staff and more importantly, Brit. Brit would not like the fact that Bernard was fucking his personal assistant and second in command. Bernard acted quickly.

The door key to Brit's office was obtained the first night Lilly slept over. Bernard already had the code and the gallery front-door key, as he often would lock up on the weekends. Two late weekends, and he had the information from the Rolodex completely copied. The need for Lilly was through.

The most important thing in breaking up with a woman was to somehow make it her fault. The perfect exit came when Bernard was able to pry out of Lilly her true relationship with Brit. She sobbed after admitting that she had many years ago had an affair with Brit but she had broken it off, as Brit was married.

This was Bernard's exit. He waited a couple of days and then told Lilly the infidelity bothered him so much that he just couldn't work at Brit's Fine Art anymore and he had lost respect for both her and Brit. He had had a very painful childhood with an abusive stepfather secondary to an unfaithful mother, and it had scarred him deeply. He just couldn't handle infidelity and even though he loved her it was a betrayal to the sanctity of marriage that he would never be able to get over. Bernard quit the day he told her. He also told Brit the same day, adding that he would keep this to himself and was not out to destroy anybody's marriage. He simply couldn't function in that environment.

Brit Currency knew better. He realized something else was going on. Bernard was a clever dealer and had potentially lethal information about his marriage. Brit was quite aware that Bernard could become a serious competitor, but he would have to do so after a two-year hiatus. The most trouble he could manage would be to work for another gallery, which also would put in their own non-compete clause in his contract. Many galleries would shy away from Bernard, not wanting to anger Brit Currency. Bernard would have to leave New York to open his own gallery, and if you're not in New York, who cares? Unfortunately for Brit, he didn't understand who he was dealing with. If he had realized that Jim Callahan was Bernard's father, and he had helped train his son for the last year and unknowingly given him his Rolodex and information to blackmail him with, Brit would have been terrified. He should have been.

CHAPTER 26

THE CUTTING EDGE

The critical factors for success as an art gallery are artists and location. The space has to have enough road visibility that collectors can find you, but also keep its air of exclusivity. First floor is a must. The best buyers don't like to wait to take an elevator, and a second-floor location translates to second rate. A gallery showing contemporary art has to have high ceilings and good light. In New York, it helps to situate where the next happening spot will be. For Bernard, luck was on his side. Chelsea was just starting to be found. He didn't have to be the first, but was early enough to get a deal on a long-term lease.

A great 4,000-square-foot, first floor rental had just come available at what would soon become a central location for art galleries. It was 1986 and the art market was just getting ready to make a bull run. The space had been one of the first galleries in Chelsea. The owner, a very wealthy gay man, had done $75,000 in renovations and only been opened for one year when he came down with a rare cancer usually associated only with older individuals: Kaposi's sarcoma. No known cure and he failed quickly. Years later, it would be obvious this was one of the early cases of AIDS. The space had been empty for almost a year, and when Bernard offered to pay a year in advance on a 20-year lease, he got a screaming deal. The landlord was older and figured the guarantee would get him through his life and he could let the kids worry about the lease afterwards.

Fredrick Marsh signed the rental agreement and the $35,000 for the first year's lease was paid up front. The space was ready to go. Great birchwood thinly planked floors and high, white walls with professional track lighting already in place. An excellent security and sound system were part of the package.

The Cutting Edge was born. A copper sign with the gallery's name in bold letters just slightly tilted to the right was fitted above the front door. It was backlit so the letters popped at night. You couldn't miss seeing it from all four corners of the intersection.

The first order of business was to lock down the Warhols. The importance of these paintings was critical to Bernard's plan. Without the paintings, he was probably fucked. He knew Marsh's cavorting nudes would be extremely hard to sell, even for him. The graphic nature was so shocking it was just too hard to wrap a plausible story around them about how this work would ever be valuable. His "Paint by Numbers" sales pitch would never fly, even for him. If he got Warhols on most of the walls, a few other good artists would be sure to follow and he could make money, especially with the Rolodex and Marsh's capital.

With Warhol's work, he would have something of quality to advertise that qualified him as a player. It was possible to have a splashy grand opening, hopefully with Warhol in attendance, and minimize Marsh's presence.

Bernard came up with a genius idea. He broke the gallery into two sections. Up front was a very public Warhol area. In back he hung huge black-satin curtains in front of a small aluminum opening fashioned after an igloo. To get to the cadaver paintings required entering the igloo that had the words "Really Cutting" above it. Bernard's pitch to Marsh was that his work needed to stand alone, and not be tainted by Warhol's. After all, Andy was simply an illustrator and Marsh was a true artist. By making it ultra selective, it was like standing in line to get into a hot nightclub: the Studio 54 effect of the late 1970s. Marsh loved the idea. It made him feel special, like a star.

In reality, Bernard wanted to keep the public from seeing the work if possible so as not to damage his reputation as a dealer with a good eye for artists. He explained Marsh's work was disturbing and one had to understand that fully before entering. He might even be able to spin it to some collectors who liked forbidden fruit kind of art. Bernard was the master when it came to fruit.

If you warn most reasonable people they won't be able to handle art like this, that it takes a special, open-minded person to understand disturbing imagery, the majority of art collectors simply will avoid what is going to be very distasteful, not wanting to upset their artistic harmony. But there are people who want things they are told are not good for them. They have to have it. For this rare freaky person, Marsh could conceivably be a match. Purchasing a Marsh was like considering a camper eaten alive by a grizzly bear as art; it could literally damage your aesthetics for life.

Warhol's Factory in midtown Manhattan consisted of an amazing group of misfits and geniuses. Assistants made silkscreen prints while Warhol focused on major paintings. The place ran at full tilt to satisfy the many gallery orders, but didn't overproduce. You can't flood the market. Andy Warhol was an astute businessman. When Bernard Phillips, who had sold over a million dollars of his work in barely a year at Brit's, came looking for more art, Andy had to listen.

"So Bernard, why did you leave Brit's? You seemed so happy and you sold so much of my work. Brit told me you already were working at another gallery. He said it was some little mom and pop start-up. I don't get it?"

"I enjoyed working at Brit's, and as you are aware I sold more of your work than all the rest of the staff put together, but an opportunity came up I couldn't ignore. I found a great gallery that is well capitalized and they love your work. Which is why I made the move from Brit's. They get you. This gallery will be a powerhouse and a market maker in the art world in short order. All art purchases and the artist stable are my decisions, and of course you are my favorite artist on earth, so I want the main focus of the gallery to be on your work. You know I believe in you and can sell the work, and now I have the money to back up my passion."

"Well, thank you, Bernard. I appreciate your kind words and all the artwork you have sold, but you know I can't show with you. I've been with Brit since the Soup Cans." Andy Warhol's Soup Cans were some of his earliest work and brought pop art to the forefront of the art world in 1962. At the time you could buy one for a few hundred dollars, although they didn't sell well at first. Andy added, "You know I'm very loyal to Brit for his help and believing in my work when no one would pay for it. Why would I want to potentially damage our great relationship? It's not like I'm sleeping with you and have to give you work, am I?"

"That's true, Andy. You do have a special relationship with Brit. I wish I could sleep with you, but I'm afraid I like the opposite sex so far. What I can do is make you a lot more money and promote you with big splashy ads in a new trendy area of the city: Chelsea. I'm not even considering asking you to leave Brit. Just allow me to purchase some fresh work from you and here's what I think you will find interesting."

Bernard paused, and then made his final pitch: "I will buy all your work at 20% off retail, nothing on consignment. My first purchase will be for $50K including your Cowboys and Indians series which I love and think needs better exposure. My second purchase in three months or less will be for $100K. My third purchase in six months or less will be for $200K. All at 20% off retail. That will make you, at a minimum, an additional $75K in your pocket as well as massive free advertising exposure. And your work will hang in a hip young gallery in up-and-coming Chelsea. I will advertise in two major art magazines each month for a year, half the ads with your choice of artwork to be promoted."

Warhol was a businessman and he knew this was a sweet deal. Brit's Fine Art, like almost all galleries, took 50% of the profits and would not purchase the pieces outright. That meant the artist had to wait to get paid and only after the sale, and then usually an additional 30 days before payment. Also the dealer often would have to discount the artwork 10% to get deals done, which meant less money. Bernard was taking a big financial risk and Warhol knew it. Brit could simply discount Andy's work by 20%, but Bernard couldn't make any money if he did that. Warhol would only let Brit discount his end by 10% and the other 10% or more would have to come off Brit's end only, but Brit wouldn't care, he was still making 40% and would be killing many of Bernard's deals. Bernard Phillips couldn't sell for less than 20% off or he would lose money. For Andy, it meant Bernard probably would have to price things above the market, which might help bring all his prices up if he could get the premium for the work.

"Bernard," Andy decided, "I hope you have a lot of money because I would guess Brit might come after you on price pretty hard and there's not anything I can do about that. It's his call. I don't care if you want to price my pieces above the current market. I will expect you to keep your end of the bargain in regards to the additional purchases or you won't ever be getting anything from me. Not even a little drawing of a pear, if you get my drift."

Bernard knew this was a reference to the little drawing Warhol had traded him for some fruit. Also Andy was saying in not so many words, "If you screw me, I'll screw you and not in the literal sense."

"Yes, Andy, I fully understand what you are telling me. And I also understand Brit will not be happy. But business is business, and Andy, I mean business. Brit will understand. Really, what choice does he have? He will never want to lose you. I've got enough capital. I can outwait him and then you'll have two strong galleries representing you in New York. With my hip location, we'll develop new collectors. All parties win, including Brit."

"OK, then I will put my name on the line for you. Just don't expect a lot of my early '60s canvases. I have to let Brit have most of the good stuff. I will give you one of my Soup Cans that I still have and a Marilyn or two of the less popular colors, but the majority of my best work has to be at Brit's. He's going to be mad enough at me as it is. He will agree to let me show with you, but he needs a carrot."

"I can live with that, Andy. I just need a couple of early works each installment to help with the discounting I will be expecting over at Brit's."

"I hope you have a few good clients who will follow you over to the new place while you develop your own clients, and they aren't worried about price. By the way, what's the gallery name?"

"The Cutting Edge, and yes, I feel confident my client list will want to buy from me."

"I like it, a real scary name, with a sharp edge one might say." As Warhol began to laugh at his little joke, he had no idea how accurate his description truly was.

CHAPTER 27

TAKE NO PRISONERS

Brit Currency was not a happy camper when Warhol gave him the bad news. Having been in the art business for 30 years, he had seen it all. Artists jumping ship, fucking the dealers who had carefully built their careers. Employees had left before and ultimately competed against him. However in the past he had always been able to continue to work with those individuals and they were never a real threat. Bernard Phillips was different. He was handsome, a great salesman, and understood the business of art. He had managed to partially steal Brit's most lucrative and well-known artist, and worse, had offered Warhol very disturbing terms—all in less than a year on the art scene.

Brit knew he couldn't or wouldn't compete with Bernard's generous compensation for Warhol's work. Brit needed to get Warhol's paintings on consignment. He didn't want to tie up precious capital on a living artist's work, even an exceptional artist like Warhol. After all, Warhol was still alive and could make more and besides it would set a dangerous precedent. Brit Currency needed the money for the dead guys. Obtaining deceased paintings required one to purchase them, rarely securing them on consignment. Deceased artists had the best margins and were the easiest to sell.

The fact that Bernard Phillips had managed to secure a great location and apparently plenty of capital—all while secretly screwing Brit's personal assistant and stealing who knows what—plus that he knew about Brit's affair, was all extremely unnerving. Brit realized Bernard was not a person to underestimate. Bernard might destroy Brit's marriage if he wasn't careful. It was obvious Bernard would not hesitate to use his ace in the hole if he were pushed too hard.

Brit decided he had to be smarter than Bernard. He would never let Bernard know how much he hated and feared him. Brit also had to make sure Bernard didn't steal any of his other artists. Brit personally talked to each of his gallery artists and explained he would take it very seriously if any defections to The Cutting Edge occurred, a personal insult. All the artists knew Andy was double dipping, but he was Andy and they were not. Brit Currency would ax and destroy any other artist's career that tried to do the same.

Brit cut off all the other artists from Bernard. He then sent spies over to The Cutting Edge to see what Warhols he had been able to get out of Andy. Brit planned to discount those pieces that were similar to Bernard's by 20 percent. If The Cutting Edge wanted to sell Warhols, then they would do it for nothing. It was war, and Bernard Phillips had fired the first shot.

CHAPTER 28

1986

The Cutting Edge opened July 7ᵗʰ of 1986. No expense was spared. The gallery advertised in two national art magazines featuring slick professional ads of a Yellow Marilyn, the one great Warhol that Bernard had for the grand opening. Andy had sold Bernard 10 works and given him one set of his relatively new Cowboys and Indians series on consignment, a good luck token. Warhol consigned his western series at 35% off retail; Brit on the other hand always received a generous 50% discount from Warhol.

Bernard was thrilled to get them at any price on consignment as it preserved his capital and he was happy not to have to buy them, especially since traditional western subject matter, even by Warhol, could be a tough sell in the East. Warhol wanted these to move; he loved the series and needed them to get into his collectors' hands so he could raise prices. He had just ended an exhibit featuring his new Cowboys and Indians series at The Museum of the American Indian in New York City. He hoped by giving the works to Bernard it would continue the buzz he had generated through the museum show. Warhol understood by allowing Bernard a little more margin in the consigned screen prints there was no way that Brit could screw Bernard. It was their secret. Brit would figure it out the first time he discounted 25% and Bernard would match it. No way would any dealer lose money. It wasn't like a gallery was some grocery store that had loss leaders, no matter how deep the dealer's pockets.

Bernard Phillips decided to test his limits with Brit right off the bat. He invited every important person in Brit's Rolodex. It would be quite obvious to Brit his confidential information had been stolen, and Bernard could be sued. What Bernard Phillips counted on was the importance of Brit Currency's long-lasting marriage. The scuttlebutt was his wife came from money and she provided all the income for the major art purchases.

Bernard personalized Brit's invitation. It came in a plain brown envelope marked "Personal: Brit Currency, Brit's eyes only." Brit Currency was not happy with Bernard's little welcome package. The 4 X 5 slick card inside the envelope featured an image of a classic early Andy Warhol, a Yellow Marilyn. Printed at the top were the words ANDY WARHOL, and then at the bottom was The Cutting Edge, its location, opening date, and the words "Now representing Andy Warhol." If this wasn't confrontational enough, there was an inscription in Bernard's hand, in neat bold letters printed directly on Marilyn's face: "Dear Brit, I do hope you and Mrs. Currency can make our grand opening. Please also invite Lilly, as I'm sure we can all have a nice discussion about our common interests." He signed it Bernard and made a happy face. If his "fuck you, happy face" didn't cause retaliation, Bernard knew he had Brit scared and would not need to worry about his old boss in the future. The happy face was for his dad. He wanted to staple the stolen Callahan Rolodex card to the invitation, but knew he was already pushing his luck.

Brit Currency was livid. He went directly into Lilly's office and told her if she ever mentioned their relationship to anyone in the future she would be terminated. Bernard Phillips was not a man to trifle with and Brit knew it. He and Mrs. Currency would not be in attendance.

The gallery had the 14 Warhols in the large front exhibit space. Eight of the 14 had been sold in the initial mailing to Brit's clients. They all had small red stickers on the price tags, which indicated the piece had been sold. It was a very good sign. The gallery would do well with Warhols. Once the actual opening occurred, Bernard would be able to close out the rest of the pieces. The gallery would need additional artists; it couldn't prosper on only Warhol. Other good artists would follow, assuming Marsh didn't scare them all off.

Marsh was a potential big problem and Bernard knew it. He somehow needed to placate Fredrick's ego. After all, Fredrick was footing the entire bill and didn't seem to give a shit about any of the money the gallery made. Bernard, like most good salesmen, understood what Marsh was looking for: lots of praise and an occasional painting sale. Bernard would deliver it.

For the opening night, four actors were hired to help stroke Fredrick's fragile ego. They were told not to ever let on they were anything but serious collectors and now fans, and to fawn all over him. They could bring a few friends to do the same, but these extras were not to say much. Let the professional actors do their job. The friends could eat and moderately drink and most importantly make the little igloo-like back room feel full and happening. Lots of head nodding and cooing when viewing the art. Bernard knew the Warhol room would be all abuzz, especially since Andy had decided he would make a quick appearance. Once he had come and gone, Marsh's room would seem the more active and this was important to Bernard. Keep him happy.

Bernard made all the actors sign legal agreements that they and their friends would never divulge any of the privileged information. If they ever were to run into Marsh accidentally, they were still just fans. The contracts had stiff penalties for breaking the stipulations, and Bernard paid well and promised additional gigs for a long time.

The opening was a huge success. Marsh was thrilled. He had never had an admirer before. To have so many individuals who were so interested and genuinely impressed by his work was gratifying. It was apparent to Fredrick after his first opening even if it wasn't a solo exhibit he would be a star. He was surprised none of his works sold, but Bernard told him this was not unusual with a new artist on the New York art scene. He would find his own collector base once the word disseminated through the Warhol admirers. Marsh was relieved to hear Warhol at his first opening of Soup Cans in L.A. had not sold a single work the run of the show. Dennis Hopper, the actor, had bought the group, but returned them later, or so the story goes. Finally the gallery owner had to buy them all on layaway, which of course turned out to be a great move once Warhol found his audience.

After the great opening in which all the Warhols were sold, and to Brit's clients, Bernard went back to refill the walls. Bernard knew he would have to find additional artists to cultivate. He hoped to be able to spot some young star before he or she hit. Bernard was a better salesperson than he was a finder of original talent. He realized this was a weak part of his art dealer's skills but figured it would improve with time. He hadn't had his own gallery before and it would take exposure to refine his eye and understand what makes an artist sing to an audience. Bernard asked Warhol's opinion when he came to filling the second $100K order earlier than scheduled.

"Andy, do you have any suggestions for an important artist to add to my stable? I know there is only one Warhol, but how about a close second or third? Who would you like to hang next to?"

Warhol thought carefully about the question, his eyes darting back and forth like a pinball machine that had a ball stuck in a bumper. As he continued to contemplate the obviously intriguing question, he scratched his white wig, moving it ever so slightly with each twitch of his hand.

"I love Jean-Michel Basquiat's work. He is a terrific artist; in fact he's brilliant. I used to be very close with him but I'm afraid we are very much on the outs. I know he likes me but I doubt we will be speaking much again and this bothers me. Maybe you could act as a kind of mediator between us? Tell him I was hoping he would show next to me, that I recommended him to you. It may help mentioning my name or could make it worse, I couldn't say, Bernard. He does have original thought, which is what I love about him. You know he started by doing graffiti around town and used his God-given talent to turn it into something else. He was even on the cover of *The New York Times Magazine*."

Andy continued, "You know, I do very much believe in God and I think he has spoken to Jean-Michel. It shows in his work. I'm afraid he does have a major issue that will be a problem for you sooner or later. He is addicted to heroin and I've heard it's become serious. I am afraid I will outlive him, and he is not even 30 yet. I won't tell you how old I am, but you probably already know. You dealers make a nasty habit of knowing all your artists' little secrets. I guess I'm too vain when it comes to my age.

"If I were you," Andy advised, "I would try to approach him—either sober or very high—if you want to get his work, probably high. He might find my concern amusing enough to sell you something."

"Thanks, Andy. I'll give it a try. How does he sell?"

"As far as I can tell, he sells pretty much everything he makes. He doesn't need dealers. He's lucky in that respect." Andy smirked as his dissed his art dealer.

"Excellent. That means he's just like you at least when it comes to selling everything you make, and I appreciate the fact you let me handle your art as I know you don't need an art dealer either." Bernard, the concerned salesman, never missed an opportunity to sell. This time he was selling to Warhol's ego. The artist enjoyed the compliment and simply replied, "You're welcome."

CHAPTER 29

BASQUIAT

The word on the street was Jean-Michel had a daily need for heroin. He could occasionally skip a day to paint, but of late was stoned a good part of the time. Bernard figured the best way to a junkie's heart was through his drug habit. Bernard, like all resourceful art dealers, could find drugs. In fact, in the eighties some of his best art buyers were dealing drugs and they paid in cash.

Drug dealers needed a way to launder their money and the easiest way was to buy art. Many art dealers would simply never declare the cash and the drug dealers don't negotiate. They pay the full sticker. Once the drug dealer has the art, he can enjoy it, then if need be sell at auction years later, the new money coming from one of the legitimate auction houses. Then it's all above board.

The dealer of choice was Big Boy Jones, a huge Columbian who got his stash directly from his South American source. He had bought art from Brit's and he only would work with Brit and always alone. It was obvious by the suitcase that accompanied B.B.J. (as he was known), which went into Brit's inner sanctum and never came out, that there were some serious money dealings going on. Bernard figured it was a drug deal. Maybe Brit bought and sold drugs, too. It was not unheard of. Many good art dealers started in the drug trade. More than likely the suitcase was cash and maybe a little blow and that was that.

Bernard called B.B.J. and was blunt about what he was looking for. "Hi, B.B.J. I worked for Brit and we met once six months ago. I'm Bernard Phillips, the tall guy who worked the Warhol room. Brit told me you were the man to get some horse from if I ever needed?"

"Yah, I remember you. Yep, I can help you. What's you need?" B.B.J. said into the receiver in an almost unintelligible Columbian accent.

"I want the most pure heroin you can sell me; nothing stepped on. It's only for local consumption, my art clients. I'm not looking to get into the drug trade. I'm willing to pay. If you want I would trade a nice little Warhol if you like. I represent Andy now."

"That's very cool, I like his stuff. Especially the kind with money in them. Got any of those?"

"Yes, in fact I do. How about we make a trade? I can come to you or if you want, come down to my new gallery in Chelsea, it's The Cutting Edge."

"I like that name, very gangsta. How about today. Give me the address and I'll bring you something you will be able to really wrap your head around. But remember, self-use only. No dealing or I will have to hurt or kill you."

Bernard believed the imposing drug dealer by the way he emphasized the word *kill*. "I understand. I'm an art dealer not a drug dealer. This is strictly for me and special art clients. So I'll see you soon."

"Get ready to have a real drug experience. You will love my shit. See you."

The drug deal to Bernard seemed no different than most of his other art deals, just a little easier. Neither party haggled over the other person's price. They both paid retail. B.B.J. warned Bernard to be very careful with the pure heroin. It should probably be cut by 75 percent, or he might end up with a dead art collector. If you were to slip a heavy user something much more powerful than they were used to, they would OD for sure.

Bernard thanked Big Boy Jones and traded a Warhol money print for $2,000 dollars of pure white heroin. The print was a 20 X 16-inch screen-print of a red-and-yellow-colored dollar sign on a purple background, number seven in an edition of 25. It seemed appropriate that the money print by Warhol that Bernard had just traded would get him real money from Basquiat.

Jean-Michel Basquiat had a huge group of collectors and dealers who tried to buy everything he made. The only way for Bernard to get anything was to buy it outright. Basquiat wouldn't give him anything on consignment. It didn't matter though, because art is an imperfect market. Bernard could buy a piece and mark it up 30 percent and someone would pay it because they just couldn't get Basquiat's work.

It was rare. They would know it was overpriced, but didn't care. They just wanted the art.

The heroin was Bernard's calling card. He showed up at Basquiat's studio and offered him the free drugs that he had stepped on by half. He warned Jean-Michel that his little gift was quite powerful and to take it easy. Jean-Michel thanked him. He didn't want to OD, so took half his normal dose. Once Basquiat was quite high, Bernard went in for the kill.

"Jean-Michel, Andy loves your work and told me you were the only artist he would show with. He thinks you're brilliant and hoped if you would sell me some paintings it might help repair your relationship. Andy is getting older and he doesn't want to have bad blood between the two of you."

"Wow, I didn't realize he felt that way. I would love to hang next to him. What's your gallery again?"

"The Cutting Edge. It's in the new hip area of Chelsea. It's a great space; plenty of room between the works and very high ceilings."

"Cutting Edge. I could use that in one of my paintings." With that, Basquiat went over to a large white canvas against the wall he had stretched ready for painting and wrote Cutting Edge and then drew a large black figure, arms outstretched, fists clinched. He then wrote the initials A.W. in red, washing them out with white paint, and then writing the initials A.W. again in blue letters.

Bernard was in awe of Basquiat's talent. He could now see the genius. Even stoned, he was remarkable.

"How's that? I believe Mr. Warhol will like this one. I'll take $3,500 dollars. You can mark it $10K," Basquiat suggested.

"I'll take it. Great. I'll let Andy know." Bernard considered keeping the Basquiat painting for himself, but he sold things—not a collector's heart.

With great finesse, just like in his juggling days, Bernard Phillips had managed to wrangle in two of New York's most exciting contemporary artists and he had only been open for two weeks and selling art for a year. His father would have been proud, especially about how he fucked Brit. If only he didn't have to handle Marsh's work. But showing Marsh's work was the least of it, Bernard would soon find out.

CHAPTER 30

TOO MANY COOKS IN THE KITCHEN

Seven months had gone by and only three works by Fredrick Marsh had sold. The front room was all Warhol, primarily his latest work, and occasionally a Basquiat, which always seemed to fly off the wall. The Warhols and Basquiats were at huge prices compared to Marsh's cadaver paintings. Bernard kept telling Fredrick to be patient. It took time. Warhol was an established artist and Basquiat was a fluke of nature.

On February 17, 1987, a turning point came in the relationship between Fredrick and Bernard. Fredrick was going on and on about the excess space Warhol received. If his own works would be moved to the front window with better exposure, Fredrick insisted they would sell. It seemed as if it was a Warhol gallery now, not Fredrick's. He reminded Bernard it was Fredrick's money funding the gallery and Fredrick's name on the lease.

Bernard explained to Fredrick that Andy would not be able to give him much work for the next month as his doctors had told him he had to have a gallbladder surgery in the next couple of days.

Andy Warhol had two fears: being poor and hospitals. His fear of hospitals had been exacerbated after his near-fatal shooting 10 years earlier by Valerie Solanas, a deranged 29-year-old man-hater and founder of SCUM, the Society for Cutting Up Men. Warhol had noticed an ad in a newspaper about her organization and thought she was perfect for one of his movies. He didn't realize she was serious about her hatred of men. Solanas wanted Warhol to make a film she had written. He refused. She shot him twice, once each in the chest and abdomen. He barely survived.

Warhol didn't like talking about his fear of death and hospitals. Only his dealers knew of the upcoming surgery and he wanted to keep it that way.

What Fredrick Marsh said to Bernard after learning of Warhol's upcoming surgery instantly concerned Bernard.

"So if I understand you correctly, Bernard, if there is no Warhol work you will be putting me in the front gallery?"

"Yes, if I don't have enough of Andy's work then I would be able to put up a couple of pieces of your work. It just depends on how long Andy's out of commission."

The next part of the conversation was what disturbed Bernard Phillips greatly.

"I don't think you will ever have to worry about having available space for my work again. In fact, this I'm sure of."

Bernard for once in his life didn't know what to say. He looked at the dark puddles of Fredrick's eyes, which were darker than he had ever seen, and wondered what he was planning. It was almost as if he was telling Bernard that Warhol wasn't coming back after his surgery, and he would make sure of it. Bernard didn't answer. There was nothing to say. He was a businessman not a soothsayer.

Bernard decided to take the threat seriously and protect his asset. He didn't know what Marsh was planning. Maybe he would frighten his star artist off, or destroy his studio while he was in the hospital. Maybe something much, much worse.

All of the money in The Cutting Edge's bank account that had been made to date was withdrawn. Bernard visited Andy Warhol's Factory at 22 East 33rd Street.

"I know you will think I'm out of my mind, Andy, but I have $300,000 dollars and I would like to spend it all today on what you have in your current inventory. I'm afraid it will pretty much wipe you out of your latest work. I'm also hoping for a couple of your early works as well."

"Now you are freaking me out, Bernard. What? Are you afraid that I'm going to die in surgery? You know I've got a great fear of dying and this isn't helping my phobia at all. Do you have some sort of premonition?" Warhol's eyes focused on Bernard's face looking for any sign of confirmation.

"No, nothing like that. I just figure you may be out of commission longer than you think, and I want to make sure I'm well stocked. I would rather have too much inventory than not enough. I figure if you can't produce, your prices will go up and I'd just as soon lock in at the old price level. I'm hedging the market. Just being a smart businessman. I'm kind of surprised that Brit hasn't contacted you."

"No, just you," Warhol said, moving closer to Bernard, analyzing Bernard's aura as if he somehow could detect some underlying motive for lying.

Bernard didn't flinch, even though he was a foot from Warhol's face. "What do you say, Andy? With $300,000, you can have a lot of fun buying stuff once you're up on your feet. Nice to be able to take a painting break and just go spend money, don't you think?"

After a long hesitation and still intently looking into Bernard's eyes, Warhol cocked his head to one side and replied, "OK, Bernard. As long as you promise me that you're not feeling some weird vibe that I'm going to die?"

"Nope, scout's honor. I have the extra cash and figure this is a great investment. I can't make money if I have empty walls while you are recuperating."

Bernard cleaned out Warhol's Factory of most of the fresh work and a few great older pieces. He had a courier pick them all up that day and deposited the funds into Warhol's account. Bernard felt badly that he couldn't be straight with Warhol about why he wanted to purchase so many pieces. Bernard Phillips definitely did have a feeling of doom for Warhol. Fredrick Marsh was possibly crazy and there was a strong chance he was going to burn down the studio or maybe worse. But business was business. Bernard didn't tell Fredrick he now had enough Warhol paintings to keep Fredrick's work off the main floor for a long time. He figured Fredrick would do what he was going to do and anything he said was not going to stop him. Let the painting gods decide.

CHAPTER 31

PRACTICING MEDICINE

Hospitals have a specific smell that is indigenous to all of them, no matter how large or small the institution. It's an aroma of antiseptic washes and dying people. The Navajos avoid these places of death, believing they trap the dead spirits of all those who have perished within the walls.

Andy Warhol and Fredrick Marsh had one thing in common: they both disliked hospitals immensely. Andy was afraid he would die in one, and for Fredrick it was a reminder of his sadistic dead father. The unforgettable aroma induced mental images of the sick and dying for both men.

The hospital register had one Andy Warhola in for routine cholecystectomy (gallbladder removal). He checked in the evening of February 20th and had the procedure February 21st of 1987. It was successful. Cholecystectomies in 1987 required a complete abdominal incision that would run the length of the abdomen. For Andy, who had already had a significant abdominal injury with scarring, the operation would take some additional healing time including a couple of days in the hospital. Andy told his doctor before he went under the anesthetic, "Dying is the most embarrassing thing that can happen to you, because someone has to take care of all the details."

The night of February 22nd, a new doctor was practicing at Warhol's hospital. He was a middle-aged physician who looked much older. His yellowing white jacket, embroidered in faded red thread, said Dr. Marsh, Extern.

Fredrick Marsh had never practiced medicine till that night. He had spent many days as a student suffering through clinical procedures. He understood hospital vernacular and settings, but was glad he had never been forced to make it his profession. Now for the first time in his life, he was excited about the prospect of practicing medicine, even if it was only for a few minutes.

Fredrick knew the night shift in hospitals changes at 11 pm. The staff arriving gets a briefing from the nurse regarding his or her patients, then checks vitals and goes and reads a book. That is the plan for most of the late-night staff. Working the graveyard shift is never fun. It is often done by the unmotivated or unlucky. Marsh understood if he was going to make a little unannounced visit to Mr. Warhola's room—Andy's real name—he should wait until the shift had changed and the vitals had been completed.

At 12:45 am, Fredrick Marsh slipped into Andy's room, 707, and looked at his victim, peacefully sleeping. As Fredrick stood over him like an executioner who was pronouncing his final judgment, he quietly whispered: "Yes the great maestro, you always flew in with your entourage for your openings. Your adoring fans all oohed and aahed at your little white ghost of a figure. Yet you never ventured into the back room to see *my* work. It was all about Andy. Now it's going to be about me. Good-bye, Mr. Warhol, your 15 seconds of fame are way over. My turn at art stardom."

Marsh then slipped out of his pocket a small vial that contained potassium and injected it into the I.V. bag next to his patient. Then he opened the I.V. line wide open, which sent a flood of crystalline solution overloading Warhol's cardiovascular system in a matter of minutes. Marsh knew the nursing staff would not check on Warhol for hours and by the time they did he would be in cardiac failure secondary to overhydration and dysrythmia. He would be dead. Piece of cake, thought Fredrick. A part of him wanted to wait till Andy's death and take out his antique blade and follow the line of the original surgical opening the surgeon had made to remove the gallbladder, but he knew this was a fantasy, at least this time.

CHAPTER 32

WARHOL DIES

The front page of *The New York Times* read, "Andy Warhola dies, age 58, after routine gallbladder operation." The article went on to discuss his career and finally that the cause of death appeared to be a postoperative cardiac arrthymia. Bernard Phillips knew better.

The entire art world was shocked, especially in New York. Warhol was relatively young as artists go, and though he was prolific he still had much to accomplish. Bernard Phillips was interviewed by numerous papers and art magazines around the country for the inside scoop on how Warhol's death would impact the price of his artwork. This of course, for Bernard, was like getting honey out of the beehive. He loved all the attention and the free money that would come with it.

Bernard told his story about the little pear drawing he had received from Warhol, and how it hung in his office. How this one object had set the course of his life, and the importance of Warhol to not just his collectors but personally. He was shocked and saddened by his passing. He had visited Warhol just days before the routine operation and purchased the bulk of his recent works. Bernard predicted the Warhol market would change dramatically over the next few years and he was fortunate he was still able to offer great works reflecting all the Warhol periods, at least for now.

What Bernard didn't mention was that he had tripled his inventory of artworks and would increase the paintings' prices one by one as they sold. He would need to work this thin vein of gold till it played out. The remaining Warhols would be his main source of income, except for the few Basquiats he owned. No more Andy. The money had to last him, because no one wanted a Marsh.

The day after Warhol's death, Fredrick came to talk to Bernard about when his artworks would move into the front room. But Bernard was one step ahead of his so-called partner. He just hoped he'd always be able to stay there.

"Fredrick," Bernard remarked blithely, "it seems that you were right. Mr. Warhol won't be making any more work. Luckily I took you at your word and bought most of Andy's inventory, which will keep the walls filled, I'm afraid, for at least a year, maybe longer. I would like to thank you for this information. Do let me know if any other artists will stop making art soon as I would also like to purchase their art inventory. I guess we are about done with this conversation, then."

The fact that Bernard obviously understood what had happened and didn't seem to give a shit actually scared Fredrick. Bernard Phillips liked Warhol both as an artist and a person, yet didn't flinch at his death and actually profited nicely on the information. Fredrick understood the significance of what his dealer was capable of. He would not take Bernard Phillips lightly. He also knew Bernard would be very successful in his profession as he was obviously ruthless in business. Fredrick figured he should back off on asking for the front space for now. He didn't want to end up like Warhol at the hands of his own art dealer. Maybe Bernard and Fredrick were more similar than Fredrick had realized. They both knew ice in the veins was a prerequisite for success, and the goal always justified the means so long as you were clever enough not to get caught. Fredrick retreated to think this all over, while Bernard pressed forward.

CHAPTER 33

THE GROWING EMPIRE

The year 1987 was a banner one for The Cutting Edge. Most of Warhol's collectors bought at least one piece during the year. By the summer of 1988, Bernard was starting to get worried he might run out of inventory, even at four times the prices he had paid. It was as if there was a never-ending appetite for Warhol's work. It reinforced his "Paint by Numbers" theory. When great artists die unexpectedly, values go up. The earlier Warhol works had been the best sellers and he was down to his last Soup Can. This piece was priced two times above the current market; he would just wait till the prices caught up. Without Warhol to ultimately keep the walls filled, Bernard would need additional artists. He had managed to get four nice Basquiats for sale before Basquiat went off the deep end.

Apparently Jean-Michel had not done well emotionally after Warhol's untimely demise, and was stoned even more of the time. Bernard figured it was the perfect time to get as much work from Jean-Michel as he could before something happened to him. His works were already bringing a small fortune. One could only imagine the value if he died young. The key was to get him to sign on as an exclusive, to let him know how Warhol would like it that way.

The secondary art market is comprised of those pieces which become available not from the original gallery or artist, but from a secondary source. Obtaining pieces from this market is not uncommon as people die, get divorced, or have tax bills that require them to sell their art collection. Amazingly Bernard could find hardly any secondary market inventory for Warhol or Basquiat. The rare pieces that came up were priced where it was impossible to resell them and make any profit. Warhol wasn't making any more, so Phillips needed more of Basquiat's work, a buffer of sorts until he could come up with some new artists or by a miracle Marsh changed his style.

Bernard had been forced to start secretly buying Marsh's works himself and storing them. It was the only way he found to placate his psychopathic artist so he would just paint and stay away from the gallery. Luckily Fredrick was extremely slow in his production. Soon Bernard could get his name on the gallery license as owner as his non-compete with Brit would have finally expired. For now, The Cutting Edge needed sales, and Jean-Michel was it. Fredrick's act of rebellion last year—as Bernard had come to think of it—had upped the stakes for both partners, and Bernard needed to press his advantage.

A simple one-page contract was drawn up stating Basquiat would show only at The Cutting Edge and the gallery would buy all the artwork. Bernard tried to see Jean-Michel twice but was stood up both times; Jean-Michel was too stoned to make it.

For the third meeting, Bernard brought the same stash of heroin that he had cut with pure cocaine as a little incentive. B.B.J. had come through with the added delight of cocaine. It was known as speedballing. The word on the street was it was Basquiat's new drug of choice.

"Hi Jean-Michel. I'm glad you could meet me today," Bernard began. "I wanted to discuss your considering an exclusive with my gallery. I could really get your work the exposure it deserves."

"You know man, I don't give a shit about galleries right now. I just want to paint and feel good. Too much pressure having to work the gallery scene. I've only got two paintings right now and that's all I plan to do for a while. I'm supposed to have a show in Europe and I don't even know if I can get my act together for that."

"I'm sure you will Jean-Michel," Bernard said. "I know Andy would want you to continue to paint. He loved your work showing next to his in the gallery."

"It was cool when he was alive, but he's dead now and it seems kind of morbid. I'm not over that whole death thing yet. The thought of ever going to your gallery and seeing his work next to mine would be too emotionally draining. If you want to buy these two pieces it's cool, but I don't want to do any more work for you right now that's going to bring me bad memories. Hanging with dead Warhols is just too much for me. I'm sorry."

Bernard suggested, "You wouldn't have to hang right next to him. I could make a little room that was separate, your own."

"Forget it, I can't deal with any of this. I've got to go. You want the paintings or not? They're $15,000 each. You can take them now and pay me later. Next week's fine." Jean-Michel lost his balance, steadying himself before he fell into his canvases as he explained his terms to Bernard.

This is when Bernard made a decision. He had not killed Warhol, but he could have saved him. Basquiat was as good as dead with his severe drug habit/depression, so it was time to let life make the decision on Basquiat's fate. Ice in Bernard's veins, something else in Basquiat's. We all make our own deals with the devil, Bernard thought. "Sure," Bernard agreed, "I'll take them both. Could you write something on a piece of paper as a receipt? And I've got a present for you, a sort of thank you. A little stash of mine, speedball mix. Hope it's to your liking."

"Wow, you're not like my other art dealers. They always are so concerned about me, harping on me to get help. Don't they know I'm in pain?"

Now that he'd decided, Bernard went all the way oblivious of Jean-Michel's cry for help. "You seem fine to me, but if you're hurting then this will help. Enjoy—I hope it's strong enough for you. I don't think it's near as potent as the last gift I gave you." Bernard reached into his coat pocket with his still-gloved hands and tossed Jean-Michael the little saran-wrapped bag.

"Thanks. I will see you around, but not at the gallery. Too weird for me. Maybe at my next opening, come by."

"I will, thanks for the pieces. I'm sorry they will be the last ones I'll get from you for a while."

The next day, August 12, 1988, Jean-Michel Basquiat was found dead in his Great Jones Street studio. Cause of death was an overdose of cocaine mixed with heroin.

The two Basquiats that were purchased by Bernard and never paid for, were put away for another time, once the Warhols ran out. An insurance policy of sorts... the prices had already tripled overnight.

CHAPTER 34

TIME PASSES QUICKLY

Seven years had passed since The Cutting Edge first opened its doors. It had become known as a top-flight gallery for contemporary art. The Warhol mystique was still the golden touch for its reputation. Bernard had been very careful in doling out the Warhols he owned, making sure he always had one for the wall. Unfortunately as with all good things, they have to come to an end, and for Bernard that was in 1994. He would be out of Warhol's art by the end of the year no matter how he priced it. He still had one of the two Basquiats he had purchased but never paid for in 1988. He could get a great premium for it now.

The art market had been in the doldrums for the last three years but was poised for another bull run. Bernard had managed to sign a couple of fairly important established artists, but he knew they just wouldn't ever have long-term staying power. Even Fredrick knew it. They were easy on the eye and priced at a level one could sell. They just weren't exceptional.

Fredrick, like a prisoner in jail, had adjusted and become comfortable with his exhibit space. He got the entire back wall of the gallery and every so often a painting would go away to some unknown collector who always wanted to keep their identity secret. His work had evolved into even a more graphic nature, with intertwining lovers having transgressed into vicious death scenes of decapitated bodies in grotesque positions. Marsh called his latest series "Final Embrace." Bernard heard one of his clients refer to it as "pornographic gore," a term he found fitting.

Bernard had made it clear the work could not be shown in the front window. He had tried it in the past with less disturbing work and had too many complaints from passersby. One mother's child was so upset they had threatened a lawsuit for emotional distress. Fredrick's response was, "Let them sue. They don't have taste. I would love to have the press coverage."

Bernard finally convinced Marsh he could lose his gallery and all the good press he had received, so The Cutting Edge's back wall became the Fredrick Marsh death wall. Fredrick could handle it as long as none of the other artists were superstars and unfortunately for The Cutting Edge, this was the case. At least it was until Craig Lendskip surfaced. Ironically, it was Marsh who alerted Bernard to the remarkable talent.

Lendskip had been showing for seven years. His fame was starting to be noticed by the art world at large, with numerous pieces in museum collections. He was only 27, yet was obviously going to be an artist for the ages.

One day Marsh was complaining about the gallery space to Bernard as usual. This time the problem was that the gallery interior seemed to be missing something. It was too one-dimensional, except for his paintings, of course. Marsh blurted out, "Why don't you get a sculptor to fill the holes? Maybe Lendskip's little twine balls would fit nicely. You know he's having a group show this month at that sculpture gallery. RAD. I believe his floating twine sculpture would contrast well against my intense paintings, like magnets pushing against each other somehow. Those unseen forces inspire people." A lack of intelligence had never been Fredrick's problem.

This was a golden opportunity for Bernard to acquire a new artist for whom he didn't have to fight. Marsh had handed him a great artist on a silver plate, and one he had pre-approved. Bernard had heard of the artist Lendskip, who had been receiving great accolades in contemporary art circles. He was apparently a modest person. That was a rarity for a soon-to-be-superstar; undoubtedly Craig was someone of whom Bernard could take advantage.

How to steal an artist away from another gallery can be a delicate process. Sometimes it requires years of schmoozing the artist, leaving clear hints every time you run in to them, like, "I love your work. It's so fresh. It would really be great in my gallery," or, "If you ever decide to leave your gallery, I would love to show your work. I know I can sell it, it's just magnificent; my cup of tea."

Then there are the less subtle ways, more in line with what Bernard's method would be, such as submarining the opposing dealer using deceit as the main weapon. A couple of possibilities he had seen used effectively included: "I heard he's in trouble—something about not paying his artists. There's talk of artists jumping ship," or, "Apparently the owner has a significant drug problem," or, "Don't tell anyone you heard this from me, but supposedly the gallery you're showing in is up for sale, very quiet and all. That's what the word is."

Then there was the best way of all, the use of pure brute capital mixed with massive promises and lots of praise for the unsuspecting artist. Nothing gets the attention of an artist so much as when a dealer collects their work and keeps it in their own house. Spending money to collect rather than for resale shows an even bigger commitment.

Bernard decided this would be his plan of attack. First he learned everything about his prey: where the artist was from, what he cared about, and his weaknesses. Once well informed, he was then able to go in for the final kill. Bernard decided the ambush would be the group opening of RAD. Bernard brought along his personal secretary and his gallery's longest employee, Sally Smith.

Sally was as plain as her name. Bernard didn't want to ever be attracted to his secretary and screw up his gallery like Brit had done. This would never happen with Sally Smith.

Her out-of-proportion bangs were meticulously rolled daily using a single extra-large curler. This left an acutely odd hair design on her forehead, like a giant tunnel traversing a painfully extra large frontal lobe of her face. She had short brown hair with a streak of gray in a very out-of-date twenties flapper-style cut. Small blue eyes that had invisible eyelashes and blondish eyebrows made her eyes seem to just appear out of nowhere on her face. Her nose was small and turned up like a pig's nose, but only at the very tip so the entrances to her nostrils were clearly visible. Sally had no neck. She very well may have had a mild genetic syndrome like Turners because she looked so odd.

While her looks were unappealing at best, her demeanor was just the opposite. Sally Smith was loyal, smart, and had a great personality with the gift of gab. These last social qualities were the only characteristics Bernard cared about. The uglier she was, the better. Less chance of him slipping up one night after drinking too much, which seemed to happen the more time he spent around Marsh.

Sally accompanied Bernard to the opening. Her job that night was simply to keep the gallery owner away from him, so he could work over Craig Lendskip and close the deal.

Finding Craig during the busy group opening in the cramped space was easy. Lendskip looked like the typical artist, entranced by one of his works, which he was enthusiastically describing to a potential collector. Bernard slipped into the milieu, listening to Craig's elaborate explanation about how the miniature ball sculpture got its title and the intricacies of how he made the piece and its deeper meaning.

Bernard forcefully said to Craig, "Mark that one sold." Craig Lendskip was caught off guard by Bernard's emphatic decision to purchase the piece. No price was discussed.

"Oh I'm glad you like it so much! It's yours. My first sale of the night. I'm Craig Lendskip. It's nice to meet someone who has good taste in twine." Craig giggled at his little lame twine joke. Typical Minnesota humor. Mr. Johnson would have laughed, but Bernard could only muster a weak smile.

"I'm Bernard Phillips. I own The Cutting Edge and yes I do love my twine," he said, trying to give a little humor back at Lendskip. Bernard gently touched Craig's shoulder, and guided him like a dance partner from his enthralled collectors to a somewhat secluded corner. "I'm thrilled to finally get one of your pieces, Craig. I've always loved the media of twine. I'm actually a fan of Francis Johnson's. He was quite an individual."

"Wow, now I'm impressed. Mr. Johnson was such a gifted artist, in the truest sense. A real inspiration to me. Have you had the opportunity to see his life's work?"

"Yes, I most certainly have," Bernard said, lying so naturally it sounded genuine. "I snuck up to Darwin one summer night before he died in 1989 to get a look at that amazing feat of creativity. If I can be frank with you, I've also always been a great fan of yours. In fact my assistant Sally is in the process of purchasing your entire show. She's over there with the owner." Bernard discreetly pointed over at his secretary, trying not to draw attention to himself and what he was really doing, stealing RAD's best artist.

"I can't believe it. You're buying the whole show? For resale?"

"Yes. I'm purchasing your entire body of work. I plan to keep half the sculptures for my own collection, and the rest for my gallery to resell. You know that your sculpture prices are terribly undervalued, in my opinion."

"They are?"

"Well maybe in a little boutique gallery like this they are fully priced. In fact I'm sure the gallery owner is thrilled to make such a big sale. He probably figures he's making a killing and soon will be bragging about his prowess as a dealer. But the truth is I feel like I'm stealing them from him and unfortunately you. Each piece should be at least two times the amount I'm paying. Not that I'm complaining." Now with the prey interested, Bernard went in for the jugular, his vanity.

"Craig, you are a rare artist, one I recognize is destined for greatness if you can find the correct gallery to help you achieve that next level, as David Smith was able to do. I would like to offer you a position in my gallery. You would be with the likes of Andy Warhol and Jean-Michel Basquiat, both of whom I represented when they were alive. You are as good as they were, if not better."

"Jeez, that's amazing. You think I am that good, and you could get twice as much money for my sculptures? Business has never been my strong suit. This is where I could have used my dad's advice. I have always taken the word of my dealer that these prices are right. I honestly don't have a clue how to price my pieces or market my sculpture." Craig's fingers began pill rolling as if an imaginary piece of twine was in-between.

"Craig, I'm very good at business and have been extremely successful. Let me fill in for your father and help you make the right decisions. This is why people like Warhol came to show with me. They trust me. Andy was a great businessman and he wanted someone ethical with keen business acumen to exhibit his work. You can ask anyone. They will confirm this." Bernard went in for the hard sell. "I can guarantee I will get twice the money for your works, and I'm prepared to back it up with my pocket book. I will purchase every sculpture you produce outright at full retail, the same amount your dealer is getting right at this very moment from me. You can have top billing in the gallery as my star sculptor. I don't care what types of sculpture you produce. As long as you believe in the piece enough to put it on the market, I will buy them all and increase the price I pay you by 10 percent a year. What do you say now, Craig? Care to make art history and leave something of significance for the world as Francis A. Johnson did?"

Craig was flummoxed. "Wow, I'm shocked and elated. I think I would be a fool not to accept such a generous offer. I feel bad leaving my gallery, though. I love it so; they have been so supportive. But with the added income I will be able to concentrate on making more important works as Mr. Johnson did. How do I tell them I'm leaving? I've never done this before."

"I'll take care of everything. From this point on we're family," Bernard assured. "Come by the gallery tomorrow and I'll get you all squared away. I can handle all the unpleasantness of what needs to be done. They will be sad, but don't forget I'm leaving them a big fat check which will help ease the pain a bit." Sad was a sentiment to which the Minnesota boy would no doubt relate. Staying one step ahead of the Midwesterner was going to be a cinch for Bernard.

CHAPTER 35

I LOVE SCULPTURE

The next day, after Craig was signed, Bernard dropped the hammer on RAD. He explained he now had an ironclad exclusive with Lendskip, and not to use any of Lendskip's work in any advertising or he would sue.

Adding Lendskip to the gallery was pure genius. He had added a breath of fresh air to the gallery that had been missing since Basquiat. In fact it took the last Basquiat selling to have enough money to insure there was plenty of money to purchase anything Craig Lendskip sculpted. Lendskip's reputation from RAD was that he was very slow. He didn't make many pieces. Often this type of gallery talk is just propaganda. Collectors think they are buying something that is rare if not many pieces are made. As it turned out, it was true in Lendskip's case. It was as if old Johnson had taught him the art of being patient as well as the love of twine. Lendskip was never finished until he meticulously numbered each piece he constructed, signing all of them with a small, almost invisible C.L. somewhere on one of the balls. This final step alone could take up to two weeks to perform, depending on the number of twine balls involved.

Craig Lendskip would scrutinize every piece of yarn as if it were a cardiac stent whose form was critical to the patient's survival. Each strand was caressed between his hands, and then slowly manipulated into a fine string once the diameter was small enough to suit Lendskip. He would then work it between his thumb and index finger, first licking the whole length of string with his tongue, then sliding it between his digits for the final preparation before making one of his sculpture balls.

The tens of thousands of hours of yarn manipulation had caused his fingertips to lose their identifying ridges. Literally he had no fingerprints. It was as if they had been erased. His tongue also had been transformed. The repetitive sliding of the twine had formed a large, smooth groove running at a right angle to the body of the now meaty tongue. He could pull numerous strings through the groove in rapid fashion wetting the yarn perfectly, never lacerating the tongue muscle, similar to the Apache Indians who used the hard, spiny devil's claw plant in making their fine basketry. The huge callus gave Craig the hint of a lisp due to the nature of the slightly deformed tongue muscle, which also accentuated his Minnesota accent.

As promised, for every piece Craig brought in, Bernard wrote a check for the full old RAD retail value. The number of balls that were involved, and their relative sizes and complexity determined the price. Craig was very happy in his new arrangement. What he didn't know, was that the contract he had signed was not in his best interest. It did call for a 10 percent raise of his prices yearly as promised, but it also gave Bernard an ironclad exclusive for all his sculpture, twine or not. In the fine print, Bernard had inserted legalese that he had the power of attorney in case of any catastrophic injury to Craig. The sculptor had no parents or anyone of real significance in his life, so he figured it didn't matter. If he were that incapacitated, he wouldn't care. All he asked was if something unexpected happened to him, Bernard would be sure to send one of his pieces back to the museum in Darwin, Minnesota, housing the Johnson Greatest Ball of Twine Museum.

CHAPTER 36

POACHING ANOTHER ARTIST

Bernard's gallery, with the addition of Craig Lendskip, was once again turning a positive cash flow on its living artists. Warhols had gotten them through the early nineties' art recession and Marsh's money had provided capital in the last two years, but with Lendskip's twine balls, money started to flow. The new funds allowed Bernard to resume the opulent lifestyle he had experienced a few years earlier. The recession was over, and Bernard was intent on charging ahead. He never would allow himself to be poor again.

The other contemporary artists in the gallery started to make more sales because of the draw the wunderkind was providing. Fredrick Marsh tolerated the mini-superstar because, as he put it, "Twine balls, while fun, will never be considered lasting art, not like my death series. Just a phase kind of thing."

What Bernard Phillips needed was a powerhouse painter, someone he could sink his teeth into and believe in, someone who, once they had died, the art world would embrace. He found his savior in the most unusual place, the travel section of *The New York Times*.

Bernard Phillips' daily routine was the same, never changing: 45 to 60 minutes on a stationary bike each morning. He would read *The Times* cover to cover. Starting with business, then arts, style, and front page, and on Sunday, maybe the travel section.

The travel section was of minor interest since Bernard rarely traveled. He preferred to stay in New York and work, make money, and keep an eye on the gallery and Marsh. He was going to throw out the travel section that day as he finished his minimal mileage requirement—12 miles—when an image caught his eye: a painting, and it was exceptional.

The cover story was about Santa Fe, New Mexico, the second-largest art community in the country by some counts. Only New York City was larger. The article highlighted the varied art scene, spotlighting Canyon Road and Native American art. They had chosen an intricate, colorful Willard Yellowhorse painting to illustrate the Indian art portion of the getaway. Yellowhorse, a full-blooded Navajo Indian, was the featured artist of a gallery, Bloom's, which specialized in contemporary Native paintings and sculpture. The article told of how Yellowhorse was the most expensive living Native artist in the country and how all the work would sell out immediately. Yellowhorse's style was contemporary and unique from other Navajo artists or any other Indian artists for that matter. Santa Fe was best visited during the third week in August when Indian Market weekend occurred. Willard Yellowhorse would have his annual one-man show at this time each year at Bloom's. "An event not to be missed," the article boasted.

Bernard was amazed at the complex images of color and figure-like people. He was also surprised Willard's prices were already substantially high while being represented by some unknown gallery in Santa Fe. Even from just the single work it was apparent he was gifted. It reminded him of Basquiat's work but with some sort of Western twist.

To Bernard's knowledge no gallery in New York represented any Native artists, and if one did it was in some obscure place and not of merit. The great part of handling a Native American artist was that Marsh wouldn't care. Marsh had heard Bernard complain vociferously about how New Yorkers' sensibilities never quite got Warhol's Cowboys and Indian series. They just didn't like Indians. Marsh would figure an Indian couldn't be much threat if any. After seven years of working closely with Fredrick Marsh, Bernard had learned what would set him off. Fredrick's main issue was if he felt an artist was overshadowing his work. If any one artist became the gallery's focus it was potentially serious trouble. Bernard had learned a valuable lesson with Warhol's untimely death; it had exposed Marsh's dark side and what he was capable of.

"This Yellowhorse artist would be perfect," Bernard thought. "Marsh would assume anyone from the West and an Indian couldn't be taken very seriously in the East, much less New York City. What he won't figure out, is it's the subject matter of Indians that New Yorkers don't like. This guy is contemporary and great."

Bernard decided he would need a trip to Santa Fe to poach another great artist. How hard could it really be taking an artist from a no-name New Mexico gallery? They couldn't compete against a big-city operation with lots of capital. They were small potatoes, not savvy businessmen like New Yorkers. The same routine as before, just a little different spin....

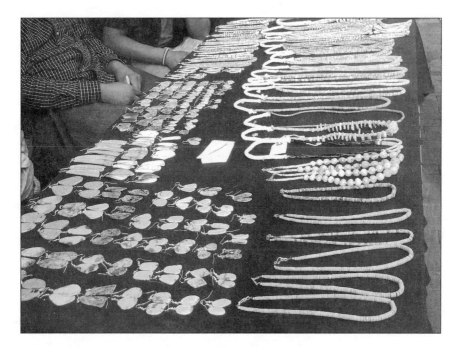

CHAPTER 37

WHO CARES WHAT'S FAIR

Santa Fe during Indian Market is an experience in itself. The city is awash in people from all over the world, all intermixing with Natives from around the country. The downtown Plaza with its usual small group of Indians under the Palace of the Governors is transformed into a huge arts and crafts fair with over 1,200 native artisans from 100 tribes. Nearly 600 wooden booths, each 10 X 10 feet, are filled with Native craftsman and artisans for a two-day period of sales. The exhibiting artists pick a handful of their pieces to enter for juried selection. Cash prizes and ribbons are awarded in each of the numerous categories. Those pieces that win a division ribbon immediately become much more valuable. If you are fortunate enough to win the Best of Show award, you are assured a good life as an artist. The Best of Show award winners are the toast of the town.

Willard Yellowhorse had transcended Indian Market and was one of the few Native artists who no longer needed to compete at the market since he was a gallery headliner now. It was at Indian Market where Charles Bloom had found Yellowhorse, who received no awards or recognition the only year he competed.

Bloom's was a huge draw on Canyon Road, with people jockeying for the opportunity to purchase a Yellowhorse work. Collectors would start waiting in line the day before and spend the night in Bloom's parking lot, just to get the opportunity to buy a coveted Yellowhorse painting. This was the yearly highlight for Bloom's. Indian Market was lovingly referred to as Indian Mark-Up, as this was the one weekend to get the most money for art work and after a sellout of Yellowhorse's work both artist and dealer could cruise for the next three months.

Bernard Phillips arrived in Santa Fe the day before Indian Market judging. The city was abuzz with activity. He had made his reservations a month in advance and still could only find a small bed and breakfast. Apparently the best hotels book a year ahead of time and any restaurant required a reservation months in advance. The spectacle was mind boggling to Bernard. One of the local dealers had told him that a hundred million dollars changed hands in a 10-day period, all art related.

Finding Bloom's was a challenge. Bernard had missed it the first time and had to snake his way back up the people-strewn, one-way Canyon Road before finally finding its little gravel entrance. No parking spaces anywhere. Another trip up the road before a spot was secured. Bernard was already sick of Santa Fe and its charm, and amazed such a shitty spot for a gallery location could do well. The narrow 300-year-old streets and endless adobe houses with chile ristras hanging from the blue porches all seemed too much like some storybook compared to the frenetic real-world pace of Chelsea.

Bloom's was having a meet and greet the day before the Yellowhorse opening, a chance to view the paintings in advance and talk to the artist. A line seven deep to purchase a piece had already formed for the next day's feeding frenzy. When the gallery officially opened for business, it would be a madhouse of people staking claim to their paintings. To be able to own a piece at this point required one to wait in a line for 24 hours.

Fourteen Yellowhorse paintings hung on the walls; each was exquisite in its own right. Bernard was convinced of the man's genius after seeing the works in person. The majority were not large: 25 X 30 inches, no frame, and an array of colors and symbolism created with a very sure hand. Each brush stroke was placed with authority. It was clear Yellowhorse had staying power. The largest painting was 48 X 72 inches, composed of a black background with fine mica dust strewn in the field, which made most of the painting sparkle when the light grazed off its surface. Large white figures reminiscent of Basquiat floated in a sea of yellow and green haze. A central dark center with no mica formed a pure black element that seemed to dictate the movement of the floating figures above. The price was $75K, a tremendous amount for a living artist in 1994.

Bernard wondered how he would acquire any paintings and steal the artist at the same time. He decided he'd rely on what works best in New York: money. The line outside the gallery was growing ever since Bernard had arrived, and it was only 3 pm. The show didn't open until tomorrow at 5 pm. Bernard had no intention of standing in line as some common collector. He was, after all, a mover and shaker in New York and had money to back it up. He flew first class and expected to be treated the same, especially when buying expensive art.

So Bernard discreetly told each person in line he would purchase any piece they were able to get to first. He would pay a 25 percent finder's fee. He would write the check for the painting and then write another check for 25 percent of the purchase price of the painting. Bernard locked down four of those in line and one other was leaning his way. For those on line, it was easy money for spending the night in front of a second-class gallery.

Yellowhorse had jet-black hair that reached to the middle of his back. A small, ancient turquoise earring bob hung from his left ear; the 100-year-old earlobe ornament was smooth and slick from its multigenerational use. Yellowhorse's sharp features and striking looks stuck out in the sea of white fans. The artist was comfortable talking to clients. Unlike most Navajos who are very reserved and don't want to engage in conversation, Willard was an exception. Years of small talk with tourists by his grandmother's side at the Toadlena Trading Post had changed him; made him more Anglo, or at least this was Willard's reasoning. It helped at gallery openings as he could start a conversation about his artworks and their meaning to him with ease. He was a decent salesman, though he hated to ever think of himself in those terms.

Unfortunately, Sally Smith was watching the New York gallery, so no one was there to help Bernard distract the gallery owner, Charles Bloom, from his prize artist. Nonetheless, Bernard Phillips, who stood above the crowd, made eye contact with his next planned superstar, smiling at the charismatic Yellowhorse. "Hi, I'm Bernard Phillips. I came from New York just to meet you and see your work. I own a major gallery in New York City that specializes in top contemporary artists. I'm a big fan of your work."

"Very cool," Willard responded. "I'm glad you made the trip. I hope it is worth your time. It looks like it may be hard to get a painting this year. I'm sorry. It's gotten a little silly these days when it comes to my paintings during Indian Market. A couple of years ago I would have been begging you to buy one of my pieces." Willard glanced out the window where the line had grown to 10 as word of the New Yorker's commitment to buy had disseminated down Canyon Road.

"Willard, I didn't come all this way not to end up with your pieces. You see I believe you are like Basquiat, a rare artistic voice of the times. Unique qualities like yours don't surface often. You know I represented both Warhol and Basquiat while they were alive. I believe you are just as special."

"Thanks. Hard to imagine I'm in their league. I studied both of them in school at IAIA," Willard offered, referring to the Institute of American Indian Art.

"How about this, Willard. I'll be straight up with you. I plan to show your work in my New York gallery and I would prefer it came directly from you, not having to buy it from shows like this. I believe your dealer doesn't have a true grip on your potential market or what kind of superstar he has. Yes it is very gratifying to see people line up once a year to buy work at the big show, but the line should be twice as long and in New York at three times the price. I have already arranged to buy at least five works from those individuals outside and hope to get five more before the opening tomorrow. I will pay a significant premium by Bloom's standards, which is why the line is growing so quickly, but by my New York standards I just made a small fortune. I would like you to think about showing with me at The Cutting Edge Gallery. How about we have dinner after your opening?" Boom. Bernard wasn't about wasting time.

"I'm afraid I already have plans with Charles Bloom, my gallery owner," Willard demurred. "But I could meet you for breakfast on Sunday before I go back to the rez, if you have time?"

"Sure, I'll extend my stay by a day. I am very serious about showing your work. Meanwhile, think about what it will mean to be a Native artist showing in New York. It gets you to a level no other current Indian artist has achieved."

"Let's talk. I'll see you on Sunday. I'll meet you at Dominic's. It's got the best green chile *huevos* in Santa Fe. It's off Guadalupe Street, next to the old Church of our Lady of Guadalupe. If there is no parking up front, which on Indian Market weekend there won't be, head to the back. There is more room around the corner. I'll be there at 10, white man's time." Many of the Indians in New Mexico and Arizona have a running joke about Indian time vs. white man's time. If you meet on Indian time it is understood you need at least a two-hour window. Time for most Native Americans is a range, not a specific number. Yellowhorse was used to Indian time. Being somewhere at a given time required watching a clock, which he had never owned and never planned to. But on Indian Market weekend, white man's time ran the show.

"Great. I'll see you tomorrow at your opening, and Sunday for breakfast at ten o'clock, white man's time." Bernard didn't have a clue what *huevos* or white man's time was, but if it helped get Yellowhorse he was up for both.

By the next day, word had gotten around Santa Fe that some crazy New York gallery would buy any of the Yellowhorses and pay a 25% premium. Numerous locals had shown up on line to get the bounty on the Yellowhorses, pushing out most of the collectors. There were more people waiting in line than there were paintings for the show.

Any opening at a major gallery during Indian Market weekend in Santa Fe can be a zoo, but for Bloom's major once-a-year Yellowhorse show, the scene was chaotic. Bernard Phillips showed up 15 minutes before the scheduled opening and threaded himself through the unruly crowd. Upon being recognized, people began

141

shouting at him, mostly trying to confirm his purchase agreement. A few irate collectors standing on the outside of the designated line yelled at him, berating him as a cheater and a thief of paintings from true collectors who cared about the artist's work.

Time to take charge. Bernard walked to the front of the line and reiterated his offer, this time out loud with no discretion: "Yes I will pay the premium if you choose to sell to me. Please bring your painting slip to me if you would like me to purchase the piece, and I will pay you a 25% buyer's premium." With that he turned sharply around and walked through the front door as if he owned the place. Those about to make a profit started clapping.

Charles Bloom, who had been prepared for a blockbuster show, was dealing instead with an avalanche of criticism from collectors about to be submarined in their efforts to buy one of Yellowhorse's works. "Duplicitous behavior," cried out one collector, accusing him of running a scam show.

When Bernard came strolling through the front door, Bloom heard the clapping and knew this had to be the tall, dark dealer from New York who was ruining his show. Bernard was dressed anything but Santa Fe casual. He was wearing a complete black Ralph Lauren suit with a red French silk tie. His expensive matching black silk shirt was covered in Northwest Coast totem pole designs obviously manufactured by someone who didn't understand what a totem should look like. Bernard thought the Indian motifs appropriate for Indian Market weekend, not realizing most of the Native Americans at the market were from the Southwest. He looked totally out of place in between the cowboy hats, turquoise bracelets, and blue jeans the rest of the crowd was wearing.

Charles intercepted Bernard just as the New Yorker started talking to Yellowhorse. "Hi, Charles Bloom. I own the gallery. Could I talk to you in private for a moment?"

"Sure, I'm happy to. If you will please excuse me, Willard, I'll be right back." Still without looking at Charles, Bernard added, "Oh by the way, Willard, do you have a favorite piece in the show?"

"Yeah," the artist answered. "I like the big one. It's called THE CREATOR. It really worked for me."

142

"Great, I'll make sure it ends up in my possession." Still making eye contact with Willard, Bernard reluctantly followed Charles to his back cubby of an office.

As Charles Bloom ushered his unwanted guest into his office to discuss his problem, all he could think was, "I fucking hate retail. Why do people always have to make life so hard? It's always about what you can get with money. Why can't it be simple and just be about the art?" He knew his face must be beet red, his telltale sign for extreme displeasure.

"Hi, I'm sorry, I don't know your name?" Bloom began.

"I'm Bernard Phillips from New York and you are Charles Bloom, correct?"

"Yes, I am. Let me get to the point. You see, Mr. Phillips, many of my clients have complained that you are trying to get a monopoly on the show, offering to buy all the pieces from people in line."

"Well, it's not a monopoly. It's just simply business. No one, including your clients, has to sell me anything. I may not get a single work. Your rather crude method for selling art, having people stay in line all night long, is not the way I purchase important artwork. If you care to make it a more civilized method, I'm happy to listen."

"I'm sorry our `crude' way of selling art is not for you, but it is the only way we have found to try to make the process fair. You're encouraging individuals who are not collectors to wait in line to buy for you essentially as an agent. This does not make it fair for all, I'm afraid," Bloom explained.

"Mr. Bloom, I don't know any of these individuals. In fact this is my first time in New Mexico. And those so-called agents are strictly collectors as far as I know and are strangers to me. Anyone can make a similar or better offer than mine, including your so-called upset clients. Let them pay for the pieces if they want them. It's simply supply and demand. Anything else, Mr. Bloom?"

At this point, Charles literally wanted to punch Phillips right in his arrogant New Yorker face. He also knew he would get sued and probably get the crap kicked out of him, judging by the rather large size of the man across the table from him.

"I'm asking you," Charles reasoned, "if you insist on buying works from those in the line, please limit it to just a couple of paintings. It would make my life a lot easier and keep my clients happy. I can try to get you a piece or two from Willard later, once things get back to normal during our off season."

"Mr. Bloom, my job is not to keep *your* clients happy or to make your life easier. That would be yours. I will purchase as many paintings as I am able," Bernard retorted. "This is strictly up to those individuals in line, not you. As I have already mentioned, I may not get any, but that's not up to me, just like you ordering me not to be a good businessman is not up to you. If you would like me to conduct business outside the gallery I understand and am happy to do so. If you try to make a production out of this and not release the paintings, I will sue you for damages and the paintings and you will lose a lot of money. Are we finished here or is there some other `fair' thing you would like to talk to me about?"

"Yes, we are finished, but here are my rules in *my* gallery. I will not accept your check for any of the pieces, unless you get in line and are first to purchase one, and then you are limited to only one piece, just like everyone else. Any individual who does want to sell you a painting must first purchase it with *their* check and then I will release the painting to *them*. If they are not a dealer with a resale number, they will be responsible for Santa Fe sales tax, and I will charge them for it unless it's an out of state sale and I am shipping it to them out of state. I hope I have made myself clear."

"Crystal. Not a problem. I look forward to my many purchases, just not from you." Bernard stood up and walked out the door, heading directly over to Yellowhorse, who had a crowd of admirers around him.

"Well Willard, your gallery owner apparently doesn't want me to have any of your paintings. He told me not to try to buy any, and that he would not take my check," Bernard announced.

"I don't know what to say. Charles is a very reasonable guy, as far I know. Do you want me to talk to him for you?" Willard responded.

"That's not necessary. I'll just pay a premium to those individuals who want to sell me one of your works. I feel badly that you don't get all that extra money I'm going to make when I sell your pieces, not to mention the premium I'm paying now. You know what I will do? When I sell any of the pieces I purchase today, I will give you 10% of the profit. That's how much I want you to come with my gallery. Don't limit yourself to just Santa Fe and this quaint gallery. To have the long-term staying power as an artist and make it to the big time you need to be in the Big Apple."

"That's very generous of you, Bernard. I hope you get a couple of my works. It would be great to get a little more cash. I know my grandmom needs a new pickup," Willard said.

"OK then, let me see what I can do. I've got to go and make some new arrangements if I hope to get any pieces." Bernard shook Yellowhorse's hand. Willard had the typically light grip of so many Native Americans. The lack of grip strength actually surprised Bernard. He had never touched the hand of an Indian before. Bernard smiled widely as he thought to himself, "Next time, easy grip. Willard Yellowstone will be my artist and I need to remember his cultural differences. I don't want to crush his painting hand, which is going to make me a bunch of money!"

Walking out to the now 30-person line that had snaked its way out to the main entrance off Canyon Road, Bernard stood up on an old wooden chile box Bloom used to prop open the door in the summer. Cupping his hands like a megaphone, Bernard yelled to the crowd, "Mr. Bloom has told me only those persons who pay with their own checks will be allowed to purchase a painting. He will not allow me to pay for it directly. So for those of you who would like me to purchase any paintings, you will be forced to pay for it first. I will pay you 35% of the price to alleviate any inconvenience this may cause you. I will set up an office at my hotel, and cut checks on the spot that can be cashed at your Bank of Santa Fe. If you are interested in my offer, I will give you one of my personal business cards now and am happy to provide you the name and number of my banker, who will attest to my ability to purchase all these pieces. Also please have the painting sent to the address on the card. Otherwise, Mr. Bloom will be trying to collect sales tax from you. And for that individual who purchases the largest painting for $75K, I will include an additional

145

five percent. I want to own this piece, as you might guess. Now would anybody care for one of my cards?"

Twenty hands instantaneously went up, including a couple of those people who had just been shouting "cheater, go back to New York." Phillips, remembering his fruit days of entertainment, quickly replied to those naysayers, "I'll take it those screaming `Cheater' decided they could use the money, so welcome aboard the money train. Who else needs some free cash to spend in Santa Fe?" The crowd laughed in unison at the showman, and yelled back at the few collectors who were not going to cash out, to lighten up and have some fun.

CHAPTER 38

HOT HUEVOS!

Every business has a situation somewhere in its development where there is a definite turning point. Recognizing that moment is the key to the business's survival. For Bloom's, the fact that 10 of the 14 paintings were being shipped to Chelsea, New York, including THE CREATOR, Yellowhorse's best painting, was such a moment. It was the beginning of the end for representing Yellowhorse, and Charles Bloom unfortunately knew it. How to stop the exodus of Yellowhorse pieces, much less the artist himself, seemed an unsolvable predicament. It was like watching a football replay: the football gets tipped and the receiver tries in slow motion to catch the misdirected oblong ball. Its unpredictable pattern is unrecoverable. No matter how hard the distraught receiver tries to correct for the ever-changing ball, it's impossible. Bloom saw his own poor handling of the whole Yellowhorse incident. His slow-motion blunder was playing out in front of him and badly.

Willard Yellowhorse had already told Charles he was considering showing at The Cutting Edge Gallery. His contract with Bloom was only not to show in any gallery in the West, so New York City was fine, and Charles knew it.

Bloom had tried in vain to explain the bind he was in when longtime Yellowhorse clients were being shut out by hired guns brought in by the New York gallery. Charles reasoned with Yellowhorse, "Not wanting Bernard Phillips to purchase paintings was me trying to protect your clients and keep another dealer from manipulating your market." Charles explained he didn't want some outside force to dictate price structure for Willard's works, especially if Willard wasn't going to receive anything from all the money Phillips would make on his work. This was the tipping point for Bloom and Yellowhorse, a point at which Willard Yellowhorse stopped thinking of Charles Bloom as his only dealer and Bloom had done it himself.

Yellowhorse gazed down at his feet. He knew if he looked in Bloom's eyes he would betray his new lack of confidence in his old dealer. He reluctantly said, "Charles, Mr. Phillips actually promised me part of the profits he makes on any resales of my work in his gallery. It seems that maybe he does have my best interests in mind."

Charles didn't have any response. What could he say? Bernard Phillips had out-dealered him on his finest artist whom Bloom had discovered and nurtured. His only hope now was not to lose Willard completely. Charles recognized the key moment and tried to salvage what he could. "That's great, I'm glad to hear this. It makes me feel better about his intentions toward you. You know, Willard, I truly care about not only our business relationship but also our personal one. I think you are an amazing individual and hope you understand I want you to be very successful, not only in your art career but also fulfilled as a person—happy. If you feel this New York dealer will help your career, I will support your decision. I would only ask that I could still receive the bulk of your work as I have been there from the start and would love to continue to see your career grow. You and I have a great working relationship, and up until this weekend we've really had no problems. If I can help you in any way or guide you in coming to an informed decision about Bernard Phillips, I am happy to make a call or two."

"OK," Willard said, "I'll let you know what I decide on the whole New York deal. But right now I'm leaning toward giving it a try. After all, what can it hurt?"

148

Bernard Phillips had purchased a great group of Yellowhorses for inventory. He figured Willard would be having some serious misgivings about selling through Bloom's after watching $50K being paid out in bonuses just to get his pieces. He must figure Bloom's screwed up on pricing when Bloom left so much on the table that Bernard could re-sell including a new premium, and give Yellowhorse money he wasn't obligated to pay. It was a brilliant gambit and it had been played out to perfection. Juggling had helped focus Bernard's mind in situations of stress. The artist, dealer, and buyers were all just pieces of fruit being tossed in the air. Bernard loved the control he had. He could manipulate a solid dealer/artist relationship and basically destroy its inner fiber with his sheer willpower and money. Bernard loved money. When he had been deprived of his wealth by his father's destruction, it had injured Bernard permanently. He got real pleasure from the fact that he had screwed another dealer who had gotten in his way. "One for the old man," Bernard thought.

Bernard showed up 30 minutes early for his Sunday morning breakfast meeting. He wasn't sure what white man time was and wanted to secure a parking space and table in the maddening Indian Market crowds. Surprisingly, he was able to get both rather easily. Lucky, considering the high price of gasoline and thousands of oil-rich Texans who had shown up to buy Indian art.

Dominic's was nothing special from the old adobe brick façade outside, but inside there was a charm. Each wall was covered with oil paintings of forks, spoons, and knives. The knife images brought Bernard back into his New York mindset. For the first time on the trip he thought of Marsh. He hoped Willard would work out, and not intimidate his so-called partner. He was well aware of Marsh's capabilities when his dominant pecking order was threatened.

The restaurant's staff was as eclectic as the old building. Most had numerous piercings and Chinese-lettered tattoos. It was an "order it as you come in" place. Then you waited for someone to find you with your little number sign that they handed out as you paid. Bernard was beginning to think he had been stood up when Yellowhorse came lumbering in. His long hair was now in a tight ponytail with a hat on that said REZ POWER. His eyes were hidden behind dark eyeglasses. Normally an individual like this would stick out, but during Indian Market weekend it seemed everyone looked like Yellowhorse. Bernard didn't recognize him; Yellowhorse had to find him.

"What's up, Bernard? Sorry for being late. I forgot and switched my internal clock back to Indian time now that I'm done with my required art duties for a while," Willard chuckled, thinking to himself he was back to being the stereotypic Indian.

"That's fine. It gave me a good chance to review the menu and think about your future. I thought I might try your recommended dish, the *huevos rancheros.*" Bernard incorrectly pronounced the "h" sound instead of pronouncing it like the muted Spanish "j," having never heard of the exotic dish before.

Huevos rancheros are a popular breakfast dish in New Mexico and Mexico. It translates to eggs ranch style: eggs sunny side up over refried beans, with green or red chile sauce slopped on a fresh-made blue corn tortilla.

"The *huevos* are my favorite here," Yellowhorse said, correctly pronouncing the "j" sound. "I like them smothered in a salsa *verde*, or green sauce. It's got the best bite to it, especially here at Dominic's. You can also have it Christmas, which is red and green chile sauce combined. Hope you are up for it; very tasty."

"You only live once, right Willard? I'll go with the Christmas version. Speaking of only living once, have you come to a decision on my offer to show in on of the finest galleries in New York?"

"Yeah. It's a big decision for me. I've only shown at Bloom's, and I'm very close to Charles so I feel bad if he doesn't get as much work. I know he depends on me a lot, if you know what I mean."

"I understand and admire your loyalty. But look at it this way, if your prices quadruple he can get 75 percent less paintings and he will still make the same amount as he does now, and more importantly you will get 75 percent more. Seems like a no brainer to me. Crystal clear," Bernard pointed out.

"Putting it that way, Bernard, makes it seem like an easy decision. OK, let's go for it. Tell me what I need to do."

Bernard sealed the deal. "I will want to plan a large opening event, so unfortunately for you we need to get you back painting. The 10 paintings I just purchased I'll put in the back racks and sell later. That way you can be assured all the works you paint for my show sell before any of these I bought at Bloom's and you'll make more money that way. I will do a press release nationwide and would like you to come visit the gallery when you can. I have a feeling you will like the works of one of my sculptor's a great deal, Craig Lendskip."

"Oh, I know his stuff, very cool. I read about it in one of those counterculture type magazines. He does those string inspired balls. They remind me of my own works in some kind of weird way, very spiritual."

Bernard didn't know about spiritual, but the stuff sure sold. "You two will make a great fit and the cornerstone of the gallery's up-and-coming artists. I'll arrange travel and hotel if you let me know when you can get out. You might find New York is to your liking and want to live there for a while. You're still single, aren't you?"

"Pretty much. I've got a girl I see some back on the rez, but nothing too serious yet. All right. I'll break the news to Charles. He will be disappointed but I think he knows it's coming."

"Yes probably so," Bernard concurred, "especially after he ships 10 of your paintings I just bought to my New York gallery. Let's order. I'm starving."

The only miscalculation Bernard Phillips made during his weekend trip to Santa Fe was his breakfast choice at Dominic's. He would remember those burning green eggs for the next two days. They had a bite in more than one way. For Willard, it was a whole different story. He was now headed down a path where he would lose all bearings.

CHAPTER 39

A NEW LIFE

Getting Yellowhorse on board may have been the easy part for Bernard. Now it was convincing Marsh that Willard was not a threat to his artistic insecurities. The spin was a Native American artist would add a different feel to the gallery, a spiritual bent. This would bring in a new kind of clientele, one that could also get exposed to the marvelous death paintings of Fredrick Marsh.

Bernard practiced his speech on the drive in from Kennedy Airport. "Now Fredrick, even though Yellowhorse's price structure is high compared to yours, remember he's an Indian and will never be taken seriously by the New York art world. All we care about is that a different crowd of collectors visits our gallery that has money and will be exposed to your death series. Besides if he does sell, the extra income helps us promote you better. He's young like Lendskip, and hanging next to your work will be such an honor for them considering your New York notoriety."

The plan from Bernard's view was simple. Once the money started rolling in for Willard, he would then pressure Willard to move to New York City. Bernard had already established a nice studio for Lendskip close by so he could bring potential clients over to see the latest piece in progress. Willard Yellowhorse was a fan of Craig's, so when the timing was right he would move him in right next door in the adjoining studio already waiting for him.

Once Yellowhorse was in his new studio space, Bernard would squeeze out Bloom somehow, probably just price him out of the Yellowhorse market. Willard, as a nouveau riche, would live above his means and be forced to paint only for The Cutting Edge to bankroll his now-luxurious lifestyle. Maybe a coke habit would develop or a pretty little rich white girl who was used to spending daddy's money would come into the picture. He would soon be trapped by the white man's ways and boom! No more Bloom, No more Indian time.

As it happened, seeing New York City for the first time was overwhelming for the small-town boy from Toadlena, New Mexico. The only stone buildings Willard had ever seen were the trading post and some old Anasazi ruins. New York had hundred-story buildings on every block made from stone.

The city bothered Yellowhorse's primary senses: the constant noise and the lack of stars in the night sky. On the reservation you can hear the call of the coyote a mile away. You can tell when a front is blowing in by the quality of sound slicing through the tall ponderosa pines on the nearby Chuska Mountains. Nighttime, you orientate direction by the heavens, which tell you the time of year and guide parts of your spiritual life. Willard wondered if his grandfather Hastiin Sherman would be able to function for just one night in the *bilagaana*'s city before becoming disoriented by what man had done to his Mother Earth.

It was impossible to see any stars, just the moon and only at its highest point in the sky. The winds swirled in all directions through the large cascade of buildings, as if they had lost their soul from the creator and were forever trying to find their way back to the mountains from which he was born.

There was only white man's time in the city. Everyone seemed to be in such a rush for something or someone. No time for contemplation or healing of one's soul. Yellowhorse was afraid of what the city might due to his *hozho,* that balance all Navajo try for, but he also recognized somehow that he was destined to take this path. Following his river of life and being true to himself were paramount concerns for Willard. He'd always felt in his art a fateful force that funneled into him, and he respected that.

The Cutting Edge Gallery was nothing like the viga ceilings and adobe white walls at Bloom's. No squeaky wooden floors; instead, gray-scored concrete with a hint of purple at its edges. At Bloom's, natural light streamed through the old multi-pane glass windows, New Mexico's bright illumination everywhere. In Chelsea, the light was only on paintings, nothing in between. No light entered the building. All was controlled at the aerostat, an unnatural habitat for Willard.

He did like the energy of New York. It was as if all humankind lived in one large hogan. The gallery clientele was different than in Santa Fe. Most were well dressed in suits with expensive furs and jewelry. No turquoise, just gold, diamonds, and black clothes. Yellowhorse was used to seeing blue and green velvet calico shirts and tanned skin. These people seemed more like funeral-home directors or vampires in their dark clothes and white skin. Even the sounds of the click, click, click of the stiletto heels seemed odd compared to soft moccasins sliding on hand-hewed floors.

The questions the collectors asked were as strange as their appearances. No one seemed to care about the spirit of the piece, just ruminating among themselves, "I think he thought this," even though the artist was nearby and could be asked if it had some special meaning. It was more entertaining for the Eastern collectors to declare their thoughts as to why something had been made, instead of asking the maker what he was thinking.

Price did not seem an issue, and it was amazing to see Bernard work his magic. He would interject just the right word or phrase, his rhythm of selling dictated by the client. Fast, slow, even pulsating until the piece was gone. Yellowhorse wondered if the same technique had been used on him. Probably, but it had worked and now the paintings were all selling at a breakneck pace, and for ever-escalating prices—$150,000, $200,000.

Willard had never planned to stay in the city. He simply meant to visit and then go home to the rez and paint. But The Cutting Edge was like a web, and Bernard the spider. Once you check in, you can never leave. Bernard had given Willard a nice little loft with a studio below for free. Craig Lendskip was next door and Willard loved his sculpture. He found himself lingering, watching for hours as Craig spun and twisted the yarn, much like his grandmother had at the Post with her own sheep's wool. It made Willard feel as if he were back on his own pace, Indian time. Somehow Lendskip had achieved what few whites do: the ability to lose the sense of time. Artificial measures of light and dark did not control him. Craig controlled himself without concern for a manmade entity, time. Yellowhorse found without this complete lack of a conceptual time barrier, he could not paint. He needed, almost required, to be in tune with Lendskip, to ground himself and get back into his own Nativeness. The two artists developed a relationship of creativity, each feeding off the other's energy. It seemed like fate had ushered Willard into this artistic cocoon in New York City for its own reasons, so Willard did his part.

Willard, who had in the past used stars as the basis of his paintings' background, started to use small, round objects from Craig's sculptures. These were the new stars of New York when none could be found. The elements of bending time and claustrophobia became recurrent themes. In New Mexico it is not uncommon to be able to see a mountain range 80 miles away, with long, open horizons of horizontal lines. In the city, the lines were all vertical: the buildings. It was if the world had been tipped on its side in a new orientation.

Embracing his alien world allowed the creative juices to flow. Yellowhorse's work, unlike Lendskip's sculptures, started to evolve. His painting basis was still Diné in concept. Yellowhorse's celestial markers had become figurative interpretations of his surrounding environment: the city and its buildings and the foreign elements that flowed through its veins. Small additions from the studio's physical space were added to the piece to give the canvas a sense of life's transient nature. It could be a spider's old skin casing left on the wall, or a fingernail snipping found on the floor. Small pieces of Willard's own hair would be cut and incorporated into the piece if it seemed appropriate to the work. The painting literally became a piece of him. Those paintings that contained small elements of his own being were the most popular with Bernard's clients.

The irony was that these insignificant elements of Yellowhorse's humanity that he had incorporated were not meant as some preconceived selling point. Instead, they were a way for the artist to say, "I am still alive in this city. Diné live even in a hostile environment. You cannot take my soul as I protect it within my on design."

It was Bernard Phillips who had noticed the odd artifacts in the paintings and asked if this was done purposely. When Yellowhorse explained his need for some kind of connection with the painting, Bernard encouraged the behavior. Bernard instinctively understood from his sales background that people would be able to relate to this need for a connection and would feel their own link with the artist. The more visible the inclusion, the easier it was to sell.

Charles Bloom had been completely cut out of the art picture by the end of year one in New York. Willard flew out to talk to Bloom and explain everything he was producing was being bought by The Cutting Edge at near retail, no matter how big or small. He was free to paint what moved him and not worry about what would sell. He had hoped Charles could somehow also buy some of his paintings. He would not even charge Charles as much as Bernard, but Willard now knew it would never happen. Charles Bloom was simply too undercapitalized to handle the kind of artist Yellowhorse had become.

So Yellowhorse said his good-byes, thanked Charles for everything, and disappeared on the next plane back to New York City to return to his new life of fame and ever-increasing fortune, never to be seen by Charles Bloom again.

CHAPTER 40

A BULL ART MARKET

The Cutting Edge Gallery found its rhythm as an art force. Excluding Marsh, all the gallery artists prospered. The big draw was the two wunderkinds: Yellowhorse and Lendskip. Their charismatic pull allowed the other artists to get exposure they would never have had. Bernard kept Marsh happy by giving him his own area in the gallery with great lighting, fancy lettering on the wall, and a small well-done book simply titled "Death Embraced." Marsh loved to talk about his work to those who had the stomach for it. He rarely sold a book and often Bernard had trouble just getting people to take one for free. Marsh never seemed to worry about sales. When he would start complaining, somehow one of his paintings always seemed to sell. Pressure off.

Bernard only put out 40 percent of what his two wunderkinds produced. The rest he stashed away. This created the perception that inventory was nonexistent, which led to a clamor for pieces by the collectors. Bernard was buying outright all the works the two artists made, a rarity for the art world. Bernard kept both artists' money in an account he controlled, and doled out money as they needed, which was rare as neither had any real wants. By promising to purchase all of Willard's work, Bernard convinced Willard to sign an exclusive for all works produced. As with Lendskip's contract, a power of attorney was snuck into the small print. Willard, whose first language was Diné, never understood the implications. For Bernard, the clause was a long-term insurance for if and when it was needed. With a partner like Fredrick, one had to be prepared. Bernard had no idea at that juncture what dire circumstances would trigger that clause, and how soon.

It had been two years since The Cutting Edge had stolen Willard from Bloom's. Willard's prices had gone up five-fold. Amazingly, Yellowhorse didn't increase his production, even though he had every piece sold to Bernard. He only painted what his creative juices would permit. Bernard decided it was time to take his two protégés —and himself—to the next level: Art Basel in Switzerland.

Getting The Cutting Edge Gallery into a major contemporary show was a coup. The fact that he had shown Warhol and Basquiat while they were both alive qualified Bernard as an important dealer, and the fact that he had been able to acquire two hot young artists of immense talent solidified his place. The only problem was what to do with the ever-present horrible Marsh.

The gallery was still technically Marsh's, or at least the business license and lease said so. The reality was that Fredrick could care less about the business other than the power it gave him over Bernard. Originally Marsh had said he would turn it over to Bernard once Bernard's non-compete clause had expired with Brit's Fine Art, but when that time came Fredrick refused. Bernard had considered leaving and starting a new gallery, but Marsh's money and the fact that he didn't seem to give a shit about any profits from the paintings sold made it impossible to leave. Besides, most of the legal risks fell on Marsh's shoulders. Bernard finally decided it was safer to just keep banking the money in his own account and not worry whose name the gallery was in. As long as Marsh wasn't too much of a pain in the ass and didn't kill anyone, he could deal with the occasional complaints from Marsh about his stagnant career.

Art Basel would change the balance of the gallery's power, and ultimately all of their lives.

For Bernard, it started out as business as usual. Only two artists were needed for the coveted Art Basel booth and neither spot was for Marsh. Excluding Marsh on the most highly publicized event The Cutting Edge had ever attended would not be easy.

Luckily for Bernard, Fredrick did not fully understand the importance of the seminal fair. He had heard of Art Basel and knew it was an international art show, but didn't seem to realize the terrific exposure artists could achieve at the world's greatest contemporary art show. Fredrick's main focus was what New York thought of his work.

The best way to keep Marsh out of Bernard's hair was to give Fredrick his first ever one-man show, an event that would just happen to run at the same time as Art Basel. The entire gallery would be all Marsh, a frightening thought for Bernard and for the rest of humanity, but a necessary one.

Another catalog was published presenting Marsh's most grotesque images ever. Because all the important artworks by Yellowhorse and Lendskip were en route to Basel, the gallery walls and floor were free. Marsh had now decided he would be making sculptures in addition to his paintings. The sculptures were of skinned human replicas. Their extreme nature bothered even doctors. The show was so graphic that Bernard was forced to put up a large disclaimer before one could enter the gallery, which read: "The following artistic creations by Fredrick Marsh may be deemed unsuitable due to their extreme graphic nature. No one under 18 allowed, unless accompanied by a legal guardian." The sign, which Fredrick opposed at first, was finally OK'd after Bernard explained that people love what they are told they should not see and how it would help generate a huge buzz. Of course Bernard hoped for just the opposite. He wanted the disclaimer sign to read, "This shit is grotesque. Avoid if possible. The true artists will be back in one month. Till then stay the hell away, trust me!"

However it read, Bernard hoped the warning would scare off clients while he was in Switzerland, and the Art Basel sales would be over the top to help pay for Marsh's revolting catalog and the opening of the doomed "Death" show. Secretly all of Bernard's VIPs were sent cards on the Art Basel show. Marsh's exhibit and catalogs were conveniently left off. The first book publisher refused to print Marsh's so-called art catalog, as they were afraid of some irate person suing both Marsh and the publisher. On those catalogs they did send out, Bernard made sure that Sally placed a peel-off disclaimer on the cover to avoid litigious clients who did not like the free little death gift.

That Marsh would be in the gallery selling assured no sales whatsoever, but he would be thrilled he had the place to himself and his beloved cadaver pieces. Bernard hired a part-time salesperson, Darren, to work with Fredrick and keep Bernard informed. Sally Smith and Bernard Phillips flew out four days before Art Basel to make sure all the artwork arrived safely and to hang the show, a big chore.

Craig Lendskip and Willard Yellowhorse arrived the day before the opening night festivities. Basel, Switzerland is located on the border of Switzerland, France, and Germany. Neither artist had flown internationally before so they decided to fly over together. The two had become close friends. Both appreciated the other's expertise, as well as the fact that they were true to what they determined was their inherent calling. Neither produced many pieces, only works that had creative substance. Each had learned from watching the other in their adjoining studios. Like many artists, they had traded works. Yellowhorse gave Lendskip a complicated small piece called THE BLESSING. Lendskip gave Yellowhorse a medium-size single twine ball with seven little balls of varying size inside. He had titled it UNCERTAIN.

Any major art fair is a huge production. First you have millions of dollars' worth of art, which all arrives at the same time. Over a hundred spaces have to be set up. The art must be delivered to the right booth without damaging it, and then everyone must prepare to sell to the 50,000 clients who attend.

Once the ordeal of readying the booths is completed and the clients are circulating, then the hard work starts. An art dealer's job is similar to being a triage doctor during a mass-casualty accident. You have to be able to quickly distinguish those who are serious from the tire kickers. The years of juggling fruit had helped Bernard's brain make those fast evaluations. He innately could recognize wealth and power. The aroma of Chanel No. 5 and new leather spelled money.

Individuals with extreme wealth have a peculiar disposition that says, "I made it." Unless one has spent time with the ultra wealthy, it is hard to explain. Bernard had it down. Dress was not important; it was only the accessories that mattered. A great watch, billfold, purse, hat, or shoes. The rest could be an eclectic mismatch of clothing worn with an Augusta golf hat. But always there was a subtle sign: the Rolex watch or Gucci purse.

Wealth does not try to show these things off. They are simply a part of everyday life. The best is a given. This includes the art in one's home, jet, or ship. A potential buyer may only look for a few minutes or even seconds before making a decision worth millions. If the dealer can recognize their tell and then add just the correct words of encouragement, the piece sells. It takes practice, like juggling. Push too hard and you drop the ball; too slow, you miss. Bernard never missed a ball or a sale.

The first night of the show, a four-day run, was a complete sellout except for the one unnoticed Marsh painting tucked on an outside booth wall. Fredrick had insisted on being represented in absentia at the event. Bernard brought the smallest, most inoffensive work by Marsh, an older painting done back during his Boston years. He explained to Fredrick it was more important to keep his most current fresh work with his one-man show so as not to disappoint his fans. Of course there weren't many fans of Marsh's in the first place. Bernard had hired actors again to visit the gallery periodically during Marsh's "Death" show so as to make sure he didn't decide to make an appearance at Basel unexpectedly and fuck up his event.

The Basel booth was 20 feet wide by 15 feet deep. Sally and Bernard had turned the small space into a cozy gallery setting, with just enough room to navigate easily. In the center was a 10-foot long jet-black pedestal, which Bernard had ordered just for this show. On top were smaller slate-gray pedestals of varying heights and widths, all perfectly spaced. Each had one of Craig's magnificent twine sculptures precariously perched upon it. There was plenty of room between the sculptures so numerous peering heads could easily maneuver between the little balls to view them from every angle. The varying heights of the pedestals made the overall composition of the sculptures take on a living quality, as if the large base was infinite space and the individual balls were planets in the universe. Each sculpture had two individual halogen spotlights placed so they illuminated the entire structure.

The rest of the booth's walls held the Yellowhorse paintings, which were all the same size, 50 X 40 inches, done as a series. It was called MY LIFE, 1-12. The pieces were sequential and represented what Yellowhorse described as his life from the beginning of his creation to present, his growth as a human. Bernard decided to gamble and sell it as a set, similar to how Warhol had originally sold his Soup Cans. Each painting had a small numeral bottom right that corresponded to a succinct dissertation Sally Smith had written on that particular painting in the series. The title MY LIFE was stenciled in red on the back panel.

Opening night at Art Basel is about who is seen and what is the hot booth. For anyone fortunate enough to be in the sweet spot of a major art show, it can only be compared to winning an Olympic medal. The Cutting Edge had won the gold. The crowd's energy was centered on the booth. Word quickly circulated that the two artists at the newcomer booth, The Cutting Edge, were not only amazing but the artists were in attendance. They achieved instantaneous superstar status. Sally had to limit entry to 10 collectors at a time to view the booth to avoid toppling over Lendskip's pieces. Seeing the crowd gather reminded Bernard of Bloom's just a few years back and he chuckled to himself at how far Yellowhorse had come. No dealer would be stealing his artists; he wished his father were alive to see the spectacle.

A billionaire oilman from Oklahoma who had flown in on his Gulf Stream directly from Tulsa, pushed his way into Bernard's booth and yelled, "Y'all, mark that black groupin' sold, you hear." He then had his assistant write a check for the $1.2 million-dollar price tag for the sequential MY LIFE. He shook Bernard's and Yellowhorse's hands, and announced he would send his jet to pick up the pieces at the end of the show and if Yellowhorse wanted, he could fly back with the paintings and hang them in his corporate headquarters. Yellowhorse declined politely, his hand still throbbing from the overzealous oilman's vice grip.

Craig Lendskip had seven important complex sculptures, nearly an entire year's work. Bernard limited sales to one twine sculpture per customer, which only added to the demand. Over 50 names were taken over the three-day period from individuals who wanted to be on a waiting list for Lendskip sculptures.

The highlight of the show was when *Art Forum,* an influential art magazine, interviewed Bernard about the show and his huge success. They took numerous photos of the booth and of the artists. Marsh's name somehow never came up. Of course Bernard helped make it happen by having Sally hand-deliver invitations to the magazine's editors at their Basel hotel. *The New York Times,* which always follows Art Basel for its readers, got wind of *Art Forum's* article and they decided to do a piece on the dynamic odd couple of The Cutting Edge Gallery for that Sunday's art section. Bernard worried that Fredrick would not appreciate reading about the gallery's other artists and not himself. The paper, however, believed that it never hurts to scoop a major art magazine, and the art reporter at *The New York Times* had been writing about Willard Yellowhorse since the artist was in Santa Fe. In fact, that was what had motivated Bernard to go there in the first place. Bernard had a bad feeling about this *New York Times* article, but he couldn't really stop the reporter. As it turned out, Bernard was right to worry: this story would put energy into motion that would drastically alter all their lives.

No one ever asked about Marsh's painting until the day Bernard packed up. He was almost out the door when the show's manager came frantically running up. Bernard had forgotten a painting on the outside of his wall and the manager had noticed it. Bernard simply took out one of his business cards and on the back of it wrote the address of a storage unit and said, "Ship it here and please send it on a slow boat. No hurry and don't spend much on packing material. Any used art box will do and don't insure it." Then he turned and walked out of the show, thinking to himself, "If I could only get rid of all Marsh's paintings that easily. Artists do die suddenly; just look at poor Andy and Jean-Michel. Maybe Marsh might have an unfortunate accident." A smile came over Bernard Phillip's face at his perverse thought.

CHAPTER 41

DYING TO KILL YOU

Fredrick Marsh was livid when he got to the gallery and Darren showed him the Sunday paper with the picture of Craig Lendskip holding up one of his twine sculptures. The caption underneath read, "One of the dynamic duo from The Cutting Edge Gallery." The article went on ad nauseum about Yellowhorse and Lendskip, and how they were the toast of Basel. A full shot of the booth was also printed in the article, with no Marsh painting in sight. The interview with Bernard went into great detail about the show and its ramifications for his two wunderkinds and how they were exclusively at The Cutting Edge. Also, how hard it was for him to keep any inventory and that prices were on the rise. Darren chortled, "That Bernard, what a salesman. Craig and Willard are gonna be even hotter now."

That night at home, Fredrick re-read the article for the umpteenth time. "No fucking mention of me!" screamed Fredrick Marsh as he crumpled up the paper and stomped on it with his bare foot. He was done being patient, done listening to Bernard Phillips. Power always wins out. Fredrick's dad had taught him that, since nobody has more power than a doctor who can orchestrate life and death. "Warhol, you're about to get some company. I hope you like funky ball and twine sculptures, because there are not going to be any more produced here on planet Earth. It's payback time for you stealing my leather portfolio, Lendskip. You go first. That's for getting your photo in *The New York Times*."

Fredrick Marsh's studio was on the same floor as the studios of the two wunderkinds, and he had access to both Yellowhorse's and Lendskip's work spaces.

Marsh may have been insane, but he was also extremely smart. He had known somewhere in his dark soul that it would probably be only a matter of time before he would tire of his fellow press-hogging gallery mates, and have to rid them from his exhibit space.

To kill is easy. To kill and not get caught is harder. The naïve Lendskip appeared to be the easier of the two to dispose of. Besides, to kill two well-known artists at once might be suspicious and it was Lendskip's photo that had tripped Fredrick's switch. To get rid of

Craig required finding a weak area in his lifestyle and Marsh knew what it was. He could thank *The New York Times* again for helping him in his plan. James W. Lewis had just been released from the New York penitentiary after serving 13 years of a 20-year sentence for extortion. Mr. Lewis was apparently not the actual perpetrator of what the F.B.I. called TYMURS, the Tylenol tampering case. Lewis figured he could make some quick bucks by demanding one million dollars for the seven deaths that had occurred secondary to tampering with Tylenol in the Chicago area in 1982. The unsuspecting victims all ingested poisoned Tylenol that had been laced with potassium cyanide. The perpetrator had never been caught, even after Johnson & Johnson had offered a $100K reward. It was big news in the medical world, something Fredrick remembered well. Every medical student from the early eighties knew the symptoms of cyanide poisoning and how to treat the almost-always fatal condition. Fredrick had to act quickly as the artists would be back soon.

The plane from Basel, Switzerland, arrived on time early on the morning of August 7, 1996. Craig Lendskip was ready to get to work. Unlike his comrades who had slept during the red-eye flight, Craig had been drawing out what would be his most ambitious sculpture to date. It would take months to finish. It wasn't a project like Francis Johnson's, the record holder of twine, but it was ambitious. Craig was biting at the bit to get to work and feel his twine.

Returning to his New York studio and smelling the musky scent that seemed to permeate the thousands of small rolls of twine carefully stored in bins throughout the space rejuvenated Craig from his long flight.

Rows of plastic green tubs were lined up along the studio's west wall. Each one had a black number designating the approximate yarn size and whether the twine had been worked or not. When a bin was finally full of completely processed yarn, Craig would move it to the east side of the studio and cover it with a blue top which meant it was ready to be used. When two to three bins had accumulated on the finished side of the studio it signaled that there was finally enough twine prepared to start producing sculpture.

The procedure was very similar to Yellowhorse's grandmother's weaving process. All the old grandmother weavers made their own wool from raising the sheep, shearing, cleaning, carding, and finally hand-spinning the wool on a traditional spindle. Wool preparation took hundreds of hours and represented forty percent of the entire time required to make one weaving. Willard's grandmother would never start a rug until she thought she had spun enough wool. Once all the wool was prepared, she could then begin weaving her rug.

Lendskip was no different. He had to have all the yarn spun before he could start the actual sculpture process. Sculpture drawings freshly done from the long plane trip had determined the approximate amount of finished twine he would need for his this ambitious sculpture.

His usual routine was to start with the last bin of yarn, which would be processed until it was perfect. He figured he had three weeks of spinning to do. The time could vary depending on the quality of the twine. Since all his twine came from donations of various fans, sometimes the yarn quality was better than expected and this allowed him to move along quickly. If he started working this morning, Craig figured he might finish 10 percent of a bin by late afternoon.

The yarn felt good to touch again. He had worked a little in Basel, but he had not brought much twine and the constant barrage of collectors wanting to talk to him about his sculpture had kept him from any meaningful work. It was the longest he had gone without working the twine since he was 15. The yarn texture was like an old lover's skin. It touched easily and the first twist running his tongue reminded him of Mr. Johnson's barn, even if the taste was a bit funny. Craig figured it really had been too long since working with his precious yarn as the twine's aroma also smelled slightly foreign, an odd sensation to the man who had manipulated a thousand miles of twine.

As Craig went to pull the next skein of twine out of the bin, he felt an extreme weakness and his head started to spin. His last thought before he died was of sitting next to Mr. Johnson's huge ball of twine and smiling at its image.

Death is never expected, even in the very old, but in a 30-year-old man in apparent good health whose photograph also happens to have just been published in *The New York Times*, there were a lot of questions to answer.

Willard Yellowhorse had found Craig's body the next day. He was sprawled out on the floor with his hand still clutching the twine he had just finished licking, a semi-permanent smile on his now tetanic face.

Yellowhorse had seen death before. Gallup, New Mexico, has the unenviable reputation of having one of the highest rates of people dying of weather exposure in the country. It's not that Gallup is the coldest place on earth, though in the winter with its strong winds it can easily get below zero. The serious problem Navajos have is with alcohol. Too many Navajos are afflicted by the horrible burdens of alcoholism and poverty. The combination leads to numerous deaths, secondary to exposure in the winter. Getting drunk and then trying to find a 20-mile ride home at night after the bars close can be a death sentence. Willard had seen enough dead drunks growing up. They all looked the same. A blank stare into space and pure whiteness from the lack of oxygenated blood.

Craig Lendskip was dead. Willard recognized it when he saw him and didn't want to feel what he knew would be cold skin. The only thing missing was a pure white color. His complexion was more a pink shade; something Willard assumed must be common to *bilagaanas* when they die. Little did he know that the abnormal coloration was due to the cyanide poisoning courtesy of Fredrick Marsh who had laced it on Craig's twine.

The thought of his best *bilagaana* friend, his studio mate and colleague, dying so suddenly was life shattering. The pain was intensified because of the great trip they had just had together in Basel. The autopsy would classify the death as accidental, secondary to cyanide poisoning that was found in a few of the skeins of twine. Since Lendskip used twine from numerous sources, almost all of it being reused, it was most likely that some of the old twine had come from a foreign source like a chemical company and was contaminated with cyanide. Just a fluke poisoning. Lendskip never used commercial yarn. He simply gathered it from wherever. In fact, because he was known as "the twine guy," often strangers would simply leave their old used twine off in front of the building so Lendskip could turn it into art. It felt good for all involved. They recycled their waste into beautiful expensive sculptures. He had used old twine his entire career. It was clear he had licked the contaminated twine, with the unfortunate fate of getting poisoned. Back in the mid-nineties, the world was not as paranoid a place as it would become after 9/11.

The police checked with those who knew him in Darwin, Minnesota, to see if the locals would confirm that Francis Johnson had the same twine-processing method. Originally Johnson had used his teeth to strip twine, but this had ruined his front teeth and he was forced to drink liquids out of the side of his mouth due to the open nerve endings in his teeth. He taught Craig to use his tongue instead.

Everyone bought the story except Bernard Phillips. The day Craig's body was found, Bernard had shown up to work early. But Fredrick Marsh was already waiting for him at the door. Fredrick wanted to see Bernard's reaction when he heard the news. He had a paper folded in his lap—that fateful Sunday *New York Times*. Sally Smith, Bernard's longtime assistant, was waiting for him to come in, too. She was obviously disturbed, visible shaking: "Bernard, I have some terrible news. Craig Lendskip was found dead this morning by Willard." Bernard quickly looked over at Marsh, who was drinking a Mountain Dew with a shit-eating grin on his face, *The Times* bouncing up and down on his legs. Bernard knew.

"Sally, would you mind excusing yourself. I need to talk with Fredrick in private," Bernard said. Sally left, sobbing.

"Yeah, tough break for the kid. He was just starting to make it big. I saw the big write-up in *The Times*. Nice picture of the lad, too bad it's his last. I'll miss him around here." Marsh sipped at his Mountain Dew and fanned himself with the newspaper after giving his insincere condolences.

Bernard snapped back, "I wonder what could have happened to him, Fredrick? I hope the autopsy doesn't show any foul play. It would be a shame if his career was ruined by some stupid stunt."

"I would highly doubt it, Bernard. Just probably some weird accident, something we will never be able to determine exactly. You know this kind of shit occurs all the time. It wouldn't surprise me if we see it again."

The thought of what Marsh might be planning next sent a cold shiver up Bernard's spine. Marsh was pissed about the news coverage from Basel, and Bernard knew it. Bernard had been worried about this, but he'd hoped it was just paranoia on his part. He picked his words carefully now: "Fredrick, tragedies like this can happen. But somehow it always happens to *my* artists, doesn't it? It would be a real loss if anyone else were to accidentally die. I would hate to see that."

"Yes, you're down to only two great artists, and only one of them has the capital backing and name on the lease, so I'm sure it would be horrible if I were to die. My guess is if someone were to go next, it would be Yellowhorse. Wouldn't you say?"

"I really don't know how to answer that question," Bernard replied. "I would hate to see our gallery lose one of its most expensive artists, who is so important economically."

"That's true," Fredrick countered, "but don't forget your `Paint by Numbers' theory. The dead guys are worth a lot more. You will just have to triple the price of those pieces you still have. I know you own a lot of Yellowhorse's work and I would expect we would be fine."

Bernard sighed, "Yes, Fredrick, I guess you're right. The economics of death are in our favor. I'm very sad to see my sweet Lendskip's passing, but business is business and I better triple the prices on the few sculptures I have left in my vault. It's a shame I didn't see this coming. I could have saved a few more Lendskip sculptures before his untimely demise. You know, Fredrick, they would have brought a pretty penny in today's deceased contemporary art market. I have a waiting list of 50 clients already. Imagine what it will become now that he's gone."

"In the future I will make sure you get some advance warning...." Fredrick started laughing, a deep disturbing laughter made by a very unbalanced person.

CHAPTER 42

THE RHYTHMS OF THE REZ

The warmer than expected reception Charles Bloom had received from Rachael Yellowhorse was the first happy feeling he had experienced in a half a year. It was apparent there was an immediate connection between the two. Charles hadn't expected something romantic to materialize so quickly with Willard's younger sister. He had come to answer some long-nagging questions. But connecting so strongly with Rachael had now changed the main reason for visiting. He had another purpose besides unanswered questions for staying on the rez, and it was Rachael Yellowhorse.

The impromptu dinner with Rachael and Preston Yellowhorse had led to an invitation to move from the cramped cheap hotel off the strip in Gallup to an equally small trailer home behind Rachael's prefab hogan. The offer had been heartfelt and had surprised Rachael herself at her ease in offering a basically unknown white man to move in behind her. What she knew of Charles Bloom had come from not only Willard, but also numerous Native artists who had worked with Bloom's gallery over the years. They all had said the same thing: he's a man of honor. To have honor is the highest compliment a Native person can bestow on someone, and knowing this was the tipping point for her.

Bloom lived and worked in one of the most expensive cities in the country, Santa Fe. The prospect of moving into an unfurnished, drafty 1948 Mobile Sportsman Trailer with no Internet was not the most appealing prospect, except that Rachael was only a few yards away. Then again, Bloom loved cars and recognized the old trailer model. It was the same exact year as when the ill-fated Tucker cars came out. Only 52 were made. Charles, looking at the beat-up trailer with dead weeds all around its frame, tried to imagine its pristine original condition being pulled by a brand new Tucker. He thought of the irony that a medium-sized Yellowhorse painting would sell for around $400K, the same amount for which George Lucas, the filmmaker, had sold his Tucker in 2005.

The trailer had been abandoned on the rez 25 years ago. Rachael's father had claimed it since it was on his wife's ancestral land. The trailer's tongue had nearly broken off and the original owners probably figured it just wasn't worth the trouble fixing, so they left it, a not-uncommon occurrence on the rez. Winston Yellowhorse, Rachael's father, had carefully attached the damaged trailer tongue to his old Ford and moved it to its final resting place behind his own now-abandoned hogan. The old trailer had never really been occupied since Winston Yellowhorse found it, except for the occasional distant relative or wayward raccoon.

The outside still retained its lovely aluminum covering, but there were now numerous dents so it looked more like a golf-ball cover. In a few places the underlying wood had rotted away. Now cold air or bugs could breach the trailer's inner surface easily. Amazingly, most of the original furnishings were intact. The first thing Charles the art dealer noticed was a print by the now-deceased Andrew Wyeth of CHRISTINA'S WORLD, Wyeth's most famous painting, which was also made the same year as the trailer. The image of a woman lying on the side of a field overlooking a distant horizon somehow seemed so apropos to the lonely reservation setting. The appliances included an off-white Marvel fridge that had not worked in decades. The dining room consisted of a linoleum white table whose veneer had been partially peeled away. The table's sitting bench's cushions were covered in their original paisley fabric. The worn coverings had become so hard that sitting on them caused a cracking sound, as if sitting on an old Twister game mat. The overhead lights were two long exposed florescent bulbs that took a minute before an illumination would occur, always preceded by a loud humming sound that never quite went away.

What made the trailer livable was Rachael's artwork. She had taken the one good wall that somehow was missing a poster and turned it into a mural of reservation life. Charles assumed it depicted her life's journey. One small middle panel was black except for a single little star, most likely representing the death of her brother. Rachael saw Bloom's reaction to the mural as she helped him move into his new humble abode. Like any good art dealer, he stopped and engaged when he saw an image that resonated with him; in this case, the mural. Rachael could tell he was moved by the way his eyes shifted rapidly back and forth, and his eyebrows rose up at different points. Nothing needed to be said. The mural bonded them emotionally at that moment.

Bloom's timing was excellent. Rachael Yellowhorse would be on spring break in two weeks in late March. She had offered her services as a guide if he wanted to see reservation life. Back in Santa Fe, Brad Shriver had been able to place the Yellowhorse drawing as promised, so Bloom had enough money to survive at least through April 15th, tax day. No luck on either his Cannon or Scholder paintings, though. The spring art season in Santa Fe was looking bleak, one of the worst on record, just like the snowfall. Brad congratulated Charles on finding a free place to live and the potential for adding a new artist to the gallery.

Bloom's occupation as an art dealer was all about design and decorating other people's homes. The fact was, however, that he didn't have anything for the trailer except his clothes and one small painting he'd brought with him: the gift from Willard. The painting was the most valuable possession Charles owned. He felt more comfortable having it near, even if he only viewed it in his suitcase. It was a bonus that now he would get to hang the piece in Willard's dad's trailer. He figured at some time Willard had been in this trailer. In fact he may have helped with its placement back when the rims still had intact rubber on them.

The thought of Willard having once had an intimate connection to the old weather-beaten '48 Sportsman made Bloom feel there was a reason, some power, which had led him to this place. He just had to be patient and let that force reveal itself, whatever it might be. At least he was getting closer to understanding the truth of Willard's life. Hanging the painting was the first order of business.

Preston Yellowhorse had the same facial features and long straight black hair as his deceased father. His face had started to change from a child's to a man's. He was a ninth grader, a tough time for any kid. Without a father, puberty was even more brutal, both for Preston and Rachael.

Many kids Preston's age were already doing drugs. This went against the Diné philosophy, which is to walk in beauty or *hozho*. This could be health, happiness, or even good versus evil. The Navajo way was at all times to maintain a balance or harmony in life. The reservation, even with all its natural environmental beauty and Navajo sensibilities, still had to deal with poverty, drugs, alcohol abuse, and recently, gang activities. A quarter of all the students lived with only a single female as their guardian and half of the families in the school district were under the poverty line.

Rachael Yellowhorse and her grandfather Hastiin Sherman were the only close living relatives Preston had. She had become his de facto mother after the unexpected death of his mother and father. One of the reasons Rachael had decided to take a job in the Newcomb school system was so she would have a steady income and Preston could stay in his ancestral home. She had always hoped to make a living as an artist and had for a short period of time, but the burden of unexpected motherhood was too demanding. One day she hoped to return to her first love, creating art, not just teaching art classes at the local high school.

Daily life at the Yellowhorse house embodied the rhythms of the rez. Up at 5 am. Stoke the fire, the only form of heat. Check on the sheep, and let them out to pasture. Get ready for school. The sheep belonged to Rachael's late grandmother and her mother, both of who had been known for their great rugs. Her grandfather asked Rachael to keep the animals until his death, then she could do as she liked. He had felt Rachael had the potential to be a great weaver, which she had demonstrated by the rugs she had produced as a young girl. He had hoped she would follow in the footsteps of the other Navajo women and become a weaving artist, that she'd stop making sculptures and paintings. Rachael had been blessed by Spiderwoman at birth by Hastiin Sherman who was known even then as a great medicine man. The Navajo believe that Spiderwoman instills the art of weaving in all the Diné women; it is her gift to the people. Traditional Navajo girl infants are blessed the first day of their life by the power of the spider. A medicine man finds a spider web and takes its web and stores it. When the first sun comes up in the infant's life, he builds a fire. The spider web is placed on each of the child's fingers to bless them with the rising sun so they can continue the tradition of weaving rugs. Rachael had received Spiderwoman's blessing but up to this point had not really done much with her inherent weaving skills.

Hastiin Sherman would tell her, "Remember what the coyote did to your brother. If you are not careful, he could get you too. Your art is the weaving, not the little figures or paint. Paint killed your brother. Follow in the steps of your ancestors. Walk in beauty and make rugs."

The sheep were a daily reminder of where she came from and what had happened to Willard. She made a promise to her grandfather she would take care of them. When he passed, a decision would have to be made. She felt life would show her the way and if she were to be a weaver she would know it. Until then, herding the sheep kept Preston busy after school and away from the Goth kids and alcohol.

Like Rachael and Preston, Charles slowly got into the rhythms of the rez. He now understood what Indian time meant. After 8 am he was alone for the rest of the day and had time to kill, if there was such a thing as time. It was the first period in his life he could remember not worrying about work, money, or if tourism was up or down in Santa Fe. His only concern was what to eat and when.

Lying around the trailer quickly became boring and he wasn't much of a reader. He had only dial-up Internet, which was too painful to attempt after years of broadband. He did check emails every day, but it was as if he had fallen off a cliff. Nobody seemed to care. His only real concern was whether one of his two remaining paintings with Shriver would sell so he could spend more time with Rachael, for whom he was falling. Charles didn't like being so intensely smitten.

174

He knew it would be an untenable situation. He lived in Santa Fe with a weak business and no extra money. Her home was on the reservation four hours away with a teenage boy to look after.

The facts were clear. It was a relationship doomed to failure. But he couldn't help how he felt. Seeing her black hair caress her back in the evening was the greatest aphrodisiac on earth. He was aroused constantly, even herding sheep, looking at the way she ran after them, her unfettered breasts bouncing with each step, the cold wind making her nipples erect.

He was convinced she had feelings for him too, as he had watched her watching him. He had even caught her smiling once as he had bent over to pick up a ketchup bottle that had missed the trash. The way her smile bent to one side was less about being tickled as it was about how she appreciated the view of his exposed backside. How to approach Rachael was another story. He was a guest, and up until this point nothing sexual had occurred. But it felt like it would soon, very soon.

CHAPTER 43

THE TRADING POST

The Toadlena Trading Post was built in 1909, the same year the great Chiricahua Geronimo died. Rachael's house was four miles away, so Charles figured he could get in the best shape of his life by running back and forth each day. He would take off around 9 am after the few cars had left the dirt road, running at an eight-minute-mile pace. His goal each time was to get there in less than 30 minutes. The days the temperature was below freezing he never made his goal. One day when it was snowing he gave up halfway and turned around, afraid of becoming hypothermic in the below-freezing weather and near whiteout conditions. The site of a *bilagaana* running in Navajo country seemed odd at first, but soon he was part of the landscape. Locals waved as they passed him in their pickup trucks recognizing his presence as Rachael's friend, and therefore their friend.

Once he made it to the post, he warmed himself by the old potbelly stove, the main source of heat. Often those same individuals that had passed him were there waiting by the stove. It became a daily ritual to tease Bloom about running from his *bilagaana* spirit. Diné knew better. They walked. The inside of the trading post was just what you would see in a movie. A trading post is a place people buy groceries, sell rugs, trade rugs, and spend time socializing. It is the local 7-Eleven, but instead of using cash, one's bills are often paid in rugs and jewelry.

At Toadlena, every person who comes into the trading post is treated as extended family. The trader knows their history and all their relatives' history. He knows if they are a good person, or not. Generally the reason for getting a loan is known as well. "Aunt Evelyn is ill and needs special food." The owner of the Toadlena Post had been around almost as long as the post and seemed to know everything. He told Charles that in the days of pawn he would keep a piece pawned way past its due day if he thought the person had a chance of repaying him in some way: "You don't like selling someone's only heirlooms because they can't pay for a couple of cans of Campbell's Soup."

The soup analogy the old trader had chosen was not lost on Bloom, who was a big fan of Warhol's Soup Cans series. The irony was, the same cans made Warhol's reputation and set him financially for life, while the real Campbell's Soup cans were incrementally stripping the Navajo of what little wealth they had.

Time would fly at the post, hearing the Navajos' life stories unfold as Bloom had his morning's freshly baked cookie and more hot coffee. Charles loved watching the grandmothers come in with their little brown weavings. He knew little about Navajo rugs but could tell by the glimmer in the eye of the old trader if it was a good one or not. The Toadlena trader would take the weavers back into his sparse office and sit down with them on his very worn-out leather couch to listen to the grandmother talk about her latest masterpiece. Bloom was allowed to sit and observe as the old trader felt a companionship with Charles since they both dealt in art: one with wool, and the other with canvas, but both fine art. Most of the time the conversation was in English but sometimes it drifted into Diné and would include more intimate details about what was going on in the family's life and how much this rug meant to her. How she had worked hard and tirelessly on the piece, and it would help pay for some necessity in her life. When enough small talk had occurred then the price was discussed. Sometimes there were negotiations and other times the trader would simply pay. This interaction between trader and artist had changed little during the last century, a small island of stability in a world of change.

When the grandmother left the back room she was usually smiling with money in her hand or a credit in the store. Occasionally she came out still grasping her rug, as the trader had not been willing to pay her price or the rug was just not up to snuff. In these cases, little talk occurred after the impasse. The weaver would just leave, saying something in Navajo that was not very complimentary with regards to the post and its longtime owner, or sometimes vowing to do better next time. The trader always offered a candy bar or gum to the weavers regardless of the negotiation's outcome.

The trading post was a central place for gatherings of the local families. It was clear when tourists came in. They looked so out of place, often loud and sometimes rude but always good for business. Bloom could relate to this as he had seen the same type of people in his Santa Fe gallery. Many tourists thought they were in some third-world country and took pictures of everything as if they were at a Disney attraction of the old West: the stone building at the end of creation with real live Indians. Bloom loved the interaction at the post. He also enjoyed the interplay and not having to sell. Not having to sell was a treat after being in retail so long.

Bloom was young by art-world standards: 46 years old. He had launched his gallery straight out of college. Now he had been in retail for over 20 years. He was so naïve when he first started, thinking Bloom's was going to set the art world on fire. The youngest art dealer in Santa Fe with a gallery on Canyon Road thanks to supportive family backing and his own optimism.

It was amazing how retail had taken the love out of the art the last few years. The art business is just that. A business. A product (art) is made and hopefully sold and a profit is made. This was how many art dealers felt about the business; it could have been shoes. For Charles Bloom it was different. He hated thinking of himself as a salesman, even though he knew that was exactly his title, "art

178

salesman." Relationships were what he had tried to develop, not sales technique. The fact that sales occurred was just a bonus, or at least that's how it had been, especially with Yellowhorse. He wanted his gallery artists to be close to him—a family—not just vendors of artwork.

The gallery business had changed from his initial idealism. It started when the dealer Phillips from New York stole his best artist and friend. From that moment on, things were different. He had never been screwed out of his main livelihood; it was unexpected and shocking. Not only by a supposed fellow art dealer, but also by a friend, Yellowhorse. He couldn't blame Yellowhorse too much as the money was more than he could ever hope to match, but the whole thing left a bad taste in Charles' mouth. It had changed his perception of what he envisioned a reputable art dealer was, this blatant stealing of an artist. Being a great artist was no different than being an A-list actor. Some poor schmuck finds the person, promotes them, then bang, they leave—too good for you.

Watching the post with the weavers gave Charles hope that it didn't always have to be so cutthroat. Maybe family, trust, and long-term relationships did still matter in some places. The reservation's Toadlena Trading Post seemed to be such a place. Make a deal, shake a hand, and do your best, was still the theme. Work as a team; both parties win and enjoy a piece of candy on the house.

Two weeks of running and spending most of the day at the historic post had given Charles back his *hozho*. He was starting to feel more balance in his life. It may have been the lack of stress or the increased exercise, but mostly he attributed it to Rachael. Her face was stenciled on his subconscious. A constant kaleidoscope of images came at him throughout the day. She had hooked him and it was a deep gut hook with no escape. As a confirmed bachelor he understood the ramifications of his serious predicament. Part of him just said, "Don't do anything, pack up and leave." Just like Willard, this attraction was an area not to be broached. He could have probably escaped, never having kissed, touched, or taken a step toward a new destiny, if it wasn't for a freaky warm spell.

179

CHAPTER 44

MUD FLAPS NEEDED

The day was a glorious one by late March standards in New Mexico. The sky was blue and cloudless, the afternoon temperature near 50 and the ever-constant western breeze had abated. It was the first real day of spring. Soon the plants would be coming to life.

Woodpeckers were already making their early-morning rat-tat sound on the side of the old metal trailer. Woodpeckers find their ideal mate by showing off their drilling abilities. Each male seems to try to outdo the other by finding the highest, most metallic-sounding object on the reservation. The aluminum shell trailer was the great reverberator. It was now apparent the outside looked like a pocked golf-ball cover from the years of unobstructed woodpecker mating calls.

Rachael found the whole thing a riot and never let him in on the joke. To stop the pesky little birds required a fake owl on top of the house to scare them off. Most all-metal houses had these, including hers, but she had left the trailer owl-less. The nearby sound was calming to her, but of course she wasn't inside the belly of the beast.

Despite the less-than-ideal sleep Charles had received, he had decided to make the seven-mile run to meet Rachael as she got off work at the high school. Spring break started the next day and they would have 10 days together. He figured he would start it off toning his body just a little bit more. The spring's warm air invigorating him, he set his pace at a grueling seven-mile run.

Arriving just as the teachers exited the building for break, Charles saw Rachael sitting next to an older *bilagaana* teacher talking.

"There you are, Mr. Bloom. You got here just in time," Rachael greeted him.

Bloom's shirt was completely soaked with sweat, his goal of 50 minutes met. "Great. What am I on time for?" he said in spurts struggling to catching his breath.

"You see, Mr. Speck here is one of our new teachers, and doesn't know what a good Navajo spring has in store for unsuspecting vehicles. See this nice old Volvo sitting in the innocent-looking mud puddle?"

"Yep, I see it, very innocent looking," Bloom agreed. His labored breathing was slowly returning to normal.

"Well it isn't. It leads directly to the underground third world as best we can tell. It may have been where Changing Woman herself first emerged to help make all of us Navajo." Rachael started giggling at her Navajo humor.

"So Rachael, you're telling me it's not an innocent mud puddle but something more sinister."

"I'm afraid so. The only way Mr. Speck, whom I pointed out is new to these parts, is going to ever get out of that trap is if you and I get behind and push like hell while he guns the accelerator."

"Got it, I'm good for my back, if basically nothing else."

"Yep, unless you got a truck and it looks like you just got those two dogs you ran in on…."

"No truck, but good dogs. Let's give her a go."

Both Rachael and Charles took off their shoes, and stepped into the recent snowmelt that was just barely above freezing. They got ready to push. Charles's head had a fine steam rising off his overheated body. Rachael was only a few inches from him. Her arm, which was covered in goose bumps, ever so gently touched up against his. A small electrical shot went up Charles' spine.

Mr. Speck got in his '87 Volvo sedan and yelled, "OK, start pushing and I'll give her a little gas."

Just as Rachael and Charles started pushing, the old man unintentionally goosed the gas pedal, his muddy wheels spinning wildly. He covered the good Samaritans in red mud from the waist up. The Volvo lurched forward from its watery bonds and with a huge WHOOSH was free of the giant sinkhole, causing the rear end participants to fall face-forward in the water. Somehow Charles moved in front of Rachael and grabbed her so he supported her whole body and he alone went face-high into the water, she on top of him. He also managed to get a mouth full of gritty cold water that he spit out like an erupting volcano, gasping for air.

"Well Mr. Bloom, it's nice to see you are a gentleman," Rachael remarked, her full body still in the pool of cold water, her long black hair engulfing his face. She then grabbed his body tightly with hers and gave him the most passionate kiss of his life. Charles Bloom never felt the sting of ice water, just the hot lips of Rachael Yellowhorse.

The two were as one after the mud bath. Not exactly a spa retreat, but it worked on the reservation.

CHAPTER 45

UPGRADING THE HOGAN

The trailer was history after the first kiss. Rachael invited Charles to more comfortable surroundings: her bed. Their first night together was the beginning of spring break and a marathon lovemaking session kicked off the festivities. The two lovers seemed to know exactly how to please the other. A two-week courtship prior to becoming a couple had helped the bonds of their union. They had already developed their common threads of art, small talk, and of course, Willard.

Originally the two were to start their vacation early on Saturday to visit the different sites of the largest Indian reservation in America. Their unplanned love affair slowed up the process. Sunday or Monday would be just as good as a new landscape was being familiarized on the rez.

Waking up early, Charles decided he would get the only warm shower of the morning while the worn-out water heater still had heat left. Stepping out of the shower, Charles noticed an unusual item of decor that stopped him dead in his tracks. The most remarkable art find of his entire life was staring him in the face, in a bathroom no less. Sitting in a cheap, innocuous soap dish next to the sink as if it were some potpourri, was a fist-sized twine ball with seven smaller balls inside. It appeared to be an original Craig Lendskip sculpture. He had never seen one in person, just in auction catalogs and online. He was familiar with the price structure, and they were terribly valuable.

The sink art, if truly Lendskip's work, would be worth a fortune; at least 20 times the house's value. As the water dripped off his stunned face and standing completely in the nude, he gently picked up the sculpture, carefully examining the workmanship. Each little ball was exquisitely fashioned out of the finest twine. It looked authentic but how in the world could a rare piece of artwork by one of the best sculptors of the 20th century end up in the middle of the Navajo reservation in a prefab hogan?

Carefully placing the piece back in the little black Walmart dish, Bloom tried to figure out what to make of this remarkable find. Nothing made sense other than that it was a reproduction. How else could it be explained? He would ask Rachael at breakfast. Charles wondered if he was losing his edge as a dealer when he started imagining such a find. He must be in love.

The breakfast meal was fresh bacon, eggs sunny-side up, and hot cowboy coffee. Cowboy coffee is the fast and cheap way to make a good strong cup of coffee. You take a cup of fresh grounds, boil them for five minutes, and then use a piece of paper towel to filter the grounds. Easy to reuse the next day, too. Rachael used an old-fashioned wood-burning stove, the same one from her childhood. The smell of fresh burning piñon/juniper mix and sizzling bacon made for a tantalizing odor. The aroma was intoxicating with the added fragrance of Rachael's slightly salty still un-bathed skin. The complex smell aroused Charles's most primitive urges deep in the recesses of his brain, hunger and sex combined.

"I see you have stolen another great breakfast from Denny's American Meals specials," he commented.

"Well my love, it's call Danny's here on the rez and we use goose eggs instead of chicken, so it's not stealing. So are you ready to see the real world, land of high mesas and golden vistas, still untouched by the hands of the *bilagaanas*?"

Charles was amazed Rachael had called him "love." He wondered if things had changed that quickly in their relationship or if it was just a Navajo way of saying good friend. "Yes Rachael, I have a couple of free days. In fact the first day I really need to be home is Memorial Day Weekend. That's about when the leaves bud out and the tourists come back. So sure, let's see a mesa or two, but be careful I might ruin it, being a *bilagaana* and all." The next question was hard to broach, as it was more dealer-like then lover. Bloom's heart rate started to race and he could feel his face turning red. "I have a question that you might find a bit odd, but it's about your bathroom art."

"I know, no good art and the towels are probably not clean enough. Or is it that you miss the outdoor shower behind your old trailer?"

"Yes, that bag shower behind the trailer was a real treat in winter. No, it's about the small twine ball that's in the dish next to the sink. Do you know anything about where that piece came from?"

"I know it really shouldn't be in there. Preston loves the little balls and probably left it in the bathroom when he was looking at it. I have found it there before. I got it from Willard. He asked me to hold onto it for him. He gave it to me the week before he died 15 years ago. He said a close friend had made it for him and he would get it when he got back home. My brother also told me after visiting our grandfather that he wanted to come back to the rez and start living his life differently. I guess the little ball was the first part of his life he wanted to leave here, something to return to. It's tragic that he never knew he also had a son waiting." As she spoke of her dead brother, Rachael's eyes filled with tears.

"I've always had my suspicions that the little ball sculpture may have been made by a very important artist," Rachael continued. "It is so well made. One of my brother's friends from art school, I always assumed. I get the feeling from your question that my hunch is correct?"

Bloom was shocked. His dealer radar was alerted. "I believe the sculpture was done by Craig Lendskip, the original twine artist."

"Yes, I've heard of him. Isn't he dead? He was a well known artist?" Rachael was only beginning to comprehend her bathroom art's pedigree.

"Yes that's right, some kind of weird poisoning related to his twine, if I remember my art history. He is very well known in the art world. So here's the thing, Rachael. If it's really a Lendskip and my eye is telling me it is, then the Yellowhorse clan just got a lot wealthier."

"Shit, really? How can that be? It's not very big, and it's just twine. It's not like one of my grandmother's rugs that took months to make. It's cool, but it's still just little twine balls."

"I know, but that's the contemporary art world. Too bad we don't have a decent Internet connection. I could look up prices. How about I call my buddy back in Santa Fe and let him do the work? What do you say we find out what your potpourri look-alike really is before we freak out?"

Bloom gave Brad Shriver a call. Brad was working, as always, his 20th Saturday in a row.

"Mr. Shriver," Bloom launched in. "Got a small favor. I'm trying to do research on a small sculpture I think could be a Craig Lendskip."

"A Lendskip? You're fucking with, me aren't you? You found a Lendskip out in the middle of the rez, because that's where all the Lendskip collectors live...."

"Did I mention that this call is on speaker? Let me introduce you to a friend of mine, Rachael Yellowhorse."

"Hi Rachael, be careful with Bloom, he's one of those nice guys. He's easy to fall for, not your typical asshole art dealer. So what's this about a Lendskip? April 1st is not till tomorrow, you know?"

Bloom explained, "No this is no joke, Brad. I think it may be a Lendskip. It's a round twine sculpture, six to seven inches in diameter, and exquisitely made. It was a present from an artist to Willard 15 years ago, so we think it's possibly his work. Could you look up Lendskip on Ask Art and see what the auction records show, and if he ever signed his pieces and if so how."

186

"Sure thing, let's see what the old database has in store for you. OK, getting there, hold on. Looks like Lendskip signed each piece with a very small `C.L.` If it's a multiple ball piece, he also signs one of the balls `F.J.` Apparently the F.J. stands for Francis Johnson, who inspired him. From the poor reproductions they show here, it must be hard to see the inscriptions. Looks like they blend in. The last five multi-ball piece sold for $450K at Sotheby's a year ago May, during their contemporary sale."

Bloom and Rachael exchanged meaningful glances. "Brad, is there any history about where Lendskip showed 15 years ago?" Bloom asked.

"Let's see. He died unexpectedly at age 30 from cyanide poisoning. Looks like he would lick the yarn and apparently some of the twine he used was contaminated and it killed him. Not much work was ever made. His last gallery was The Cutting Edge. Hey, isn't that the same gallery whose dick dealer screwed you over? I didn't know he handled him."

"Yeah, that makes two of us," said Bloom. "Shit, I can't believe it. That's where Willard must have met him and gotten the piece. When did Lendskip die?"

"Looks as though it was 15 years ago. August 1996."

There was a pregnant pause while Rachael and Charles took in the information. Her bathroom art was worth hundreds of thousands and Lendskip had died just a few months before her brother, and both were represented by The Cutting Edge. Could this be a coincidence? Charles got a very unsettled feeling. "Uh, thanks Brad. That's what we needed to know. Any luck with my pieces?"

"Nope, dead around here. I would stay put as long as possible. I didn't have a single client yesterday. I'm at the desperate phase. Got a kid handing out fliers to the few tourists along the Governor's Plaza. It's just a matter of time before one of the portal Indians finds me and kicks the shit out of me for trying to poach their clients, but that's the kind of environment we've got around here right now. Also we just went into a stage-four drought, so if you have any sculptures that use water you can forget selling them this season, and any

187

plants you liked won't be around by fall, no water for you!" Brad Shriver used his best Soup Nazi impersonation from "Seinfeld."

"Thanks, Mr. Happy," Bloom sighed. "I'll call you back in a few weeks. Let's lower both of my paintings by 20%, see if we can get some interest. I'd be tickled just to get my cost out of the Scholder. It's a great painting but I would rather have the cash right now."

"Okey dokey. I'll see if I can drum up some business at a new, kinder price. Hope to meet you, Rachael, come visit someday. By the way, I've got to ask, if you ever want to sell the Lendskip, keep me in mind. Maybe your buddy Bloom will tell you what a good salesperson I am. I have the clients for the sculpture, top money."

"Thanks Mr. Shriver. I can tell you're good at your trade, but I'm not in the market to sell right now," Rachel responded. "I'll let you know if I run out of firewood."

"Fair enough, Rachael. Talk soon, buddy," Brad concluded.

A close observation of the twine sculpture revealed a small C.L. and F.J. on two of the balls. It was for real and it had two more spheres than the one that sold for $450K a year ago. And it came with a great provenance: the estate of Willard Yellowhorse. Rachael's piece must be worth at least half a million dollars. That kind of money goes a long, long way on the rez, like a lifetime. But Charles couldn't quash the feeling of icy dread that also came with the discovery. This sculpture only solidified his original belief that Willard's death was not a suicide. Willard's passing was just too close to the death of Lendskip to be a coincidence. Charles had always suspected Willard Yellowhorse had been killed, and now he was even more convinced.

CHAPTER 46

TIME TO VISIT THE MEDICINE MAN

Rachael was feeling the same misgivings. Her world had just been turned upside down in a matter of minutes. She was having a great day up to that point: fantastic early morning sex with a man she was falling for and an upcoming free week's vacation exploring the rez. Preston had gone up to stay with his great-grandfather Hastiin Sherman and it was supposed to be a magical time. Now she was responsible for a piece of art worth more than all the generations of Yellowhorses combined, and it wasn't even hers by all rights, really Preston's, and the most disturbing aspect was the connection with Lendskip's and Willard's old gallery. Both men had died within four months of each other and under suspect circumstances.

Something was wrong and Rachael knew it. So did Bloom.

"Rachael, I don't know how to say this," Bloom launched in, "but I believe Willard was murdered and his whole final art piece and death is a sham. I have to come clean. I came up here hoping to answer some questions that have been eating at me for 15 years. I

189

hoped you could shed some light on it. I never meant to mislead you, but frankly I fell for you and now I feel like a shit, as if I had some plan, which I didn't. It just happened."

Looking intently into Bloom's eyes from a distance of less than two feet, she could tell he was telling the truth, or he was a sociopath. Either way she believed him.

"So you are falling for me?" Rachael said with a devilish smile, breaking the tension between the two. Rachael stepped a foot closer, as she teased him.

"I'm afraid so. I've gone Native."

"Nice. You better be part Cherokee as you said or I might think you're a racist."

"I'm full blooded. Well, as much as one-sixteenth can be and having no roll card yet, but I'm working on it."

Bloom retreated a foot away from Rachael so she understood his concern. "So here's the thing. I believe something happened to your brother and it wasn't by his own hand. That so-called last painting of his is nothing of the kind."

"Yes. Our family all knew it wasn't his painting, not his work. Just hype and a way for some rich *bilagaana* art dealer to make some more money off a dead Indian."

Charles wondered if Rachael ever thought of him in those terms—a "*bilagaana* art dealer"? "Right," he agreed. "That's what I've been saying for years. Just not his style at all."

"It's more than style. What you as a Cherokee/*bilagaana* don't understand is that all of Willard's work had a spiritual component that was hidden in his work. There were always subtle *yei*s somewhere, and this so-called piece not only did not have any *yei* to it or heart to it, but my grandfather had foreseen the design the week before his death and told Willard he was in trouble, a coyote was chasing him."

Charles, who in many ways thought of himself as a spiritual person, was blown away by the concept that this was a preordained event

190

Willard's grandfather had seen before he died. The fact that the family hadn't done anything about Willard's death was also disturbing. "Rachael, this is some pretty heavy stuff." He plopped down on the worn-out living room couch, rubbing his head as if looking for an answer, then looked directly up at Rachael. "You are telling me your grandfather had a vision of his grandson's death and saw the painting's design?"

"Yep. I know it sounds creepy, but old medicine men can do things like that and my grandfather is one of those men. He's the real deal, a powerful person among the Diné."

"Why didn't you go to the police? Tell them about your concerns?"

Rachael set down next to Bloom, the couch bowing noticeably. She placed her hands on top of his. "We did, the Navajo Tribal Police. They told us to have a healing ceremony because the New York City *bilagaana* would just think we were nuts. They advised not to bother pursuing it. Bad press for everyone and it wouldn't change anything. Quite frankly, I agreed. Who would believe such a story? The painting was not his because it didn't have the Navajo *hozho*? My brother was dead and that wouldn't bring him back. After the unexpected birth of Preston, it just didn't feel right to open up a fresh can of worms. The one thing that most upset us was that Willard's body stayed back East. The gallery owner, Bernard Phillips, had papers that said he had power of attorney. He alone determined the use of Yellowhorse's work and his burial. We had one of the local tribal attorneys check it out. He said there was nothing we could do about it."

"I wondered about that," Charles said. "I thought there would be some kind of service. I remembered feeling hurt no one contacted me even if I wasn't his dealer anymore."

"Yes, it was a difficult time for all of us. We had a family service up near Canyon del Muerto at my grandfather's place. Then we closed up the family hogan down here in respect to my brother's passing."

"Listen Rachael, something is really wrong with this scenario. We have Lendskip dying within a short time period of Willard's death, and they were both represented by the same gallery, owned by a guy I don't mind saying is quite slimy. I believe that Lendskip's death ties in somehow. Maybe we could go visit your grandfather and see what he has to say? He sounds like an important part of the puzzle."

"I agree. We should go. I can check on Preston at the same time. I will warn you, my grandfather is not a big fan of *bilagaanas*, especially ones who take advantage of his favorite granddaughter. It's a good thing you aren't named Carson, if you get my drift."

Charles put his arm around Rachael and pulled her close to his chest. Bloom's specialized in Native artists. He understood Rachael's reference to Carson.

The Navajos had been rounded up in 1864 by Kit Carson and sent on what became known as the Long Walk. Carson and the United States military had orders to kill any man, woman, or child who could carry a gun and showed resistance. The North had conquered the South and they had their eyes on the Navajos. General Carlton had told Carson to destroy the Navajos' food and shelter, as he had done marching through Georgia. The Navajos' sacred 100-year-old peach trees in Canyon de Chelly were cut down, and all their sheep and hogans destroyed. The Navajos were starved into submission and rounded up in Canyon de Chelly, and then sent to eastern New Mexico. It was a forced march across Arizona and New Mexico. Those too weak or young simply died and were discarded along the road. Close to 1,500 died along the way. They walked the entire state of New Mexico until they arrived at a flat, barren land near Fort Sumner, New Mexico. It was called Bosque Redondo. The prisoner-of-war camp at Bosque Redondo was brutal on the Navajo. Over 2,000 died within the first year due to a smallpox epidemic. All the Diné *hozho* was lost for four years as the Navajos were forced to be farmers on a land barely suitable for agriculture. Finally they were released in 1868 and made their way back to the sacred land surrounded by their four mountains: Mount Blanca on the east, Mount Taylor on the south, San Francisco Peaks to the west, and Mount Hesperus to the north.

The Long Walk was still recent history to Hastiin Sherman, whose grandmother had survived the ordeal and told her grandson never to forget what the *bilagaana* military had done to their people. Hastiin Sherman became a medicine man to help keep his people strong and he never forgot. In his mind, white people were never to be fully trusted.

Driving to visit Rachael's grandfather took half the day even though it was only fifty miles as the crow flies. The couple drove Rachael's old 1971 two-toned white/yellow Ford pickup, leaving the useless low-to-the-ground Mercedes 350 parked at Toadlena. Fewer pack rats there. Pack rats are the scavengers of the desert. They love to pick apart things, especially hoses on low-height vehicles. They build incredible mounds of debris of all types. If you leave any shiny object outside, it will become part of the pack rat's home.

Canyon del Muerto was the home of Rachael's maternal grandfather, Hastiin Sherman. He had lived in the same dirt-floor hogan since his birth. It was a traditional hogan, its opening to the east looking toward Mount Blanca. The doorway placement allowed the morning sun to enter the home as the sun rose. The house was made from hundred-year-old junipers his father had cut before Sherman was born. A wood-burning stove was the only means of heat, with a single bed dating from the First World War. He still had his late wife's weaving loom near his bed, the two-thirds-completed brown rug a testament to Rachael's grandmother's remarkable talent as an artist. She was in her late eighties when she recently died. Up until her death she could still see to weave without glasses. Her jet-black hair had just started to turn gray at the edges. Hastiin Sherman had kept the loom, hoping his only granddaughter would finish the weaving. All her yarn was already spun and waiting for the last of the Bear Clan weavers to take her rightful place and finish what Spiderwoman had taught her.

Hastiin Sherman was a man of few words but those he spoke were worth listening to. Many sought out his great knowledge regarding the ways of the Navajo. He knew many of the major sand paintings and had a remarkable ability as a visionary. The Navajo's Nightway tells of a visionary who was taken to meet the twelve elder gods, lesser gods, and divine birds and animals. The visionary teaches the Nightway to help in the curative powers of the Navajo.

Hastiin Sherman, who performed the Nightway Ceremony, was respected for his ability to see things others could not. His own grandson had sought him out and he had told Willard of his impending doom if Willard continued on his chosen path. Willard had believed his grandfather but the bad coyote spirit was more cunning than Willard had expected.

On the drive to Sherman's hogan, Rachael explained her grandfather's life and beliefs. He would undoubtedly have great trepidation about any white person coming to him concerned about a Navajo, especially a dead one. "He may assume you have some hidden agenda and are trying to take advantage of his people and will be hesitant to help, even with me there," Rachael warned.

Bloom was not looking forward to Rachael's grandfather's racial dislike as he had experienced this in the past. New Mexico is a racially diverse and tolerant place, probably more so than any other state, but there are pockets of hatred one comes across that no amount of love can change. No matter how hard you try, it is often impossible to break through centuries of racial mistrust.

The ride over to the backside of Canyon del Muerto was a series of ever-increasing beautiful vistas. The desolation was palpable. Buttes of varying size and coloration as far as the eye could see, all dotted by hearty junipers, large pine trees, and a solitary red-tailed hawk whose presence seemed to follow the old Ford truck. The radio was a mixture of static and Navajo. Charles had never felt such isolation but somehow Rachael's closeness helped him feel at ease. He was a foreigner in a foreign country even if it was the United States. There were no other vehicles on the road. The unusual warm spell of just a few days ago had disappeared completely, a false hope. The clouds turned gray and snow showers periodically followed the route to Rachael's grandfather's hogan.

"Charles, I know this will sound crazy, but please promise me that whatever my grandfather tells you, no matter how unbelievable it could sound, you will heed his words. He is a spiritually gifted individual and his visions are for real. I understand it is not your way, but it is mine and even though we have not known each other long I feel a closeness I can't explain."

"I promise I will pay attention to any guidance he may give me. I feel the same way about you...." Charles said, gently touching Rachael's hand as she drove the old truck toward their destiny.

CHAPTER 47

HOLY BOY AND BIG FISH

Hastiin Sherman had just finished splitting a week's worth of piñon pine, his great-grandson Preston helping him with the chores—a welcome relief for a man pushing 100. That he could even lift and use an ax was a testament to his virility. He insisted on living alone and knew when his time was up he would die in his ancestral homeland, not in some hospital like his wife. The thought of his spirit being trapped in a hospital in Chinle was not in his plans. He knew his time was short but he still had important things to finish and needed firewood to see him through the rest of the cold spring still ahead.

Preston was staying 15 miles away at his great-aunt's house. She had a three-bedroom home with electricity and plumbing. No such amenities at Hastiin Sherman's hogan. Rachael called her aunt's house to let her grandfather know of her arrival. She failed to mention Charles as she figured it would be better to explain in person.

The little dirt turn-off leading to her grandfather's hogan had its usual tire out. This was equivalent to saying, "I'm home and come over." It was rare for the old man to leave anymore and if not for Preston's great-aunt, he would probably have starved by now. He hadn't driven his old pickup in over a year and was unable to ride his horse anymore. He refused to move in with any relatives and just waited for a relative to bring groceries. Rachael had stopped at City Market in Shiprock to get some staples for her grandfather, as she knew his routine.

As she pulled up to the little brown wooden structure, a steady thin stream of gray piñon smoke was curling skyward from its center chimney with a welcome smell. The aroma of wild-animal meat cooking took her back to her own childhood when she would come up for the summer to help tend her grandmother's flock—the predecessors of that same flock she continued to look after back in Toadlena.

She could see her grandfather through the hogan's one window and he was chanting, unaware of her arrival. She would wait outside in her truck until he noticed their presence. Finally the chanting stopped and she decided it had been long enough for him to regroup and pick up whatever he felt he needed to.

"I'm going to go in first, Charles, see if I can't butter him up a bit before he sees my *bilagaana* boyfriend."

Rachael had used the word boyfriend for the first time in describing him and the thought not only did not bother Charles, it made his heart race and palms sweat.

"I'm glad to hear I'm your boyfriend. I was afraid me being part Cherokee might blow the deal, interracial couple and all...."

"The Cherokee have always been our friends so you're cool, even if you do have that bad streak of *bilagaana* running through you." Rachael's little joke caused her to start laughing a deep hearty laugh, just the right medicine before confronting her conservative grandfather.

Opening the door of the old truck let a wave of freezing air and snow flurries blow into the vehicle. No spring anytime soon here. Rachael cracked the old wooden hogan door and yelled to her nearly deaf grandfather. "*Yatahee* Grandfather, it's your granddaughter."

The old man slowly worked his way up from the small metal unpainted chair that was across from the wood-burning stove and gave his granddaughter a huge hug. Rachael noticed immediately how weak her grandfather's grip had become, a sign of his short time left.

Speaking in Navajo, Hastiin Sherman greeted her knowingly. "My granddaughter, you have come for a reason. What is it you seek?"

"Yes, I have brought a friend of mine. He is a good friend and I hope you can like him as much as I do. He was also a friend of my brother's. You may remember this man. His name is Charles Bloom."

"I know of Bloom. My grandson told me he liked this man, a good *bilagaana*, a friend of the Navajo."

"He's also part Cherokee, Grandfather, just so you know."

"I will be nice to your Cherokee/*bilagaana*. I had a feeling someone important was coming to visit me. I now know it was your good friend Bloom. He is welcome at my home. You know, much warmer in here and I can't bite anymore since most of my teeth are gone." The old man smiled, showing his missing teeth.

Rachael returned with Charles. She decided to take a chance and grasp his hand as she entered; no mistaking her intentions with her *bilagaana* boyfriend.

"*Yatahee*, Mr. Bloom," said Hastiin Sherman, speaking in English with a thick Navajo accent. "It's nice to meet you. I can see my granddaughter likes you. I hope you will treat her with respect and let her follow her path in life as a Navajo."

"Yes, Mr. Sherman, I always will. She is very special to me as well." Charles looked over to Rachael as he said the word special and winked at her. "I knew your grandson Willard very well and was his art dealer in Santa Fe. He was my friend and I hoped you could give me insight about the design you had seen."

"You know, Mr. Bloom, we Navajo don't like to talk by first name about those that have gone to the next world. Our ways may seem strange to others, but if this "insight" means to explain, then I will tell you what I can. Would you like some coffee? I just got a pot going."

Bloom had jumped in so quickly about Willard that he had shown a poor understanding of the Diné way, which is to slowly broach a subject only after ample time has passed and all small talk has been completed. Charles realized his *faux pas* and felt embarrassed at both his lack of sensitivity and his use of confusing words in his opening conversation with Rachael's grandfather. He dealt with Native artists in his business and knew better. He was so anxious to quiz her grandfather that he had not used good judgment.

"I would love a strong cup. I hope it's like your granddaughter's." After saying this, Charles realized it sounded like, "Yeah, after we sleep together I like my morning coffee strong." His face turned even redder at the thought of his potential second *faux pas* in less than a minute.

Hastiin Sherman's cowboy coffee was identical to Rachael's. It was obvious where she had learned to make it. After pouring his guest a cup, Sherman carefully sat down on the military-style cot whose springs had worn out sometime in the early sixties. Skipping all the required small talk, Hastiin Sherman began to relate the events that Charles had come to hear about. "Mr. Bloom, my grandson came and visited me the week before his death. He was very disturbed about a friend of his who had died unexpectedly. He told me he had lost his balance in the big city and didn't think he could make art no more. He was making lots of the white man's money but something was wrong with him. He was unhappy and worried.

"I held a Male Shooting Way for him, to help him find his way. I drew the Male Shooting Way sand painting and chanted to clean him of anything sharp that may have entered his life and to help heal him from the death of his friend. During the ceremony I had a vision. A dark design came from the spirits above and I showed it to my grandson so he would know what I had seen. I told him that the Shooting Way was not enough. He needed to break from the dark one who was stalking him. His life was in danger and I told him if he continued on this path this design would swallow him and he would die. I should have tried to stop him from going back to that big, dark city but I didn't. This will be something I must address in my afterworld when I see my grandson again, which I hope to do soon."

"Mr. Sherman," Bloom asked, "do you have any idea who killed your grandson, or why?"

"It was coyote, a bad spirit. He is not of this world, and will try to kill again if he is threatened. It was coyote that caused the design to appear in my vision. The holy people showed me his dark ways. I think that is all I have to say."

The old man and Charles sat, slowly drinking cowboy coffee and contemplating what would happen next. Finally after what seemed an eternity, Bloom said, "I know you don't want to think about the past, as I don't either, but I must get to the bottom of what happened to Willard, I mean your grandson. I have decided I am going to visit the big city and find out what happened to my friend. The design you saw and which was found underneath your grandson after he died is going to be sold at auction as one of his artworks. I think this piece holds the answers to his death, which I believe was a murder. I feel I must track down the bad coyote."

"No one can tell another human what they must or must not do," Sherman responded, nodding. "If you are going to follow your heart then I must protect you from this coyote spirit as best I can. He will try everything in his power to stop you, including killing you. I will perform the Holy Boy is Swallowed by Big Fish ceremony in the morning. I have not done this in many years. I must rest now so I can remember and help you. Rachael, take my new friend to the sacred Canyon de Chelly and tell him why we Diné are how we are to outsiders."

Rachael was shocked her grandfather called Bloom a "friend," and that he was going to perform the elaborate and one of the most sacred of all the Navajo sand paintings on a non-Navajo. Her grandfather knew something. He must have had another one of his visions and understood her boyfriend had a quest and he was to help him. The Canyon would help solidify his beliefs about what it was to be Navajo.

CHAPTER 48

CANYON DEL MUERTO

The Navajo nation is larger than 10 of the 50 states in America and covers over 27,000 square miles. Its terrain is immensely varied, but in Canyon de Chelly it is unique. This defensive natural wonder has been home to Native populations for thousands of years. The Navajo were latecomers to the region, arriving according to anthropologists in the 1300s.

Numerous houses of stone and large cliff dwellings dot the region. This was one of the last stands of the Navajo against Kit Carson and his men. Many Navajo died here at the hands of the U.S. Army. For Rachael's grandfather, it was the most sacred of places. His father and his father's father were both buried in the crevices of the canyon walls.

Rachael's grandfather had given her a directive, which was to make Charles understand the Diné roots so he might better understand their spiritual base.

Canyon de Chelly is one of the wonders of the world with straight-dropping, 500-foot cliffs of orange, red, and gold that change color as the sun touches their walls. The floor is fertile with the small Tsaile Creek providing nourishment for its sparse human population for thousands of years. Access is by truck or horse, and those lucky enough to visit must be accompanied by a Navajo guide.

Rachael knew its walls well, having spent her summers as a child wandering the floor with her grandmother's sheep. The Anasazi—a Navajo word for ancient enemy—lived for over 500 years here before her family arrived. The numerous large caves and overhangs were perfect for building rock homes for the inhabitants. The Navajo do not believe in disturbing the dead, even those of a long-gone culture. Their aversion to bothering any of these sites has left many prehistoric ruins nearly pristine, just as if they were there yesterday. The Anasazi abandoned the area probably after outstripping their resources and undergoing a drought. Their descendants are the Pueblo people. The Diné have lived in the canyon for nearly 400 years. The walls of the canyon have petroglyph drawings made by the Anasazi, Hopi, and the early Diné inhabitants.

One cave in particular had special meaning to the Navajo. Its hidden entrance is located in the Canyon del Muerto, which translates literally into the Canyon of the Dead. This cave has been a sacred place since 1805 when a group of 100 women, children, and elderly Navajos were massacred by a band of Spanish marauders. The hidden spot high on the canyon wall was discovered by the garrison who discharged their weapons into the cave until they had disposed of their enemies. The bodies remained untouched for nearly a hundred years until 1903 when a half-Navajo, Sam Day, rediscovered the cave and brought it to the attention of local anthropologists. The cave held the remains of the Navajo and their clothing that became the earliest documented examples of Navajo textiles. For those whose ancestors were slaughtered there, it also became a reminder of what had happened to their people at the hands of outsiders.

The Sherman family sheep hogan was located near the cave. It was a special place for both Rachael and her grandfather. The small hogan was made of stones from the surrounding canyon, many recycled from previous buildings of early inhabitants, the Anasazi. Hastiin Sherman's father, who built the remote structure, constructed the roof from juniper logs that were hauled by wagon 70 years ago from the Chuska Mountains. The metal roof had been added one summer when Rachael was a teenager. She fondly remembered the symphony of sounds bouncing off the canyon walls as the hogan roof expanded and contracted in the early morning and evening. The pinging metal was nature's alarm clock signaling the temperature changes of the canyon floor.

Charles Bloom understood the importance of what Rachael was sharing with an outsider. He would never be Diné, but her family was allowing him to experience their cultural heritage, something few *bilagaana* knew about. Rachael explained to Charles the importance of the cave and what had happened. She also went into detail about her own experiences spending summers herding sheep and becoming one with nature. The gods of the Diné's ancestors overlooked all who entered this sacred place. Because her grandfather had welcomed him to their world, he must have something important in store for Charles.

The spirituality of Canyon del Muerto infiltrated Bloom's soul. He felt different, as if he were being baptized into a new religion. Rachael's openness with her own life also added a new dimension to their relationship.

Hastiin Sherman decided Bloom needed help in his quest to find the truth about his grandson's death. The old medicine man had to equip Bloom in case he had to battle the bad coyote spirit, the Ma'ii ni.

A specific sand painting from the Male Shootingway was chosen: Holy Man and Holy Boy, which are trapped by supernaturals. This was the most intricate of the Navajo sand paintings in the old medicine man's arsenal of treatments.

Hastiin Sherman, Rachael, Preston, and Charles all met at grandfather Sherman's hogan early the next morning and took the old four-wheel drive Ford to the summer sheep hogan in Canyon de Chelly. The landscape was magnificent from the canyon floor. High red cliffs with occasional streaks of cobalt blue intermixed with stark white bluffs. As the Ford drove deeper into the canyon, the cliffs got higher and Anasazi ruins more numerous. It was compelling yet not a single word was spoken during the hour-and-a-half bumpy trip. Charles was starting to understand the Navajo way of introspection. He respected the seriousness of this journey. The air was a crisp 20 degrees at 7 am, but the sun was shining so the temperature felt warmer.

The hogan was in a remote side canyon far removed from any perceivable road. It would have been easy to miss even for a Navajo. The narrow passage of steep cliffs opened up to a small cottonwood-filled pasture with a few stray brown corn plants from years past. The small structure was adjacent to a sheer white cliff stained with zebra-like black lines, insignificant in size next to the giant wall of stone. Once inside the old stone hogan, Hastiin Sherman readied the structure for his patient's treatment. To make room for her grandfather's intricate sand painting, Rachael and Preston's job was to move the hogan's 1910 heating stove that took up most of the center portion of the eight-sided room to outside the hogan. Once the stove had been removed, a fire was started to heat up the surrounding area. The smell of piñon filled the canyon floor, the cold air keeping the gray smoke low as it slowly drifted into the still canyon air.

Hastiin Sherman uttered his first words of the morning: "Mr. Bloom, what I will perform today is for my late grandson, who I hope you will bring home to me soon. Even though you may not be Diné, your heart is open and I believe can be touched by my medicine. I need you to help my grandson get the proper burial and follow with me to the afterlife." As he spoke, Sherman pointed to a red northern-facing canyon wall above, the little crypts barely visible on the distant rock face. The medicine man then looked to the heavens and repeated his wishes in English and Diné: "Mother Earth, hold the crypts of my ancestors and they will hold me soon. I ask for your help to bring my Ma'ii Yaah back so he can join me in my final travels."

Charles had not noticed the multitude of small, round stone crypts that dotted the high walls above. He could barely see the little square openings on each dome. Squinting now, for an instant he imagined he almost saw into them. "Hastiin Sherman, I promise I will not return until I have helped recover your grandson and my friend, to his proper burial ground. I thank you for any help you can give me in this journey." The ceremony and his newfound alliances on the rez were strengthening Bloom's resolve. He was no longer alone in his intuition that it was his fate to solve the mystery of Willard's death.

"Rachael," Sherman directed, "would you mind getting your Charles, Preston, and me some food for a late lunch. We will be in the hogan for quite some time. Charles will also need his clothes, bedding, and lots of warm blankets. He will be here for four days."

When the old man said *four days* Charles suddenly felt panic at the thought of that many days of some unknown Navajo treatment and it sounded like he would be alone. He began realizing how dangerous his mission was, if it was going to require four days of girding himself in a freezing hogan.

Hastiin Sherman's direction was Rachael's cue to leave. She understood she was not to come back anytime soon. Her grandfather was on Navajo time and he would stay in the hogan until he had completed his sand painting and vision quest. She gently gave Charles a squeeze of his hand and in his ear whispered, "Charles, keep your mind and heart open and let my grandfather show you the way. You will need to stay as long as it takes for his medicine to work."

The old man slowly moved into the sheep hogan, bringing with him various colored bags of sand. He made the trip four times, lining each of the bags in a neat row. He gave instructions in Navajo to Preston, who started emptying large bags of brown sand on the hogan floor. Once all but the very perimeter of the hogan was covered in three inches of fine brown sand, Hastiin spoke again.

"Charles, I need you to sit in the middle of the sand painting. I will be working on your piece for many hours, so if you want to go relieve yourself, now is your chance."

Charles took advantage of his last potty break and got himself prepared for a long day, which he expected to be both mentally and physically challenging. He had no idea what to expect, but hoped no bear claws were involved. Charles' mind flashed back to an old movie from 1970, "A Man Called Horse" starring Richard Harris. Harris, a white man, was indoctrinated into the Sioux tribe and was hung up by sharp bear claws piercing his chest for days waiting for visions.

Charles was not Navajo and had never attended any kind of Indian ceremonial other than a couple of feast days at Santo Domingo Pueblo, an Indian village near Santa Fe. Pueblo feasts were fun with lots of dancers and smells of cooking bread. This, he felt, would be very different. He was open to new ideas, and was certain he could use help when it came to confronting the mystery of Willard's death.

Carefully, Hastiin Sherman sat down on the dirt floor and prepared himself for the most intricate sand painting in the Navajo repertoire. For a man in his 90s, it would take all his energy to be able to properly prepare the daunting piece. Young Preston, who had been training with his great-grandfather since he was 10, was used as a go-fer and allowed to fill in simple parts of the evolving piece.

Generally these types of curing rituals are attended by many people and are costly to those being treated. A four-day ceremony could run many thousands of dollars to have a great medicine man like Hastiin Sherman treat you. The old medicine man had no intention of charging Charles. He needed Bloom's help and didn't have enough time left in his life to do a proper ceremony with lots of participants. This ceremony would be very intense: just Charles, Preston, and Hastiin Sherman would be involved.

The sand painting background was first laid out on the floor using light brown sand against the century-old, hard-packed, chocolate-brown dirt floor. Methodically, an image next came to life under the sure hand of the medicine man. On the north quadrant was Holy Man captured by Thunders while hunting mountain sheep. Holy Man, his black body covered in white lightning bolts, was surrounded by Big Fly and Otter. The southern design depicted Holy Boy, who had been swallowed and was in the belly of Big Fish. Holy Boy held a flint knife in his right hand, which he would use to escape Big Fish, and in his left hand was the medicine to heal wounds.

During the process, which took seven hours to prepare, the old man chanted nonstop in Navajo. It was apparent where Willard and Rachael got their artistic acumen. Hastiin Sherman's dexterity with the colored sands was no different than any accomplished artist with their paint and brush. He seemed as if he didn't need to even look at the painting; it just appeared with each new sand lot. Sherman's eyes seemed more closed than open. No words were spoken to Charles during the entire process. Bloom sat and watched in amazement. Only Preston moved, and that was to stoke the outside fire and fill in areas his great-grandfather had finished. The air was filled with chanting and the occasional raven's cawing.

When the sand painting was completed enough to satisfy the old medicine man, Sherman looked up to the heavens so the gods would be able to know they could look down at his powerful medicine and bless his patient. Then Sherman turned his attention to Charles, whose eyes were as wide as saucers. Bloom had no idea what to expect but kept Rachael's words in his mind, *be open*.

The medicine man took an old Navajo basket that was covered in corn pollen and gently felt its rim. The basket was turned ever so slightly so the spirit break in the basket now faced east. The basket makers know that the break is hard to see in a dark hogan all covered in pollen, so they always end the basket's rim right at the spirit break so it can be found by those without sight. Hastiin Sherman took little pinches of the precious yellow pollen and applied them to Charles' head, shoulders, hands, and the soles of his feet. Once just the right amount of powerful pollen had been placed, Hastiin Sherman gently grasped Charles' hands and started chanting at a much louder volume. The light pressure seemed to give some kind of heat from the medicine man's hands to his, especially to his wrists and spine, which began to tingle with excitement.

Finally the chanting crescendoed. Then came silence from the medicine man. Hastiin Sherman's eyes shut with only the tiniest of trembling noticeable in the old man's hands, his eyelids fluttering back and forth. Bloom's mind was completely clear and he had no thoughts other than of Willard and Rachael.

As if coming out of a trance, Hastiin Sherman's grip lessened then he let go of Bloom's hands and shared, "I have seen your path and it's filled with much danger. Your journey will not be easy and if you are not of one with Holy Boy you too will have my grandson's fate. Like Holy Boy you must escape Big Fish's grasp if you hope to return to the land of the Navajo."

Charles had no idea what all of this meant, but he understood innately that what Sherman had said was true. He would be in grave danger if he went back to New York City looking for answers. Surprisingly, this revelation made Bloom want to pursue the truth even more. It was something he was meant to do. It was his duty.

The medicine man slowly worked his way to his feet, and then as he sang a low song he shuffled over the painting, his deerskin moccasins mixing all the colors of blue, red, green, black, and white until there was nothing left but a gray hue on the hard-packed dirt floor. Preston and Hastiin Sherman pushed all the sand to the middle around their patient. Bloom felt frozen in space and time. The sand was scooped up with care and distributed outside around a small piñon tree on the east side of the building.

"Charles, I'm ready for lunch and some water. You can get up now. I think Rachael will have something for us. Let us go." As if by some magical Navajo watch, Rachael drove up at that instant in the yellow

Ford, bringing a selection of sandwiches, drinks, and Bloom's supplies.

"Rachael, my granddaughter, I'm ready for a little food. I'm getting old now and can't go so long without nourishment. It's going to be cold soon. We better get back to my hogan. I think the weather is about to change." Just as Hastiin Sherman finished saying *change,* the perfectly calm air started to blow, the temperature dropped, and lines of dark clouds appeared on the cliff tops.

"Charles," Sherman directed, "you must stay in my sheep hogan for four days. You cannot make any heat. No breaking or cutting of anything. You cannot touch hands, as when you shake hands, or you will lose the powers I have given you. Rachael can talk with you when she visits, but the two of you must not be alone. Preston should be around. I know this must seem strange, but it is the way and if you want the power to stay with you it is important to follow what I say. You will need all the power on your upcoming journey. Rachael has brought you plenty of clothing and blankets. You will be safe in my hogan, but it will be cold the next few days. I'm sorry you can't have heat but it is important to follow our rules. It is for your own protection from the coyote's jaws."

The three Navajos drove away. No words were spoken in the truck, but the mood was markedly different than on the ride out. Charles was left alone at the old sheep hogan to let Hastiin Sherman's medicine percolate. Rachael could see in her grandfather's demeanor that he was genuinely worried. He had seen something, and it wasn't good. Her Charles was in real danger. During the slow drive back to Sherman's hogan, the weather completely changed. Snow flurries came out of nowhere and the temperature dropped 15 degrees. "Rachael," Sherman advised, "you and Preston need to get back to your aunts before the snow comes. You better have Preston stay with you tonight. I'm afraid you can't get back before the winds come."

Now left alone in the remote backcountry of Canyon de Chelly, Charles tried to soak in what had transpired over the last eight hours. He had been a patient in an ancient Navajo ritual practiced in a foreign language. He had felt things—physical sensations he couldn't classify in any logical terms. The next four days were to be in near isolation and very, very cold. He didn't know what he was supposed to do, if anything. Bloom figured this was what being on a deserted island must feel like. He was Tom Hanks without Wilson the soccer ball in "Castaway." If Rachael for some reason didn't come back, he could easily die.

The first night was arctic cold. The little hole in the roof for the stovepipe let in frigid air and copious amounts of snow. Finally at around 2 am, Charles decided freezing to death was not part of the ceremonial and took an old box and standing on his tip-toes, plugged the hole with one of his woolen blankets. He slept in little fits of 30 minutes each. His dreams that night were full of images of being eaten by Big Fish and running, always running, and lightening all around.

As the sun broke over the cliff's walls, Charles heard Rachael's old truck sputtering onto the canyon floor. The sound was never so reassuring: human life. Rachael brought him cold coffee and a sandwich. Rachael also looked tired, as if she had not slept. It was obvious she was concerned about Charles for her to be at the canyon so early, and especially with nearly a foot of new snow. Preston was sound asleep in the cab and never moved for the next four hours. Rachael spent the day with Charles, parceling out more food and blankets. She explained her grandfather had made it clear that Charles had to spend the next three days alone if he was to get the full benefit of his powers. No human contact. She would be back on day four at noon.

No human contact was all Charles could hear in his mind. He had been attached to his Blackberry so long that it felt odd. He could empathize with how Barack Obama must have felt when he lost his phone after moving into the White House. At the time he thought it was so odd. Why wouldn't he be happy not to have the added distraction of the phone? But now he understood. It was the isolation. No human contact with those you wanted to touch. No way to escape the loneliness. He knew he was no president, but he did relate to the president's emotional mindset. Charles was learning what Rachael's grandfather's treatment was about. Self-awareness and understanding of the interconnectedness all humans have, even with presidents.

During the next three days, time started to bend. It was about introspective thought, hunger, and contemplation of the future, including death. Art, nature, and humanity blended together. The ancient crypts of the Sherman and Yellowhorse clans' voices became relevant. The hundred *chindi* from the sacred Massacre Cave were heard. The wind and snow were their voices telling of life's journey and end. Charles, for the first time in life, thought of his own mortality and path in life. What had he done to make the world better and his own life enriched? He was a salesman basically, but he also affected lives in many positive ways. The art he enjoyed and shared with others, the artists he helped support, and how Willard Yellowhorse had in an oddly circuitous route brought him his first and maybe only deep love, Rachael. Charles was a handsome man at six-one, but most of his life had been spent as a loner with his gallery dominating his thoughts.

Without his art career, Charles would not be in this cave or in love with Rachael, and maybe that romance would grow into more, a new generation of Blooms and Yellowhorses combined.

The last day was peaceful for Charles Bloom. He had no sense of time. He ate and slept only when his body's rhythms dictated to do so. He rarely moved and when he did it was purposeful. No wasted energy. He was in balance for the first time in his life and now

210

understood the true definition of tranquility. He almost didn't hear the hum of the glass-pack muffler on the old Ford truck as Rachael pulled up with Preston on the fourth day of his Navajo treatment.

✳ ✳ ✳ ✳

"Hi, Charles," Rachael greeted him. "I see the bad coyote hasn't gotten you. I'm happy to see I will still have a friend tonight. It's supposed to be cold again, and my feet miss yours."

Bloom was surprised at Rachael's forwardness, especially with Preston so near. He was also excited by her voice. He replied, "You won't want me too close, I can assure you, until I get a nice, warm shower. I think I've lost a pound or two. The Navajo Diet Method works almost as well as my No Painting Sales Art Dealer Diet I've used in the past."

Charles, Preston, and Rachael spent the next hour replacing the stove in the hogan and reattaching all the parts and closing any cracks in the ceiling. The ride back to Hastiin Sherman's home was one of laughter and joy; it was as if Charles had been away for years, not just four days, and now he was more Navajo than white in Rachael's eyes.

Arriving at Hastiin Sherman's hogan, the old man was nowhere in sight. Rachael ushered Charles into the hogan and told him her grandfather wanted to see his patient. The old medicine man looked as if he had aged greatly in the four days Charles had been in treatment. The elaborate ceremony had used up most of his remaining life juices. His earth time was short.

"How are you feeling, Charles?" Sherman asked.

"I actually feel very good. The best I can remember."

"Yes, that is how you should feel. You walk in beauty. You didn't light a fire, or break or cut anything while you were in the hogan?"

"No, none of those things. I did plug the hole in the roof. It was quite cold. I hope that was OK?"

"Sure, if you hadn't you might have frozen, so you pass the don't freeze to death part of my test," the old man said, smiling to himself at his *bilagaana* humor. "Charles, I have something for you. It will help in your journey." The old man shuffled over to his worn-out antique pine bureau, bent down to the last drawer, and carefully pulled out a brown deerskin purse fringed on both ends. As he did so he began to softly chant. Charles assumed the item the medicine man was retrieving must be very powerful.

Inside the worn fringed purse were three smaller leather pouches, all tied with sinew and each dyed a different color. The pouch painted ochre, Sherman set over to the side. Then in one of the other hidden compartments of the purse he carefully removed a six-inch-long flint blade, which was covered in a separate tan animal-skin hide.

"Charles, this blade is like the one Holy Boy used to free himself from Big Fish. You will need its presence if you try to fight the evil coyote spirit. Keep it close at all times. This small bag is medicine if Big Fish hurts you. My medicine will heal you. I wish you luck. May the holy people look after you." And that was that.

CHAPTER 49

TAXES ARE DUE

The rest of the week with Rachael flew by. Rachael took Charles to visit distant relatives near the base of the Chuska and slot canyons in unnamed mesas. Charles grew more in tune with the rhythms of the rez. When it was time for Rachael to return to work as spring break was over, she picked up Preston from his great-aunt's house and the three made their way back to Toadlena. Nothing had been spoken regarding what Hastiin Sherman had seen. Rachael knew it must not be good and she didn't want to dampen their spirits with talk of bad demons. She knew such discussion would come soon enough.

The night before Rachael's school started, Charles decided they needed to talk. The mood was somber, as if Charles were heading for war and shipping out the next day. He explained to her what her grandfather had shared with regard to Holy Boy and the danger awaiting him. He also showed her the knife. Rachael burst into tears. This was serious stuff and the knife solidified her worst nightmares. Her concerns would only intensify in a few weeks when her school email account brought more mystifying information.

In the midst of all their planning, Brad Shriver resurfaced with great news for Charles. He had mailed a receipt for a bank deposit made for Charles' Fritz Scholder painting that he'd sold. He also included the most recent Sotheby's Art Catalog for the upcoming May 7th Contemporary Art Sale in New York City. Lot 47 was Willard Yellowhorse's STRUGGLE. A rare and expensive single-item addendum catalog had been printed solely on the painting to go along with the main publication. The thin but well designed addendum, which was printed on glossy heavy stock, told the story of Yellowhorse. It even mentioned Bloom's gallery as the site of his first one-man show. Shriver had put a yellow sticky on the page as if to point out the obvious to Charles. The addendum included the prerequisite chronology of Yellowhorse's life, beginning with his birth at his family hogan in Toadlena and ending with his suicide and the "magnificent last work," as they were calling it. The estimate was $2.5 million to $5 million. It portrayed a watered-down version of the painting's gory origins and why the experts thought Yellowhorse had made it in such a disturbing fashion. No mention was ever made about Willard coming back home to the rez and his plan to leave The

213

Cutting Edge Gallery. And definitely nothing about his grandfather's vision of Willard's death was mentioned. The catalog had a long quote from his dealer talking about the importance of this final work as Yellowhorse's *piece de resistance*: how Yellowhorse had given his life to enhance his short but overall important body of work. Somehow even in such a horrific ending as hanging himself, Yellowhorse had hoped his color senses and rhythmic pattern of painting would live on after his own struggle with depression.

Phillips' bullshit quote and quack diagnosis of depression made Bloom want to throw up. Bloom knew it was crap and it was now even more obvious to him that STRUGGLE was nothing like Yellowhorse's work. Bloom had had deep suspicions even before he met Hastiin Sherman, who explained about the celestial bodies and his own vision of the design. Yellowhorse's paintings always had subtle images hidden somewhere in the background, and Rachael's references to *yei*s were nowhere to be found. This was a death painting all right, but one that was done to help cover up his murder. Bloom, upon seeing the catalog, knew he had to stop the sale of the work somehow, even if telling the crazy story of sand paintings and medicine men in New York meant he would be thrown out and banned from the auction house for life.

The painting was the key that could unlock the hidden truth of Willard's death. Bloom just needed to find the lock and the answer was in New York. Thanks to Brad's outstanding salesmanship, there was now enough money to pay taxes and go to the Big Apple to sort out what had really happened to Willard Yellowhorse. The tribal police might be right in saying it would be a lost cause, but the Yellowhorse family needed closure. Willard's remains belonged here on the rez, and the last so-called Yellowhorse should never be included in Willard's *catalogue raisonné* of paintings.

Rachael was worried for her lover. She wanted to come and help. Charles explained to Rachael that as much as he would cherish her company, she had a job and what's more, Hastiin Sherman had only seen him fighting the coyote spirit. He must accomplish the task on his own if he hoped to stop the painting sale and find out who had killed Willard. The medicine man had imparted strong power. He would be safe. Bloom didn't share the substantial risks her grandfather had told him about. It was frightening enough when he thought about it, and he didn't want Rachael to worry.

The plan to stop the sale and expose Bernard Philips could ruin Charles as an art dealer. The man selling the death painting was very rich and a well-respected contemporary art dealer. But Charles felt he now embodied the spirit of Holy Boy and somehow must triumph. Hastiin Sherman had prepared him for battle and he had to be a warrior, fighting the Thunders and the bad coyote spirit.

The extra money from his most unexpected painting sale would more than allow Bloom to fund the New York trip. Everything seemed to be falling into place for the trip. Nonetheless, for the first time in his life Bloom was seriously thinking about his own mortality. His time at the sheep hogan had begun the process. If he died in New York, any money he had left from the Scholder sale would go where? No need for money if you're dead and no real family concerns, except now there was Rachael.

Most of Charles' wealth was in his small Yellowhorse painting, Willard's gift. The irony was not lost on Bloom. He decided it should stay with Rachael next to the Lendskip for safekeeping. He told her if for some reason he did not come back, it would be hers to do with as she liked. Just one caveat—if he weren't able to stop the sale of STRUGGLE, then under no circumstances was she allowed to sell his Yellowhorse at Sotheby's. "Take it to Christie's instead. Teach 'em for selling a fake," he said. He attempted a faint laugh with his weak Sotheby's joke, hoping to ease the serious subject of his possible death. But when he looked at Rachael, tears were streaming down her beautiful high cheekbones. His attempt at levity had failed miserably. Rachael buried her head in his chest and vowed, "No sale, ever!" Bloom's own eyes filled with tears. He wasn't used to having somebody care this much about him.

CHAPTER 50

VISITING BURIED BODIES

Leaving the reservation was one of the hardest things Charles ever had to do. Its remote qualities had allowed Charles to turn off the rest of the world, with its time, art, and money. It was a foreign concept for one who made his living in retail.

Since it was already nearing mid-April, he went back to Santa Fe first. He was intent on organizing the gallery for another departure, this time for the East Coast. He felt he had lost his retail edge and was without his old drive to succeed in business. Bloom's had been hanging on by a thin margin anyway. The current art recession had already taken down some very good galleries. It was interesting to him that his main concern was not the loss of his potential income nor seeing his name on the gallery, but what it would mean to the artists who depended on him to help support their lives. Most of his artists relied on his summer sales to help keep them afloat. It's a hard road being a Native artist, creating objects people don't have to own, as art is not a necessity of living for most. One needs allies to survive in this landscape of creativity, and Bloom was one of their best.

He headed to the East Coast in early May. Bloom had plenty time to develop a plan of action during his long solo drive. His concerns about whether he could handle a retail environment anymore could be a moot point, depending on this trip's outcome. If the New York City auction of the Yellowhorse piece went off as scheduled and he made a huge commotion attempting to stop the sale, he was toast. At best he would get sued and at worst he would get sued and be blackballed by the contemporary art dealers in New York City, spearheaded by Phillips. There would be many unflattering articles written about the art dealer who went Native.

Then there was Hastiin Sherman and his visionary predictions. Those four days at the sheep hogan seemed very real at the time, but now, weeks later, driving cross-country in his old Mercedes, they felt surreal. Almost comical. He tried to keep in his head Rachael's words: "Listen to what he says. He is a powerful medicine man."

Rachael was a smart 21st-century woman, and yet she truly believed what her grandfather had told him. Bloom believed as well. He had decided to drive to the East so there would be no issues with airport security and no chance he would be separated from the flint knife's power. He had a small bundle of herbs of some unknown source with no doctor's prescription and what appeared to be a very sharp, long, ritualistic black-stone knife. To try to explain these to any airport guard in this day and age was asking for federal time. So, a 2,200-mile road trip was on the agenda. The blade stayed near.

The first stop was not New York but Boston, to visit Willard's grave. Hastiin Sherman wanted him to bring his grandson home, so Charles would have to see where Willard was buried and what his options were as far as removing a body.

Discovering where Willard's body was buried had taken some good old detective work. There was nothing on the Internet about the location of Yellowhorse's grave. Charles found this strange. He could Google almost any famous artist and generally find where they were buried in a couple of searches, but not Yellowhorse, and even more disconcerting, not Lendskip. It was as if these two artists were lost to mankind. The obituaries on both men read as if they had come from the same hand: information about their art and tragic early deaths, nothing about where they were buried. Regarding services it read: "Private, family only."

The reality was none of the Yellowhorse family had gone to the funeral and none of them were invited. A certified letter came from Willard's attorney saying the executor of his estate, Bernard Phillips, per Mr.Yellowhorse's wishes, wanted no services and his body had been cremated. The Navajo tribal lawyer looked into the validity of the letter and determined there was nothing the family could do. The coroner's autopsy had determined death as a suicide, no foul play. No further investigation was needed and the body was turned over to the executor of the estate, per Yellowhorse's wishes.

It occurred to Bloom to just call Phillips and ask him outright about the body's ashes. But if Phillips were involved in Yellowhorse's faked suicide, then he would be tipped off. Bloom didn't want this, nor did he trust Phillips.

Charles and Rachael had decided to review the wording of the death certificate, as it would have the most information. To get a copy required Rachael to submit a request on behalf of Preston, Willard's son, for a copy. The copy would take eight weeks to get there by regular mail. Time was of the essence so she paid a $35 dollar fee plus $15 dollars Internet charge, and five days later a copy was sent to Rachael at her school email account. The answer to the body's location was finally discovered and it was not what they had expected. Willard Yellowhorse had not been cremated and his remains had been sent to Boston, of all places.

Mount Auburn Cemetery in Boston was listed on the death certificate. This made no sense to Charles or Rachael. Why would Willard want his final resting place to be in a city that as far as they knew, he had never visited? So, Bloom was on his way to Boston, Massachusetts, to find Willard's grave and see if anything would help with the ever-growing mystery of his death. At least he was uncovering new information.

✵ ✵ ✵ ✵

The trees were just starting to fully bud out at the 150-year-old cemetery when Bloom arrived, two days before the May 7th Sotheby's auction. Pollen was in the air. Charles was glad not to be in Santa Fe as this was also when the juniper bellowed out their toxic pollen. The last freeze date in Santa Fe is May 17th, the day Bloom normally planted his gallery's tomato plants. He hoped he would be alive and back in Santa Fe this year for his annual spring/summer passage.

How easy would it be to find the grave? Why was Willard buried in Boston? These were questions he had asked himself a hundred times on the three-day trip from New Mexico. At each gas stop, Bloom noticed the red mud of the rez still visible under the end of his Mercedes bumper. The color, a blood-tinged shade, looked similar to the red sand that Hastiin Sherman had poured over his right hand in copious amounts. The symbolism of the dirt seeping off his body was unclear to Charles but the red color still present on the car was a reminder to be careful. Everything now had some kind of hidden meaning to Bloom. He didn't know if he had just become super sensitive to his environment or if the old medicine man had somehow changed his five senses and added a sixth one, supernatural. Either way it was freaky when he thought of the sand

and reflexively touched his little pouch of herbal medicine that now hung on a leather cord around his neck. Feeling the tiny pouch eased Bloom's anxiety, and triggered faint memories of being calm and focused.

The old Boston cemetery was a beautiful place. Its charm was not lost on Bloom's aesthetics. He could see why somebody might want to have their final resting place in such a grand setting, much more like a park or sculpture garden than a place of the dead. Maybe Willard had thought the landscape here somehow reminiscent of his ancestral burial grounds in some Eastern way?

It turned out to be rather easy to find the grave. Bloom simply told the young woman that his best friend from whom he had become estranged was supposed to be buried at the cemetery, and he was unsure how the grave would be marked or located. It turned out it was not under the full name but under the inscription name of "W.Y." and was on the farthest seventh hill in one of the more remote areas of the cemetery. It took nearly a 45-minute walk before Charles found the marker. It was on a small knoll with a plain gray granite stone, which read, "W.Y. with all my respect, F.M."

Seeing Willard's initials and knowing his friend's body was under his feet opened a floodgate of memories. Bloom was transported in time to 18 years earlier at his gallery, reminding Willard to please put W.Y. on his drawings as collectors like things signed. Then he was back on the rez, seeing a photograph of Rachael and Willard next to their grandmother on top of Rachael's dresser. Bloom's heart started to race, suspecting he could be standing next to a crime scene and he might be next. His hands were noticeably trembling. He steadied himself on the adjacent headstone across from Willard's. Trying to focus and slow his breathing, he saw the initials C.L. and the same inscription, "With all my respect, F.M."

Bloom tried to decipher the meaning. Thoughts streamed through his head: "Who is F.M.? Respect, what respect? Oh my God, C.L. must be Craig Lendskip. Why is he buried next to Willard's grave? The dates of death are the same year, it has to be Craig."

The oddity of what he was seeing was almost surreal. As Bloom paced around the graves, he thought about the fact that both dead artists from the same gallery were buried next to each other. He wondered who else was buried nearby, and were there other famous artists? Under a large old oak with no other graves around, he found a slightly larger headstone with a name chiseled in larger bold letters: "Fredrick Marsh." There was an apparent birth date, but no death date.

Who was Fredrick Marsh? The name seemed vaguely familiar. The initials would be F.M. It had to be tied in, but who was he? What was the connection? Overloaded with mental images, Bloom said out loud, "Who is Fredrick Marsh?"

Then a voice talked back....

"Mr. Marsh is the owner of this site." The deep, gravelly voice startled Charles, causing him to stop in mid-step and look to the sky. Bloom's brain was having an auditory hallucination. He had heard it clear as day. The old medicine man must have damaged his mind. Not knowing what else to do, he answered the voice, cupping his hands as to amplify his voice.

"Marsh owns the grave site?" Bloom said, looking still at the heavens.

Then from behind the old oak tree, an elderly black man appeared from the tree he had been sitting under. Charles was relieved to see a real human was the source of the voice and he wasn't going crazy. He was surprised he wasn't embarrassed by his actions, but Charles's sense of what was possible had changed permanently out in Navajoland.

"Fredrick Marsh used to work here a long time ago," the man explained. "He worked for me, in fact. It seems like a very long time indeed. I ain't seen the man in 20-plus years, but I know he does own this here plot. That boy was a weird duck, but he sure loved this place and you got to respect that in a man. I don't know who these two graves belong to, but I assume it must be relatives of his 'cause they are buried on his plot. That man bought the whole damn hill, if you can believe that, one of the last big plots left. That was years ago. None available now."

Charles got goose bumps. He asked, "Any way to get ahold of Mr. Marsh that you might know? I would love to talk with him."

"'Fraid I couldn't help you there. Last time I talked to him he said he was heading to New York City. Going to be a famous artist, people was going to respect him—that's what he told me."

"An artist! He was an artist?"

"Yeah, I guess so," the man answered. "He said he was. Never quite figured that one out. He worked here cleaning graves, then bought one of the most expensive pieces of land in the cemetery, maybe even in all of Boston, and was an artist. I guess he must have been one hell of a painter. Hell, his plot's better than that there Winslow Homer painter, and I know for a fact he was damn good."

"Interesting, Mr....?"

"Name's Day, no problem. If you ever see Mr. Marsh, tell him old Levin Day from Mount Auburn says hi. Hope I don't have to ever clean his grave. I would think I should go first. Matter of fact, ask him if you don't mind, if he got room on his plot of land for me? Sure like this here oak tree. It'd make a great place for eternity."

"I will, Mr. Day," Bloom agreed. "I'll pass on your message."

✳ ✳ ✳ ✳

That evening in his hotel, using a laptop and very expensive Ethernet connection, Charles got the answer and it was a disturbing one. Fredrick Marsh was indeed an artist and, best that Charles could determine, a very demented one, judging from his paintings. He had had only two galleries in his career: the first was Proof in Boston, and the second was The Cutting Edge in New York. Marsh had been there since it opened.

The Boston gallery Proof was gone, but its owner still had a listing in Boston. One phone call and Charles got more than he was prepared to hear. The gallery owner, who now owned a series of shoe outlets, remembered Marsh more clearly than he would like.

"Yeah," the guy said. "I won't ever forget that nut job. I've never been so happy as I was to send his last piece of perverted art to New York to his so-called gallery there. The shit he painted used to really creep me out. Images of dead people making love. Very disturbing. He had these visions of grandeur about his work. I actually encouraged him to move to New York so I wouldn't have to deal with him any more. If it weren't for the fact that he paid part of my rent, I would have never let him into the gallery."

"He actually paid to show in your gallery?"

"Yeah. I know as a gallery owner this sounds queer, but hey I needed the dough and it wasn't as if he couldn't paint. It was just the totally bizarre subject matter and his graphic imagery that no one could possible relate to, at least no one sane. So he helped supplement my income. He probably kept me in business longer than I should have been."

"You think he did the same for The Cutting Edge?" Bloom wondered.

"You bet. I never heard of that gallery until he showed up, then poof, he's in some very successful gallery which came out of nowhere. I remember thinking how in the hell would a guy like Marsh be in a gallery that also had Warhol and later, Yellowhorse and Lendskip? The answer has to be cash. Big bucks and lots of it. The only possible way. He paid to play. Marsh was one of these rich trust-funders is my guess. They're the worst. They aren't hungry so they never give you any work and they bitch about every detail of their career. Yep, he was a trust-fund artist. I still see an ad for his work every so often in some offbeat contemporary art magazine, always well done and always full-page. The current work is even more obscene. If there wasn't a recession, I'm not sure the magazines would publish the ads. His personality was weird 20 years ago. I can only imagine what he's like now. In fact, if you talk to him please keep my name out of it. I don't want to ever hear from the guy again, even if he wants to buy a hundred pairs of shoes!"

"No problem," Bloom assured, a chill running through his spine. "I never talked to you. Thanks for the heads up."

The plot was getting deeper and darker, but at least Bloom was making progress. An art dealer who's afraid of an old artist. An artist who bought his way into The Cutting Edge. That might explain Bernard's deep pockets. This Marsh sounded twisted and his paintings reflected a troubled individual. Bloom had assumed all along that somehow Phillips was to blame for Yellowhorse's death, but maybe it wasn't him at all. Maybe it was Marsh.

Bloom muttered, "Is Marsh a killer of artists? Is he the bad coyote spirit? I have to be careful of him, it's clear. And what about Phillips? He's a dick, no doubt, I'll never forget how he screwed me in Santa Fe. Still, he didn't seem like a killer. Marsh, his paintings have psychopath written all them."

It was time to visit to The Cutting Edge, even if with extreme trepidation. Charles was going to have to outwit more than one devious New Yorker, and the last time the Southwesterner had gone up against a New Yorker he'd failed miserably. This time the stakes would be even higher.

CHAPTER 51

NEW YORK CITY

The four-hour drive from Boston to New York seemed only like 30 minutes to Charles, who was deep in thought about his strategy for confronting Phillips. The more he thought about it, the probability in Bloom's mind became that Marsh had murdered Yellowhorse and very possibly Lendskip. The question was, did Phillips know and if so, did he orchestrate or participate in their murders? There was no doubt Phillips was an asshole when it came to his business practices, but he didn't seem like a killer. The paintings Marsh had produced were deviant, even to a contemporary art dealer. The fact that Marsh had shown at Phillips' gallery for what appeared to be almost 20 years meant Phillips must know Marsh's mindset. How did two artists come to be buried in what appeared to be the Marsh family plot?

The key had to be the so-called Yellowhorse painting. Stop the sale and the coyote spirit couldn't be far behind. So first stop for Charles was Sotheby's, which had its contemporary auction in only one day. Bloom knew he was cutting it close coming the day before the sale, but he hoped if the auction house got scared off by potential authenticity issues, the painting might pulled. Maybe their lawyers would flinch. He knew there were no exact legal grounds for the family to demand that the auction house remove the painting. They had no lawyer or judge's injunction. And yet if he could muster a serious enough accusation about the piece at the last hour, he might be able to stop the sale. He rehearsed the conversation while driving:

"Yes, well, I was Willard's first dealer and I'm currently dating his sister, and Willard's grandfather says it was not an authentic Yellowhorse, but from a design he had a vision of during a healing ceremony 15 years ago. I understand it's a $5 million dollar painting, but it's a fraud and I think Willard Yellowhorse was murdered!" Actually saying it out loud gave Charles a shiver. It was not going to be a pretty scenario. He was inviting a murderer to focus their sights on him. The coyote would not be happy with his meddling.

The day was typical for early May in New York, cold and dreary. It felt more like winter than late spring. Finding a parking spot turned out to be an ordeal even though the Sotheby's website boasted "ample parking." Charles circled the block of 72nd and York on the Upper East Side three times. Sotheby's, with its 10-story modern glass front, took up a huge portion of the block. The outside window had a huge poster of the upcoming sale with, of all paintings, STRUGGLE glaring back at Charles each time he circled the block. He missed a parking opening out front the first go-around as he was so mesmerized by the painting. He couldn't help but wonder how many fake paintings could have actually been sold at such a venerable auction house, and if so had any ever managed to become the lead poster. It was undoubtedly a first, and he was going to be right in the middle of the whole mess. By the third pass at the window he was starting to physically become ill at the prospect.

Finally securing a spot a half block away, it occurred to Charles he had a six-inch, stone-age knife wrapped in a deerskin cloth in his coat pocket. The dilemma was, Hastiin Sherman had told him to keep the knife and medicine bundle close at all times. The medicine bundle was safely around his neck as if some modern-day charm, but the knife was a different kettle of fish. To confront auction officials about the authenticity of their painting with an insane story, and to be carrying a rather menacing knife on one's body might not go over so well. Bloom decided his car was near enough to be classified "close to him," so he gently pushed the deerskin package deep under his driver's seat.

The contemporary art sale was tomorrow night. Numerous serious buyers had flown in for the sale. The highlight was a major Rothko, an orange, white, and pink variation of Rothko's classic theme of large blocks of color that seem to float on a background of monochromatic color. The painting had an estimate of $35 million to $45 million, but should sell for much more. It was lot 48, one after the Yellowhorse. It was the cover of the main catalog, and also had its own mini-catalog like the Yellowhorse. The Rothko was magnificent. Under different circumstances, Bloom would be thrilled to see it in person. The entire sale's exhibit had been structured around the painting, which was centrally located on a wall by itself. The Yellowhorse was hung nearby to counterbalance the exhibit space.

Currently the head of Sotheby's contemporary art department was giving a rousing explanation of the Rothko and its virtues to a local

New York television channel. Charles watched, his eyes transfixed by the man's arms, which waved in every direction as if he had some sort of art Tourette's syndrome. His British accent matched his face. With each arm fling, his sandy brown hair bounced in and out of his long face and it looked as if he would toss his BlackBerry away, but it remained clutched in his hand. This man, whom Charles had never met but whose face he'd seen on all the contemporary catalogs, would soon hate him. Bloom knew he would completely fuck up his precious auction.

All major auctions are arranged leading to a crescendo, like a musical production. The Yellowhorse was to bring the auction to a fever pitch when it sold for a record for the artist, and then it was on to the Rothko, with the buyers primed to follow suit. If he could stop the sale of the Yellowhorse somehow, it would have the exact opposite effect: a complete downer for the auction and it would screw up the Rothko sale as every person in the room would become too enthralled with the Yellowhorse debacle to focus on the Rothko. It would taint the next lot by association, which was going to be a major problem for the auction, which meant a major problem for Bloom.

He would probably be sued for damages to the Rothko sale and his wages permanently garnished as well as being banned from Sotheby's and any other respectable auction house where he was recognized. He couldn't help but think of one of his favorite movies, "Kingpin," starring Woody Harrelson as the hapless bowler Roy Munson who blows his one big chance to beat Bill Murray. Forever after, any choker on the bowling circuit was called a "Munson." Bloom envisioned any person who bungled an auction or even an important art show would be referred to as being "Bloomed." Like, "He really Bloomed that artist's career," or, "This auction's prices were Bloomed." The image in his mind made Charles instinctively touch the pouch around his neck. His right hand started to throb. He wondered if his blood pressure was up and maybe he was about to have a stroke. He was only in his mid-40s but he was under severe emotional distress and his heart was beating much faster than normal.

Bloom focused for the first time on the Yellowhorse. It was a large canvas with a star-like spattered red design laid down on a pure egg-white canvas, interspersed with areas of yellow discoloration due to Willard's urine. He had never seen the piece in person, just in newspapers, a book on Yellowhorse, and of course the catalog. He hoped the painting would never be included in the Yellowhorse *catalogue raisonné*. An art history professor from the University of New Mexico was completing the *raisonné*. Bloom had already given the author images of all the pieces he had sold. The *raisonné* is the comprehensive chronological collection of an artist's life work. In the Yellowhorse *raisonné*, the final painting would be the fictitious STRUGGLE, something Bloom was hoping to stop somehow. Charles Bloom's hand increased its throbbing the more he studied the piece. He could feel Willard's presence; it was as if Willard's spirit was still a part of the canvas but not in a good way, there was pain and he could feel it. His right wrist throbbed as he looked at the painting. He gulped, shook his hand, and focused on what was now his path in life.

The interview had just finished and the crowds were starting to thin away from the Rothko and nearby Yellowhorse. Bloom figured this was his chance. It was time to "Bloom" the department head, anticipating his new title as art idiot extraordinaire.

"Hi," Bloom began, sticking his slightly numb right hand out to shake the hand of a Mr. Rupert, the head of the contemporary art department, who looked much older close-up than in his catalog image. Bloom kept the handshake minimal, still trying to retain any power the old medicine man may have imparted to him.

"Yes, nice to meet you Mr....."

"Bloom. Charles Bloom from Santa Fe."

"I recognize that name. Aren't you Mr. Yellowhorse's first dealer? I remember putting your name in the catalog on our lovely Yellowhorse."

"Yes, I'm afraid I am." Bloom knew in a moment Rupert really would be afraid to have met him.

"Oh wonderful. Have you had a chance to preview the piece? As you know, this is the first time on the market and we are expecting a rather pitched battle for its debut. If you need any condition reports or would like to see the piece in private, that can be arranged. Do you think you will be bidding on the piece? And if so, may I help you with advanced registration or anything?" Mr. Rupert said the word anything letting the g linger to emphasize his British pedigree and willingness to help.

"Actually," Bloom said, "there is a way you can help me but I'm afraid it's not what you might expect." Here it came, where he had to fall on his sword, the obliteration of a wonderful career in art. "You see, Mr. Rupert, as you know I am an expert when it comes to Yellowhorse's work, and it so happens that I also represent the Yellowhorse family when I say this. I have my concerns with this so-called final piece of Yellowhorse actually being considered a painting by Willard."

Rupert was stunned, it was obvious, but he kept the same demeanor even as the blood drained from his face, calmly replying, "Well, that's an interesting point of view, one I have not heard before. We will of course have to look very closely at your concerns. We do have ample documents of its authenticity if you care to view those. Rather gory police forensic photos showing Mr. Yellowhorse and the painting underneath, as well as his handwritten suicide note stating the painting's title and that he made it. The letter comes with the painting of course. What other provenance were you looking for exactly? I'm sure we have it as well?" Rupert's tone had changed from stunned to peeved, no more wanting to help in his voice, his right foot tapping the marble floor.

"It's not that I don't think the canvas was under Mr. Yellowhorse when he died. I have no question that it was. It is the circumstances under which it was made. The family and I believe Willard would never have done such a thing and his note was somehow coerced and possibly some kind of foul play was involved."

"I see," Rupert responded. "Well I can't speak to any possible murder, that was 15 years ago and it seems rather unusual such a concern only comes up one day before such an important painting is to be auctioned off. I wonder if there is something else you or the family might be looking for, some kind of financial consideration." This was his British way of saying, "Are you trying to blackmail us," in a very proper way.

"No," Bloom replied. "We are not asking for anything monetary. We would like the painting to be reconsidered for its inclusion in this sale." There it was, asking to pull the painting. The kiss of death for an auction house. He had officially just "Bloomed" the sale.

"I see, well I will take your request to the Sotheby's president and of course our lawyers. We will consider this with the utmost concern. Of course you realize without some sort of legal injunction that the piece will be sold on the 7th. I'm assuming you don't have such a document?"

"No, not yet Mr. Rupert. I was hoping we didn't have to go down that road."

"I will take this up with the consigner and make sure they are aware of the situation. They may want to pull the piece, though I wouldn't count on it. I need to get all your local and New Mexico contact information, and we will look into what we feel should be done. I would expect your lawyers to call us if you have any further requests. Of course, Mr. Bloom, you also realize any slander of the painting's reputation by you would also be taken quite seriously." Rupert quickly said his tart goodbye and walked away, punching the keys on his BlackBerry at a furious pace. His day had just been "Bloomed" and he was not very happy with the minor dealer from Santa Fe. Bloom realized Rupert's last statement was his warning shot to not screw up the auction or there would be consequences to pay. Serious consequences.

CHAPTER 52

A CALL FROM THE CUTTING EDGE

As promised, Rupert notified Bernard Phillips of one Charles Bloom and his problem with the painting STRUGGLE. Bernard was livid upon hearing the snag to his multimillion-dollar payday, his retirement check. "I know Mr. Bloom. He's just looking for money. I will speak to him and see if we can't come to some private arrangement. I think we both know no one is going to come out of the blue just one day before the auction with some cock-and-bull story which should have been addressed 15 years ago."

The answer seemed to pacify Rupert, who responded, "If there are any problems, our lawyers need to know immediately and I have to have time to notify our clients who may be flying in tomorrow to bid on the piece. We don't want a billionaire to take time from his schedule and get here and there is no painting to bid on because some irritated family member has filed an injunction. I think you understand our position, Mr. Phillips?"

"Absolutely. Crystal," Bernard assured. "I'm sure this is just a minor speed bump by a greedy ex-dealer trying to stir things up. Please plan on continuing with the Yellowhorse in the sale. Give me Bloom's cell and I'll work this out, I promise."

Bernard Phillips had a problem, which meant Charles Bloom had a problem. The fix had to be quick and complete. No screwing up Bernard's huge payday. Bernard was reaching the end of his career, and he didn't have any more Yellowhorse-like artists in his gallery and never would. The Cutting Edge was now more synonymous with a dull butter knife than a scalpel, no longer at the edge of contemporary art. No important artists to speak of and Fredrick Marsh's morbid work took up half the gallery now which meant wasted wall space. It might as well have been empty walls. Nobody appreciated or purchased Marsh's work, especially not Phillips. Marsh drove off more potential clients daily than he ever brought in. He did have his good points: he still paid the bills and was technically the owner of the gallery.

If Bernard blew town, let's say with a multimillion-dollar paycheck from Sotheby's, who would be the wiser? Bernard had been advanced $1.5 million dollars on the upcoming sale of the Yellowhorse, and that money was safely sitting in his Anguilla bank account, waiting for his May 8th arrival. Phillips was counting on an early retirement, unbeknownst to Marsh. No more retail. It would be Marsh's turn to take care of the gallery. Sally Smith, Bernard's longtime personal secretary, knew as much about any business issues as Bernard did, and she would never leave. No more dead body paintings for Bernard to stare at. Their presence had damaged Phillips' subconscious from the years of close association.

The trick was to placate Bloom for a couple of days. If he wouldn't go away peacefully, then a different tactic would be applied. Nothing was going to interfere with Bernard's May 8th exit. Marsh would also need to be informed. The time had arrived for Bernard to orchestrate his *coup de grace*.

Nobody was more aware of the crucial timing than Charles Bloom, who was having his own now-or-never moment. When Rupert had said the consigner would need to be contacted, Bloom had cringed inside. It was common knowledge in the art world that Phillips was the consigner. Bernard would be upset to say the least when the Sotheby's people called one day away from his payday. Bloom thought if he were in the same position as Phillips, he would try whatever it took to make the deal work. The difference was that Charles would rely on legal, ethical ways and he doubted seriously whether Phillips had the same playbook. If Bernard was involved with Yellowhorse's demise, Charles could be in great danger. However, the real concern currently for Charles was not Bernard but Fredrick Marsh, the unknown element.

Normally Charles would have relished the idea of taking the day to look at the great masterpieces of contemporary art that were hanging at Sotheby's main exhibit hall. This was not one of those times. He had fled back to the flint-stone knife in his car. It was part of his protection in some weird way and he could feel when its presence was absent. The only comforting thought was that his hand had stopped hurting after leaving the Yellowhorse painting. Maybe it would all work out somehow, balance restored in some way.

The call Charles was dreading came just as he checked into his boutique hotel not far from the Chelsea area. He figured he might as well be close to the art district; never know when you could do a little business. The chances were slim to none, but it made Charles feel better thinking he still had a normal life and was not performing hari-kari on his art career.

The call was from Bernard Phillips.

"Mr. Bloom, this is Bernard Phillips. I hope I'm not interrupting anything?"

Hearing Bernard's voice after 17 years gave Bloom a deja vu of his disastrous experience back in Santa Fe. His heart sped up instantaneously. "No, this is as good a time as any, Mr. Phillips."

"Please call me Bernard. We share too much in common to be on a last-name basis."

"Bernard, I'm assuming you're calling because of my concern with the Sotheby's painting," Charles got to the point.

Bernard could feel his own heart rate speed up, having to be cordial to this man who was trying to ruin his life. He thought of how his dad must have felt when he was told the Picasso was a fake. "Yes, indeed. I thought maybe you and I could meet over at my gallery for a private conversation regarding the unfortunate situation. I'm sure something can be worked out."

Charles' heart was truly racing now. Going to The Cutting Edge seemed a dangerous option. But did he have any other? "Um, OK, I'm fairly close by. How about in 30 minutes?"

"I can't today, I'm afraid," Bernard demurred. "But tomorrow, say 10 in the morning, would be outstanding. It's going to be busy as you can imagine, and it would be best to talk before all my big clients show up."

Charles wanted to scream back into the phone, "Yes I remember about having big clients coming in and some dealer screwing everything up," but he politely confirmed, "Ten, it is."

"Great Charles, I'll look forward to seeing you again."

The only way Bernard would want to see me, Charles thought after hanging up, was in a body bag. The knife had to be kept close. He would stop and pick up some flesh-colored duct tape and wrap it around his abdomen. Just in case something weird happened, Charles would be prepared. But was he really able to anticipate what coyote was planning?

Bernard clearly understood the implications of what needed to be accomplished. He called Marsh and explained the situation and how Charles could destroy the gallery if not stopped in some way, and if it couldn't be done in a civil manner then it had to be done in a very Marsh-like fashion. Bernard's lone remaining employee, Sally Smith, was given a variety of tasks to do outside the gallery for the rest of the day, and told not to show up tomorrow until one in the afternoon as Bernard had a special client in the morning and would keep the gallery closed. Bernard knew Sally was smart and might question being off on a busy day, so he explained that tomorrow, with the auction and all, she would be needed to work a very long day and be on her game. She was surprised but happy to get some unexpected "me time" tomorrow morning. Bernard used the rest of the day to get ready for the possibility of Charles not being a reasonable man. Steps had to be taken.

CHAPTER 53

A BUSY MORNING SCHEDULE

Charles did not sleep well. His room was next to a busy street and he had become accustomed to the sound of silence on the rez. No truck noises, just the occasional horny woodpecker. The city's thriving life force was compounded by intense dreams of Willard's voice calling to him from the grave, coyotes, and Willard's swinging body making the dreaded STRUGGLE. Its image had been seared into Bloom's mind from seeing it in person for the first time. The painting's three dimensionality of colors mixed with Willard's urine stains had distressed Bloom's unconscious. The image woke him repeatedly whenever he slipped into a few minutes of sleep. In the morning it took 10 minutes to get out of bed knowing what he faced. He skipped eating as he had no appetite and drank a $7 cup of black coffee as breakfast instead; it was nowhere as tasty as Rachael's cowboy-style brew. The aroma of the coffee brought Bloom's mind back to Rachael. He missed her smile and wondered if today might be his last day to think of her. He checked the knife to make sure it was secured safely before leaving the hotel.

Deciding to walk to the gallery rather than give up his cherished parking spot gave Bloom time to ponder the situation and fully awake from his sleeping ordeal. It was 8 am back home and he would have been getting ready for his morning run.

With each step now, Bloom could feel the edge of the sharp flint blade barely touch his cold white skin. The stone's pure nature made Bloom feel he could only say the truth when he confronted Bernard, and see where it took him. Maybe if Bernard were privy to Hastiin Sherman's information, Bernard would respond to the truth, especially if the painting turned out to have occurred during some sort of murder. Bernard would ultimately be responsible for the Yellowhorse's authenticity no matter when it was sold. Charles knew his logic was flawed, but he couldn't come up with any other course of action. He was a ship without a rudder. He would have to let the currents of life take him down the road and hope Hastiin Sherman's powers would guide him back home.

The smell of the gallery as Bloom entered was a mix of cigarettes and an odd antiseptic odor. Hospital-like, in a bad way. Not the typical gallery smells of paint and maybe a scented candle. The imagery of Marsh's extreme paintings stunned Bloom in their detailed horror. The most prominent piece was a large painting of a black male, his intestines hanging by his sides, skin partially removed and eyes gouged out. The face was blank as if his soul was removed along with his eyes. As an art dealer it did evoke emotion, which is what one looks for, but it was not the emotion Bloom wanted to feel at that moment. Evil, was all Charles could perceive from the images and it caused him to break out in a cold sweat. He hoped Bernard wouldn't notice.

"Charles, nice to see you." Bernard's fake smile belied the anger that was seething underneath his façade.

"Interesting gallery," Charles commented, overcoming his anxiety and attempting to connect with Bernard as one gallery owner with another. Maybe they could join forces against Marsh. "You ever have an issue looking at those images of human suffering?" He wiped his sleeve across his brow as he turned away from Bernard to emphasize the paintings he had just walked by.

"There are days I wish Mr. Marsh would paint a flower or two, but he has tremendous original thought, something I look for in an artist as I'm sure you do too. Why don't we go into my office? We can spend a couple of minutes discussing your concerns about STRUGGLE," Bernard suggested.

As the pair headed to his office, Bernard did something that bothered Charles. "I'm going to put my `Gone to Lunch' sign out. I don't want to be bothered. My secretary is coming in late today, no one to watch the front." Bernard then briskly walked to the front door and turned the deadbolt and put out a little hand-stenciled sign that said, "Back Momentarily." Charles' instinct was to turn, dash past Bernard and push him out of the way, and run out that door to his freedom. Feeling his abdomen with his hand, touching the knife, gave him the strength not to follow what his inner voice was screaming. Charles had been in retail a long time and never once remembered locking his door when he was in the building. Maybe New York was different than Santa Fe, but Charles was sure it wasn't. He steeled himself for coming confrontation.

Bernard's back office was a showplace for the people he had met. Photographs of important artists were lined up: Warhol, Basquiat, Lendskip, and of course, Yellowhorse. Each image had Bernard next to the artist with a smile. There were snapshots of openings and articles that had been written about The Cutting Edge Gallery. All were now yellow after years of sun exposure. No current images of success were anywhere to be seen. The walls were architectural white. One Geronimo Artist Proof in a burnt orange hue hung over Bernard's desk, along with a couple of unknown artists working in an abstract expressionistic style. A built-in easel was against one wall, arranged to show special paintings when it came to closing sales. Two old bomber chairs from France with dark brown patina and cracking leather were next to a clean, modern desk. The floor was scored, colored concrete with a pink cast. Luckily none of Marsh's paintings were in eyesight.

"Please, Charles, have a seat," Phillips invited, pointing to one of the comfortable vintage 1920 leather chairs. Phillips chose the other chair instead of sitting behind the desk. He plopped down next to Bloom. "So what can I offer you and the Yellowhorse family so as to not make a big scene with regards to STRUGGLE?"

Charles knew this was a nice way of saying, "How much is it going to take to make you go away?"

"Bernard," Charles replied carefully, "I'm afraid it's not a money issue, it's an ethical one. No amount of money will help. The family doesn't believe this painting was done volitionally. It's not Willard's true work."

"I can understand the piece is probably bringing up old feelings. But it is clearly Yellowhorse's piece and everyone can use money. There's no doubt he produced the note found underneath the canvas. The red paint can had only his handprints. It was a suicide and he obviously wanted his life to make some kind of important statement. Surely you are not denying that Yellowhorse made this painting?" Bernard countered.

Charles could tell this was going nowhere. Hoping to appeal to Bernard's artistic sensibilities, he asked, "Did Willard ever tell you about his grandfather's vision of the STRUGGLE design?" Bernard's shrugging shoulder demonstrated his indifference.

Then Charles asked a question that surprised Bernard: "What about Marsh? Could he have had a role in Willard's death? From what I've heard, he is quite odd. I know he buried Willard at Mount Ashton Cemetery in Boston. I saw the grave myself. In fact, Marsh's own future grave marker is nearby. Lendskip also appears to be buried there. You of all people must find these images Marsh produces to be coming from a disturbed mind?"

Bernard made his decision right then and there. Charles was a problem and needed to go. There was no way Bernard could explain about the graves. Charles was too close to discovering the truth. Bernard rose, and stepped towards the closet.

At about the same time, Charles realized every artist Bernard had so proudly hung on his office walls—Warhol, Basquiat, Lendskip, and Yellowhorse—had all died suddenly by accident or suicide. It was at that moment that Charles panicked. But it was too late.

Charles didn't see Marsh slip out from the closet. The chloroform-soaked cloth was pressed hard against Bloom's mouth and nose, the same way as it had been with Willard Yellowhorse. Charles tried in vain to break free of Marsh's grip. The noxious smell was the one he had sniffed when he first entered the gallery. Within a minute and half, Bloom was out cold.

Marsh and Bernard had to act fast. The effects of Marsh's dad's aging bottle of chloroform analgesic might not last more than 30 minutes. Bloom's motionless body was roughly dragged into a large plastic bag that was used to cover heavy sculptures. Bloom's mouth was gagged, and his hands and feet bound with duct tape. His pockets were searched, but nothing was found other than a near-empty wallet and iPhone; these were tossed in the bag with Bloom. The unconscious body was then zipped up as if it were some large bronze and hoisted onto a floor roller, then moved to the back of a rented truck waiting outside. Using a mechanical lift, the still-unconscious Bloom was pushed roughly into the back of the cold steel interior and the floor roller was thrown in the back with him. The Santa Fe art dealer with the screw-loose vision quest was soon to be no longer a problem, except for the coroner.

237

CHAPTER 54

SCALPEL FUN

Fredrick Marsh had never been to Bernard Phillips' storage area, even though he had paid the bills for decades. Dealing with used crates, boxes, and miscellaneous files was an aspect of the art business too trivial for the true owner, Marsh. The dark and isolated building was located in the meat district. Unknown to Marsh, it had been used by Bernard for years for more than storing crates. It was a special place, as Fredrick and Charles both would soon find out. For Charles, the discovery would be enlightening. For Marsh, it would be crushing.

The old building was in a rough part of town. People dragging sacks with bodies probably happened here more often than anyone would like to know. Because it was in the meat district, a steady flow of blood seemed to have permanently stained the sidewalks a sienna color. Bloom was starting to stir just as the final heave-ho of the bag into the old freight elevator was completed. Bloom's head struck the metal floor with an audible crack.

"Now that's got to hurt," Bernard said laughingly to Marsh, who just grunted in response.

"Why are we taking him here?" Fredrick complained. "You should have let me give him the whole bottle of chloroform and he would be toast. Then we could have just disposed of the body, or better yet let me have a crack at him with my surgery skills. You heard the man, I have a disturbed mind. You should have let me use it! Now we still have to kill him and dispose of his body. What's up with that, Bernard?"

"You'll see. We still need Mr. Bloom. And you can still have your scalpel fun, besides I'm going to like watching your mind work close-up," Bernard grinned at Marsh.

The elevator stopped and the two men dragged the now slightly audible sack into a dark room.

"OK Fredrick, let's have some fun with this piece-of-shit, low-life, so-called art dealer. What do you say there, my good man?" Bernard suggested.

"I'm up for it. I would love to get some new photos for my book. I could make a great painting from today's work," Frederick agreed.

"Easy there, big fellow, don't want to start cutting too quickly. Savor the moment. I know I am," Bernard cautioned.

The two men pulled Bloom out of the bag and set him up on an old metal chair. They tied his body to the rusting frame, his hands still bound.

As he came to, Bloom's eyes began jutting back and forth, like a doll with glass eyes. Bloom was becoming aware of his perilous position as the chloroform quickly wore off. The gag and duct tape were removed and Bloom reflexively turned his head and threw up, the side effects of the toxic chloroform. Having skipped breakfast, his vomit was primarily dry heaves. It was too dim for him to see exactly what was in the damp storage room, but he noticed Bernard was wearing gloves.

Still gagging, Charles began speaking in little spurts of words, addressing himself to the more reasonable of his two abductors: "Phillips. You can't do this. No one has been seriously hurt yet. Please come to your senses. Don't let your deranged artist take you down. We can forget about the painting. I'll just quietly disappear, call Sotheby's and tell them I believe the piece is real and we don't have any problem."

"It's too late now," Bernard snapped back. "You and I both know you would never let the incident go away. You're too ethical for that."

"You can't be seriously going to kill me," Charles pleaded. "Won't the authorities think it a bit strange that I complain about the supposed suicide, tell them the painting is a fake, and then I get knocked off?"

"Yes, that might be a problem," Bernard allowed. "But I have it all worked out. You'll see."

Bernard turned to Fredrick: "Marsh, would you mind showing me your skill with that little scalpel you love so much, which you brought, I hope? I'm interested to see how much blood really comes out of, let's say, a radial artery. I assume for an anatomy expert like you that would be a fairly simple procedure?"

"I've always wanted to sever that artery," Fredrick quickly agreed. "I remember doing blood gases back in medical school. It was hard to hit with a needle and the patients always seemed to jump so. Must be a very sensitive area. You know I always have my best friend with me."

As Bloom watched in horror, Marsh came over next to him and grabbed his still-bound hands. "Listen to me, Marsh, you don't want this. It's crazy. You will get caught. I'm not hurt yet. Let's think about this. Once I'm seriously injured, it makes it a whole lot harder," Bloom argued.

"Shut up," Marsh commanded. "I'll tell you when you can speak. This is an art piece in the making by a famous artisan. I will capture the moment in one of my great masterpieces, like your friend Yellowhorse. You will be long gone but your image will live on, you will be famous!" Marsh took his antique ivory-handled scalpel out of his specially made case which he had attached to his belt, and ever so slightly pressed the tip of the blade into the tender flesh of the right wrist on Bloom's arm. The cold edge precisely severed the right radial artery, which began flowing blood in pulsating spurts from the underside of Bloom's wrist.

"AAAHHH," Bloom screamed involuntarily at the pain. "What, Marsh, you trying to fake my suicide like you did Willard's? Is that it, your sick plan?"

Marsh backed away after his wrist surgery, never saying a word, just grinning and licking his lips in a circular fashion as he stared at Charles.

Bernard had slipped behind the now profusely bleeding Bloom and answered from the darkness, "Actually, STRUGGLE was my handiwork. Can't let you give credit where credit isn't due. Marsh is the artist, but I'm the real mastermind."

"You killed Willard? Why? He was making you a ton of money! I don't understand, he was a great person," Bloom gasped.

"Fredrick, I'm afraid, had a little problem with his celebrity status. When Mr. Yellowhorse told me he wanted to go back to his reservation, well that just wouldn't do. He might screw up his own art market by selling to weak dealers like you. I knew if I didn't take care of him in my own way, Marsh would anyway. Isn't that correct, Fredrick?" Bernard explained, as he rustled around behind Charles.

"Yes, I would have skinned him alive for one of my projects, but instead Bernard here got one more nice work out of Willard. By the way, I heard you like my gravesite. Isn't it beautiful? Yellowhorse should thank me for getting him to a place like Mount Auburn. He's the first Indian to get that honor. It's a great cemetery. Very expensive. If you're lucky, once you bleed out maybe I'll let what's left of you lay next to your old friend," Fredrick offered.

Still busying himself in the darkness, Bernard pointed out, "You see, Mr. Bloom, I decided if poor Willard had to go, I should at least get one more major painting out of him. What kind of a dealer would I be to pass up such a great opportunity? I didn't get the same chance with Lendskip. A real shame, there. The truth is I never did get enough work by him. He was just too damn slow. I needed a few more years." Bernard glared at Fredrick, his anger still apparent with regards to the premature death of Craig Lendskip and loss of a great moneymaking opportunity.

With each beat of Bloom's heart, the radial artery squirted a little more of its life-giving blood onto the cold, concrete floor. It was already starting to pool in places, making an abstract-looking blob. Steam rose off the red pooling mass as the icy floor sapped the heat out of the now worthless blood.

Turning Charles' chair around to face a dark drape, Bernard announced, "Now for the treat I've been waiting for. Fredrick, have you ever wondered how many paintings you've sold during your career?"

An odd question, Fredrick thought, at such a dramatic moment. "Yes. 120 paintings, I remember each of my babies. Those lucky owners or their heirs will someday be very rich because of their great taste in art."

241

"You are exactly right, 120. Do you know how I know your number is correct?" Bernard had been anticipating this moment for years.

"I can't say, Bernard. I guess you are a very good dealer and you kept accurate records." Fredrick was beginning to get nervous wondering what Bernard was getting at.

"No, Fredrick," Bernard exploded. "I know because I bought each one of those fucking pieces of shit you call art over the last 20 years." Then Bernard jerked down on a nondescript nylon cord, and two canvas drapes swung apart, revealing rows of painting racks filled with Marsh's artworks.

Fredrick was stunned. He walked over and started to pull out paintings from his entire body of work, looking at each one as if it were the first time he had ever seen them. "What the hell is the meaning of this, Phillips? Why are all my gorgeous paintings in this shitty storage unit?"

"They're here, Marsh, because they're all worthless garbage and like garbage it doesn't matter where you put it. If I didn't buy them, you would have left my gallery and I needed your money. It was your only redeeming quality! I used your own capital to buy your paintings, money by the way I could have spent on good art. But I don't need you any more. I've got STRUGGLE and it will allow me to retire. Your crappy, sick paintings which I own are going to be destroyed because the world has enough bad, sick art without the horror you have produced over your pathetic life. It will be the only really ethical thing I do!"

Ethical, thought Charles. Had Bernard really said *ethical*?

Bernard moved behind Bloom, still ranting, "Marsh, you are the only artist I've represented where my`Paint by Numbers' theory doesn't apply. You are a true outlier. Your work is so twisted that the art world will be happy to be rid of you once and for all. All these stored paintings are only worth the value of the canvases on which they are painted. Your life's work will soon end up in New York City's finest dump, the only place worthy of your presence!" Bernard glowered with fierce intensity in his eyes as he demeaned the distraught Marsh, finally uncorking 25 years of repressed anger at his psychotic partner.

The fury in Fredrick's dark eyes was equally palpable. He was on fire. His eyes' pupils completely dilated wide. With a giant scream, Marsh lunged violently at the taller Bernard with his scalpel held like a dagger to destroy the man who had just ruined his life.

A huge BANG, BANG and Fredrick's lifeless body hit the ground just in front of the still profusely bleeding Bloom.

Bloom was in shock, both mentally and physically. His head and ears were ringing from the adjacent gunshots. He didn't even realize when Phillips grabbed his own bleeding hand and stuck the butt of the still-smoking gun in it. Bernard manipulated Charles' fingers into pulling the trigger once more, the bullet hitting its mark: the back of Marsh's head. Marsh's functionless blood now intermingled with Bloom's in one last final collage of bodily fluids.

"There we go, my little meddler," Bernard taunted Charles, taking the gun back into his own gloved hand. "Just wanted to make sure you have powder resin on your murdering hand when they do your autopsy."

Bernard turned his attention solely to Charles now. "I think you will like my little story, much more plausible then your medicine man bullshit. It goes like this: the late Marsh here tied you up and was starting to dissect you when you were able to stop him. You luckily had a hidden gun and were able to kill Marsh before he finished his anatomy lab. Unfortunately though, you weren't able to escape your bindings and you tragically bled to death. Very sad, I'm afraid. The police will find the scalpel in Marsh's hand, see all these horrific images done by Marsh, and be convinced that anyone that twisted could easily be a killer."

Bernard went on, "I'll be back before I leave town to take care of any loose ends—make sure you're good and dead, leave the gun, and pick up your body-carrying case. I will need it again to put my cash in. You see, I got a very nice million-dollar-plus advance on my little Yellowhorse, and I plan to get a lot more money after tonight's sale."

Encouragingly, Bernard suggested, "Look at the positives. You won't have to be buried next to Mr. Death over there for eternity like your buddy, Yellowhorse. Goodbye Fredrick, finally you did a corpse piece

I actually liked!" Saying the words tickled Bernard, who started laughing as he turned off the lights to exit the room.

"Nighty night, Mr. Bloom," Bernard called out. "Nice doing business with you. Again!" He had an auction to get ready for.

✳ ✳ ✳ ✳

Bloom's mind was racing. He was in the dark and bleeding to death. The only sounds he could hear were his own heart, and his blood as it hit the floor. He tried to slow his breathing and think rationally. His hands were firmly bound. He was tied to a large but somewhat movable chair, and he was quickly losing his life force. As he thought of what his next move should be, his right wrist started to pulsate with pain. It was at that moment that the vision came to him. He closed his eyes to combat the fact he was in the dark and concentrated on living. His heart slowed and he remembered the old man's words. "It will save you."

With his chin and shoulder, Charles maneuvered the leather string that was around his neck holding the medicine pouch into his mouth. Using his teeth and tongue, he worked on opening the little deerskin bag. As he fought to extrude the bag's contents and not choke to death, he simultaneously sent blood spurting in every direction with each beat of his heart, including on Marsh's body. More evidence for the police that he was Marsh's murderer.

Finally after a long minute the leather pouch neck was opened. Bloom pushed the contents out with his tongue as he forced them against his front teeth, shaking his head back and forth. The herbs' gritty, bitter taste immediately irritated his mouth as some of the fine-crushed plant parts fell onto his blood-soaked lap. Charles took his injured wrist, felt for the plant parts, and then pressed the open cut hard into the Navajo medicine man's herbs. The bleeding started to slow immediately, its medicinal properties plugging the deep gash. Feeling the blood flow retreat gave new hope to Charles Bloom, who didn't know how much time he had before Phillips came back or he simply bled to death.

The flint knife was still taped to his abdomen. Charles wished he hadn't put so much tape on. Freeing it from his taut abdominal muscles took what seemed forever, even though it was closer to 15 minutes. Once the blade was freed, Charles quickly used its sharp stone edges to saw through the duct tape. He was in such a hurry and still unable to see in the dark that he unintentionally cut the skin on the uninjured wrist, which started to ooze blood. Once his binds were cut, Bloom was able to use the leather string that held the now empty pouch, to wrap his right wrist tightly. He searched for and found the remnant duct tape, and this was wrapped around the string for good measure. A little of the remaining herbs was used on his self-induced sawing wound, stopping the bleeding instantaneously. Bloom's tongue and the roof of his mouth were numb. He wondered if Hastiin's medicine might kill him or send him into some hallucinogenic trance.

His head was throbbing intensely from both blood loss and chloroform exposure, but he managed to saw through the binds holding him to the chair. He was unsure if he could stand without passing out, but he was alive, more than he could say for Marsh— who lay face down in a pool of their comingled and congealing blood.

Bloom tried to focus, remembering what he had learned from his four days in seclusion in the old sheep hogan. The one thing that stuck in his mind was to slow down, breathe, and concentrate on the present situation. He found the lights, retrieved his wallet and iPhone, and took snapshots of the crime scene. He realized he would need these soon if he was going to stop Phillips.

CHAPTER 55

MAY 7TH, SHOW TIME

Somehow, Charles Bloom staggered out of the old storage area, still stunned from his near-death experience with considerable loss of blood, all courtesy of the bad coyote spirit, which turned out to have possessed both Bernard Phillips and Fredrick Marsh. Maybe Bernard's working in such close proximity with Fredrick for 25 years had tainted him with Fredrick's pathological streak. Maybe it was the handling of Fredrick's art for so long that had done it.

Outside, the sun had just gone down. The weather was unusually cold. It felt as if it could freeze, which would be shocking for May.

Stumbling down the streets of a dangerous neighborhood covered in blood kept any potentially hostile combatants far away. Bloom finally reached the street corner and rested against a lamppost, trying to sort things out in his mind, which was spinning. What should his next move be? The rational approach would be to go directly to the police, but the auction would be starting shortly and he was sure Phillips would be there.

If he went to the police first they would interrogate him for hours, during which Phillips might escape. Someone would undoubtedly buy STRUGGLE, the fictitious painting by Yellowhorse, possibly his dick client who wanted all the free advice. The thought of Mr. Dick purchasing the painting did make Bloom crack a smile. He realized it was perverse for him to smile at this thought considering all that had just transpired but he couldn't help himself. Visualizing in his mind how his client had ridiculed him for talking about karma, it seemed apropos for the client to end up with the piece.

The auction would start in less than an hour and the Yellowhorse, lot 47, would go around 7:40. To stop Phillips and the sale would require plenty of luck, and he knew it. Bloom hoped he still retained enough of Hastiin Sherman's power to fight the *chindi*. As Bloom looked at his extremities, still soaked in his own blood, a large clap of thunder and a lightning bolt filled the air, a rare thunderstorm in New York. Charles jumped straight up as the bolt sounded like another gunshot.

The heavens then opened and rain poured down on Charles Bloom, cleansing his body and spirit of bloodstains and death. Charles looked up to the sky and filled his mouth with pure, cold rain water, which he swished around, spitting out the last of the powerful medicine man's life-saving medicine. His numb mouth returned to normal immediately. Hastiin Sherman's power pulsated through Bloom's rejuvenated body. The soaked but now halfway presentable Bloom was able to hail a cab and make his way back to his hotel.

Back in his hotel room, he organized a plan. Figuring out how to persuasively present it to Rupert was the second-hardest thing he had to do that day, although not nearly as hazardous as surviving near-death bondage. Charles had to go to the auction and this meant he would need the less-than-accommodating head of the contemporary art department to put him on the guest list and cooperate. He knew Rupert would be trying to close any last loose ends and get the fence sitters off in time to make bids. The art market had been tough lately and Rupert's last-minute efforts could make the difference between having a good sale or failure. What Bloom knew and Rupert did not, was that they had given a murderer an advance of over a million dollars on a fraudulent painting. This information should be enough to make Rupert stop his last-minute push for sales and deal with Bloom. Rupert wouldn't want Phillips leaving the country unexpectedly with Sotheby's cash, and he wouldn't want Sotheby's to be selling a fake.

Charles devised a way to avoid damaging Sotheby's sale completely and to capture Bernard Phillips—thief, murderer, and forger. To accomplish this required persuading Rupert to believe his story and to go along with his plan.

First, Charles emailed Rupert the photos he had taken an hour ago of the murder scene, with the subject line reading *Phillips is a murderer*. He followed the email with a phone message. The information he imparted, along with the appearance he told Rupert he soon would be making at Sotheby's with a lacerated wrist and pallid coloration secondary to losing 30% of his blood volume, couldn't hurt in making the point that he was telling the truth. Charles hoped Rupert was still monitoring his omnipresent BlackBerry.

CHAPTER 56

LOT 47

A major contemporary art auction is always the place to be if you are an important art enthusiast. The bigwigs arrive in their private jets from all over the world. They all show up at 6:30 to make their way up the line of adoring fans and wannabes. They are the art-collecting stars walking their red carpet. The trade magazines are all there to make notes on who buys what and for how much. Established art dealers swarm around like a hive of bees, all waiting to bid for important clients or for themselves. Rarely do artists show up. This is too much like a cattle auction. Their creative sensibilities are offended by the sale of the product: their art.

The special buyers have their spots reserved on the main auction floor. Each knows their pecking order in the art-world hierarchy. The back is standing room only, relegated to press and those who aren't going to buy anything but somehow got a golden ticket for the big show. The suites above the bidding floor are reserved for those who are either the consigners of large, important pieces or the really big buyers who don't want to be bothered or identified.

May 7th was Bernard Phillips' night. He was the consigner of a much-talked-about painting and those in the know understood he would be a multimillionaire in just a matter of an hour. He was offered a box seat weeks ago, but insisted he wanted to be on the floor close to the action. He needed everyone to see his moment, one his father had never had. Bernard was incredibly cool for a person who had just murdered his longtime artist/partner and arranged for the other Yellowhorse dealer, Bloom, to meet his demise as well. Nonetheless, Bernard was genuinely enjoying himself, coming early to meet his fans and talk up his painting, shaking hands and making small talk with those he hoped would bid on STRUGGLE.

The crowd finally took their seats and the auctioneer, a distinguished, tall man with a regal-sounding British accent, gave the disclaimers to the potential buyers. This audience had heard it all before. You don't make the main floor seating of the May contemporary art sale at Sotheby's unless you have spent a lot of money in the past and are a known entity. Each auction has its own rhythm. The auctioneer's objective was to try and gauge what the tone of the sale was going to be, and manipulate the crowd to the best of his abilities.

An enthusiastic group of bidders will start things rolling along with lots of secondary background noise, even clapping if things go well. The opposite can also be true. If a major piece fails early on, it can dampen the mood and the room falls silent. The crowd wonders if the art market has changed in some unperceivable way and maybe bidding too exuberantly is unwise that night. The auctioneer's worse nightmare is quiet in the room.

The first couple of lots were positioned to go above their estimates, which they did at tonight's auction.

A spectacular Damien Hirst butterfly painting sold for a million dollars, nearly twice the high estimate. The next lot was a large, colorful Keith Haring of a man in a box with a dog barking for his head. It brought nearly $700K, a very strong number. The auction continued right on track, each progressive lot never missing a beat, with great prices for the material being offered and the best still to come. The art market was supposed to be in a recession but not tonight. Values for paintings were strong, as were the paintings. The auctioneer was able to get the last cent, or in many cases, half-million dollars, out of the crowd.

When the Yellowhorse, lot 47, came up, the crowd instinctively silenced themselves to hear the auctioneer's impressive description of the last Yellowhorse painting ever produced. Bernard Phillips fidgeted in his seat. He felt the need to juggle something to ease the first stress he had felt all night.

The auctioneer cleared his throat and said in a most distinguished and yet firm voice, "We will be skipping lot 47 tonight, the Yellowhorse, as the family has decided to pull the piece. We apologize for any inconvenience this may have caused any of our clients tonight." Then without missing a beat and trying to keep the crowd upbeat and on the same good roll, he continued, "Now for the piece we have all been waiting for: the Rothko, one of the best of its kind!"

All in the know in the crowd simultaneously turned their heads toward Bernard Phillips, who was sitting in the coveted first row. He had been going on and on about the piece just 50 minutes before. The painting must have been pulled without his knowledge. What could have happened? Phillips himself was in a state of shock and anger. His face turned beet-red and he felt his heart rate explode.

Bernard wanted to scream, "You can't pull my painting! I took care of Bloom! Sell my fucking painting; I killed three people to get this goddamn piece here!"

But realizing something had gone terribly wrong, Bernard got up and exited the room. Again, many eyes followed his movement, ignoring the Rothko as it was reaching a near-record price. The art reporters tried in vain to get a tidbit from Bernard for their magazines, but Phillips ignored them and exited the room quickly and without a word. The Rothko had become the secondary story of the night. Bernard Phillips' omitted painting was the first.

Phillips was out the door and nearing the escalator when he saw four police officers rapidly heading his way. Behind them was the very pale Charles Bloom with a smile on his face. Bloom—out in the world? Ghostly looking, yes, but obviously not dead?

Bernard realized he was in serious trouble. He would have to make a run for it. He had over a million dollars in an offshore account waiting for him. He couldn't proceed forward. Turning backward, he saw two Sotheby's guards and Rupert had closed the auction doors and were guarding them, stopping him from returning to the auction and stopping anyone from coming out.

Phillips' gun was in the car waiting for his final plant, which was now a fast-fading memory. The only way out was to jump over the railing to the floor below. He saw himself as Harrison Ford in the "The Fugitive," jumping into the waterfall while Tommy Lee Jones looked on helplessly as Ford makes his successful escape. His destiny would not be jail like that of his late father, Jim Callahan. The still-athletic Bernard Phillips went for his dramatic final gambit.

The desperate plunge might have succeeded if not for a red Italian silk scarf around Bernard Phillips' neck, which he had worn for the unusually chilly night. The scarf got entangled in the railing's metal slats, twisting at the last moment into a perfectly formed hangman's noose, the scarf's length just long enough so his whole 200-pound body weight felt the full impact as the expensive silk textile tightened its high-quality yarn, never failing even with Bernard's heavy load, breaking his cervical spine at C1/C2. Bernard's demise was instantaneous. There was no painful struggling, his life ending in one quick pull, unlike Willard's death with its inhuman strangulation that resulted in the so-called painting. The irony was not lost on Bloom, who stared in morbid fascination.

The scene was surrealistic. The well-dressed man hanging from the Sotheby's railing by an expensive red scarf, a slow drip of urine coming off his new crimson Donald Pliner shoes. The whole event seemed like some well-orchestrated, art-performance piece done for public consumption. It would make a great story, of which Bloom wanted no part. At that critical moment, Bloom's thoughts were of Rachael, Preston, Willard, and Hastiin Sherman, the old medicine man who would finally have peace and his grandson's return.

CHAPTER 57

NO SALE EVER

It had been two months since the deaths of Bernard Phillips and Fredrick Marsh. The art world was shocked by the immensity of the scandal. Bernard's father, the notorious Jim Callahan, who had been so reviled in the early sixties, was a hot subject once more on the New York social scene. The now-retired Brit Currency had been interviewed by all the magazines for his story of two generations of deceit by Callahan/Phillips males. Numerous reporters had tried to interview Bloom, even offering money, but he was reportedly in seclusion somewhere in Arizona, according to his best friend Brad Shriver, owner of the Upper Deck Gallery. Everyone assumed it must be a place like Canyon Ranch; instead it was a small metal hogan near Toadlena, New Mexico.

The Yellowhorse market had exploded since the auction. Everyone wanted a piece. All of Bloom's old clients had called, leaving messages on his cell phone, asking if he had anything available by Yellowhorse. Bloom couldn't deal with the thought of selling another Yellowhorse, and finally turned off his cell phone. The images of

Marsh he had taken on the now-silenced cell phone had weeks ago been downloaded by the police and the case closed. Marsh's complete collection of paintings was locked up in a huge police warehouse, never to see the light of day again.

Willard Yellowhorse's body had been exhumed from Boston's Mount Auburn Cemetery and returned to Toadlena for a traditional burial. The body of Craig Lendskip was also exhumed, and taken back to Darwin, Minnesota. Lendskip was placed next to his mother and father, and in very close proximity to his mentor, Francis A. Johnson.

Mount Auburn refunded fully to the Marsh estate the money Fredrick had paid for his plot, and removed forever any trace of his evil presence. The state of New York was the recipient of Marsh's estate money since Fredrick Marsh had no heirs or will. His body was placed in a common state grave, one of many in a sea of simple wooden markers of the unwanted or unknown, a grave that was never to be visited or found again. Bernard's body was buried near his father's in the family plot.

Hastiin Sherman would never see the funeral of his grandson, but would be forever near him, as Sherman died the day after finding out the coyote spirit was no longer alive and his grandson Willard would be returned to him. Sherman had left his hogan and made a small encampment at the base of Canyon del Muerto where he died in his sleep. The family hogan could remain occupied, as the old medicine man had purposely vacated it, knowing it was now his time. He left a note for Rachael on her grandmother's loom giving her the hogan and its contents, and his blessing to be with her *bilagaana*/Cherokee, and telling her how proud he was of the way Charles had followed the Diné path.

The bodies of Hastiin Sherman and Willard Yellowhorse were taken to their final resting places high above Canyon del Muerto's wall and placed in their ancestral vaults next to each other for eternity.

The STRUGGLE canvas Yellowhorse had died on was returned to Rachael and Preston. Amazingly, Bloom had been asked about the availability of the piece as if it were something that would soon be for sale.

254

Charles, Rachael, and Preston decided Willard's death canvas still had the spirit of Willard in its essence, which would best be freed by burning it along with his boyhood hogan, which had been abandoned since his death.

The day was a cool July morning when Willard's spirit was finally set free into his ancestral sky. A large gray smoke cloud appeared on the calm Navajo vista, floating effortlessly southeast toward distant Mount Taylor. A lone eagle gently glided through the piñon smoke as the family watched and said their final good-byes.

Rachael's mind cleared of all thoughts while looking at the magnificent bird slowly disappearing into the distant horizon. An image suddenly appeared in her consciousness: it was a flock of sheep. She knew what it meant. It was time to finish her grandmother's weaving and then start one of her own.

The End

KAYENTA CROSSING

BY MARK SUBLETTE

PROLOGUE

NO NEW TRUCK

Randal Begay's vision was strong. The sweat lodge's medicine had done the trick. Now he could journey down the correct Diné path, in step with his ancestors' beliefs. The hard decision to return the money was clear in his mind. For the first time in months he felt at ease and in balance.

His grandfather, a respected medicine man, had recommended the sweat treatment to help him resolve his inner conflict. It had worked, empowering him with a newfound courage, something he had lacked for too long. Randal knew he must break his deal with the *bilagaana*. If not, he would never walk in beauty. A bad choice had been made eight months earlier by accepting the $10,000 down payment. He would not compound the mistake tomorrow. The $25,000 in cash that was to be paid to Randal for finishing the project was a deal he must back out of. If he completed the transaction, he would never be able to live the life of a good human being by Diné standards. He also might end up in jail if the truth became known. Or maybe worse.

Randal had expressed deep concerns earlier in the week to the old rancher William "Buck" Wilson, his trusted friend whose family had lived near the Begays for two generations. Buck had relieved Randal's conscience at the time. He told Randal he didn't see any problem with his arrangement with the *bilagaana*. He assured Randal that it was an honorable transaction, and no laws were being broken. Buck had influenced Randal by reminding him of his family duties, pointing out, "The money will get your clan back on their feet. Besides, there's no harm being done. You're a Navajo and you are just taking advantage of the talents your grandmother taught you. You have nothing to worry about, son."

Randal had wanted to believe Buck, but Buck was also a *bilagaana* and didn't understand the essence of what it meant to be Diné. Despite his serious trepidations, Randal had continued working to complete his commitment. The outcome was amazing, even in Randal's eyes. He was gifted, yet must destroy what Spiderwoman had helped guide him to complete. It could never be sold or he would be doomed.

Tomorrow would be a better day even if he would be poorer. Randal would face the man with the orange hat and explain why he must back out of his obligation. The man would be very angry no doubt, and demand his $10,000 back plus interest. The money was gone, but fortunately Randal had not wasted it. He had purchased a good truck. He would sign over the vehicle's title and make it right somehow, giving the man whatever was required. Randal would not cause the gods to punish his heart. Navajo spirits are not to be tested. They can destroy a man. He saw this now.

Come clean, change his ways, and have his grandfather perform a Blessing Way ceremony to cure him of his poor judgment and the *chindi* that were haunting his subconscious. So Randal vowed now. He had been sleeping poorly, his appetite nonexistent as he neared the completion of his long ordeal. Now he knew the right road. It was not too late to change, or so he thought.

Steam rose off the hot sweat-lodge rocks, producing a fine ribbon of white clouds that hugged the open mesa's horizon, the lodge's calling card visible for miles. The temperature outside was near freezing, but inside his cramped juniper hut it was well over 100. One more cup of water, and Randal would be fully prepared to handle the anger of the man in the orange hat with the bleached white teeth.

Randal stuck his head out of the hut's opening, searching for the plastic jug of water. He was ready to complete his treatment. His unadjusted eyes were temporarily blinded by the late evening sun, which caused him to reflexively turn his head away from its glaring golden light.

The last memory he had before all went dark was a flash of white and an image of Black Mesa in the distance, its sacred voice calling him home.

To be continued in KAYENTA CROSSING, *scheduled for release in 2013.*

Photography courtesy Mark Sublette